*For our children,
May the past guide
you into the future*

CHASING EMBERS

THE OARSMEN: BOOK ONE

GLENN BECK

WITH MIKAYLA G. HEDRICK

Forefront
BOOKS

MERCURY
INK

Published by Mercury Ink and Forefront Books, Nashville, Tennessee.
Mercury Ink is a trademark of Mercury Radio Arts, Inc.
Distributed by Simon & Schuster.

Library of Congress Control Number: 2024906716

Print ISBN: 978-1-63763-304-5

Cover Design by Alexander Somoskey
Interior Design by Bill Kersey, KerseyGraphics
Illustrations by Jacob Thompson

Printed in the United States of America

THE VANISHING

It was the night the scales tipped decisively in the Administrator's direction. A young couple was sitting in their unit in the half-built utopian city known as "Oasis." The city was flush with the sounds of mechanical construction—*crash, whizz, pop, smash*. These sounds were normal in Oasis. The Tenants were hardly bothered by it anymore.

As they did each night, the couple sat at the dining table, writing feverishly in a small leather-bound notebook. The wife would write for a moment, then pause, cock her head to one side, and then slide the notebook across the table to her husband, who was sanding down a small wooden sword he was making for his son. He would look at the page, pause, scratch his forehead, and then pick up writing where she had left off. She left gaps in the sentences for her husband to fill in as best he could.

Pocahontas was ___ years old when she saved John Smith. She was a member of the ___ tribe. Her father was Chief ___.

The wife usually left the numbers and proper nouns blank. Her memory wasn't what it used to be. No one's was anymore.

"Twelve?" the husband asked himself. "No, that's not it." He looked at his wife. "Was Pocahontas twelve when she saved John Smith?"

The wife shrugged.

The husband pressed his pointer finger against his forehead and circled the small space between his eyebrows. He always did this when he was unsure. He hated to get even one detail wrong.

"For goodness' sake, Adam. Just write *twelve*. Write something."

"But I'm not sure she was twelve. I'm not positive."

"Was she close to twelve?" she pressed.

He added two more fingers to his rigorous forehead circling.

Losing her patience, she blurted, "Oh, just put twelve; it's close enough."

He slapped his hand on the table in frustration. "It's *not* close enough!"

The wife pointed sharply in the direction of their children sleeping in the bedroom, warning him to not wake them. Matching her forcefulness, he leaned across the table and whispered, "It is either right or it isn't. It can't be close."

"It will be *nothing* if we don't finish it," she retorted.

"It will be nothing if it isn't *True*! How do you not understand that?"

In anger, he had thrown his writing pen across the room. This behavior wasn't like him. He was generally a mild-tempered man, but he could feel the clock ticking inside him.

The wife held his gaze for a few moments until tears welled up in her eyes, and she rose from the table to turn away from him. The baby started to cry in the bedroom. She dropped her shoulders, sighed, and went to attend to him, leaving her husband alone. He buried his face in his hands and listened to his son wail.

"It's *not* twelve," he said under his breath. But there was no way to be sure. When he had first written down this story, he had been sure. But that was at least ten drafts, multiple cycles without real food, a baby, and a war ago. The Oarsmen had secured the prior collection of drafts in a place they had *thought* was impenetrable, but they had been wrong. Like every draft prior, the last collection had also disappeared. By the time the Oarsmen realized they had been compromised, their hiding place was already destroyed. Every time the Oarsmen sat down to write, the stakes were higher and higher, but at the same time, they were all remembering less and less. Less of everything that once was before the war, before the peace made in exchange for freedom. Before their collective mind was wiped clean.

The husband was the sharpest mind left among the Oarsmen, but he, too, was starting to forget. It was driving him mad.

He decided it was time to finish writing for the night. He rose from the table and walked toward the bedroom to apologize to his wife and calm his son. Then he heard it. The Tones. He hadn't heard those since moving to Oasis.

"Tones? But the war is over," he muttered.

For years, the Tones had announced the incoming rain of missiles on unsuspecting towns. It was that deafening siren that had driven the Aaronsons to Oasis, seeking a city of refuge. When the war continued around the world, it stopped in Oasis. At the time, that was all that really mattered.

He ran to the window. The city was illuminated by the dim glow of LED streetlamps. The husband caught a glimpse of his neighbor Mr. Clark, or at least the back of his head, from across the street. The man's arms were swinging relentlessly in the direction of a large, uniformed man, who was yanking him out of his front door.

Mrs. Clark was only a few feet behind, screaming and clinging to the doorframe. Another uniformed person, this time a woman, came up behind Mrs. Clark and injected her with a luminescent teal liquid. Mrs. Clark's whole body began to contort and seize up. She screamed in pain, causing Mr. Clark to finally throw a blow hard enough to free himself from his captor. But before he could reach his wife, she had collapsed on the ground; then he, too, was injected with that same strange teal liquid. Their unconscious bodies were hauled into the street as a warning to the others about the consequences of resistance.

The husband didn't recognize the captors' uniforms. They were jet-black with teal piping, as if the wearers were some kind of dystopian theme park attendants. On the lapels were three teal-embroidered circles, stacked on top of one another. He knew that emblem.

Topos.

He heard the woman from three units down from the Clarks desperately scream, "I am not an Oarsman! I am *not* an Oarsman!"

She wasn't an Oarsman. But that hardly mattered now.

Four units down in the other direction, an older man was being led away without speaking, without resisting. As he caught the husband's eyes in the window, he noticed that the man was somber—peaceful, even. For some reason, this shocked the husband more than the scene with the Clark family. He recoiled from the window.

"Julia!" he called to his wife.

She ran out of the bedroom with their baby boy in her arms. Their daughter, only nine years old, was peeking out from behind the door her mother had only half shut as she'd rushed out. The daughter couldn't make out what her parents were saying over the sound of her brother's cries, the blaring Tones, and the growing chorus of desperate shrieks— "I'm not an Oarsman! I'm not an Oarsman!" Her mother ran to her, panicked but resolute. The daughter still couldn't hear her over the noise.

The screams were next door now.

"Hide them!" the husband yelled.

Without hesitation, the wife placed her hand on her daughter's shoulder, turned her around, and shoved her into the bedroom.

The husband sprinted through the front room, removing all traces of the children and wedging the unfinished toy sword underneath the couch cushions.

With the crying baby still clinging to her chest, the wife flung open the doors of their old wardrobe, violently whipped clothes aside to make room, and yelled to her daughter, "Ember, get in!"

Still holding her boy in one arm, she grabbed her daughter by the waist and forced her into the wardrobe. She handed her the baby, saying, "Quiet him. You *have* to quiet him."

The wife looked at her children tucked into the wardrobe and placed her hand over her mouth to stifle the scream rising in her throat. She was crying. Then she heard someone pound on the front door, and instantly her demeanor transformed. With tunnel vision, she sprinted to the leather-bound notebook still lying on the dining room table.

Although he knew it was no use to resist, the husband would not open the door. He stood just a few feet away, facing it with his fists clenched and his chest rising and falling with each deep breath. The door was being forced open as the wife grabbed the notebook from the table, bolted back to the bedroom, opened the wardrobe, and thrust the book upon her daughter all in one motion.

"Never lose this book," she whispered to her.

The door of the unit burst open, and people flooded in, shouting and brandishing syringes glowing with teal liquid. There were four men and three women. Five had on the new uniforms; the remaining two were still wearing the old ones. One was viciously eyeing the small sketch of crossed oars etched over the doorway.

The wardrobe doors creaked ever so softly as the wife shut in her children and pressed an ear to the bedroom door to listen.

A man who appeared to be the leader of the group spoke. "We are charged with removing all adult Tenants in this unit. Are you alone?"

Without missing a beat, the husband responded with a definitive, "Yes." But just at that moment, he heard an unmistakable sound in the back bedroom. So did every other person in the unit.

Perceiving that her brother was about to cry again, the daughter had begun tying a pair of her father's work pants around her brother's mouth. In the process her hand slipped and knocked against the wooden interior with a hollow *thud*. She hadn't even noticed.

One of the officers still in his old uniform said, "Who else is in here? Come out now."

"By order of who?" the husband demanded.

The officers stood silently.

He asked again, his fists clenched so tightly they were turning pale. "By order of *who*?"

After a moment of silence, the leader replied, "Topos, Inc."

The wife pressed her hands to her stomach as if she'd been punched. The husband lowered his eyes for the first time, but only for a moment. Then he spoke sternly and plainly.

"You will take me alone."

Through the doors of the wardrobe, the daughter heard a crashing sound.

Standing taller, now with his knuckles as white as snow, the husband again declared, "You will take me alone!"

Another crash followed by a thud. The sound was too muffled for the daughter to make out what was happening in the other room, but she did hear the door to the bedroom open.

"Don't," the husband warned his wife, but it was too late. The officers saw her.

The husband sighed and dropped his head. He knew what this meant. So did she.

Another crash. Another thud. Then the sound of the front door slamming.

In an impulsive act of rebellion, as the couple was dragged away from their unit, the husband began asserting facts from the past.

"We were the first nation to land a man on the moon. We became an independent nation in 1776. Our first president was George Washington, then Adams, then—"

His wife joined him. "Jefferson!"

They spoke together, overlapping each other's sentences.

"In 1492, Columbus—"

"...endowed by our Creator—"

"...dedicated to the proposition that all men are created equal—"

One by one, every Oarsmen within earshot, all the others being taken away from their units, began to shout at the same time.

"The shot heard 'round the—"

"Give me liberty—"

"…Allied Powers—"

"September 11, 2001—"

"…and we dropped the atomic—"

"Free speech, free press, free religion, free assembly, free—"

"On the seventh day—"

"…by the content of their character—"

"The Truth will set you free!"

A wave of disjointed, rebellious, and True words flooded the streets, swelling into a kind of desperate but beautiful music and then drifting away into nothingness.

Silence.

In the stillness, the sister hurriedly untangled her brother from her father's pant leg. He took a deep and terrified breath. He was not crying anymore.

Holding her brother, the sister slowly opened the wardrobe door and stepped out. She shuffled into the main room, cognizant of every sound her feet made as they grazed the floor. A chair had been turned over. Her father's writing pen was on the ground. Even one of her mother's shoes had been left behind at the threshold of the front door. Seeing the shoe, she remembered. She placed her brother on the couch, rushed back to the wardrobe, and grabbed the leather-bound book from underneath the fallen clothes.

She heard her brother scream. She rushed out and saw him recoiling from a wooden tip poking out of the cushion—his toy sword.

"Shh. Henry, you have to be quiet," she whispered, picking him up.

She held the book against her chest with her brother pressing against it from the other side, securing it in place. She drifted back through the unit and out the front door. The street was empty and quiet. She stood there with her brother and her book for what seemed like hours until another small boy stepped out of his unit into the empty street. Then another child. And another. And another. Soon hundreds of children poured out onto the streets and waited silently for their parents to return.

But they never did.

OASIS

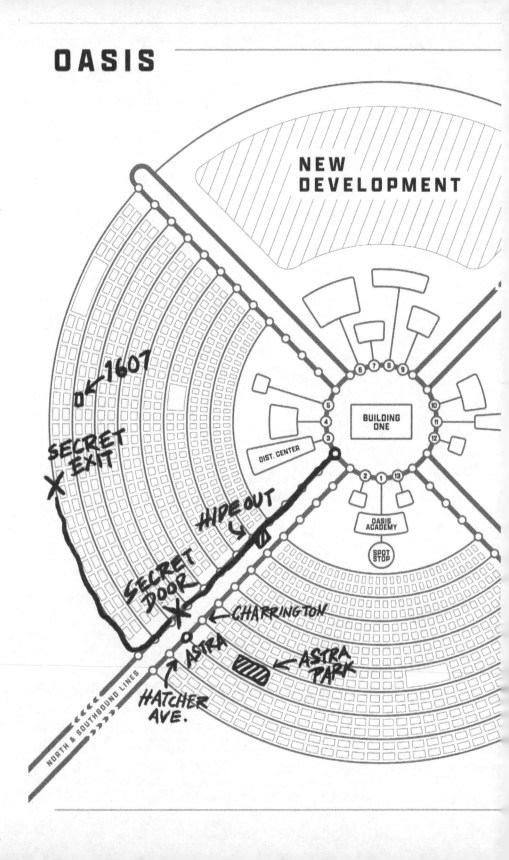

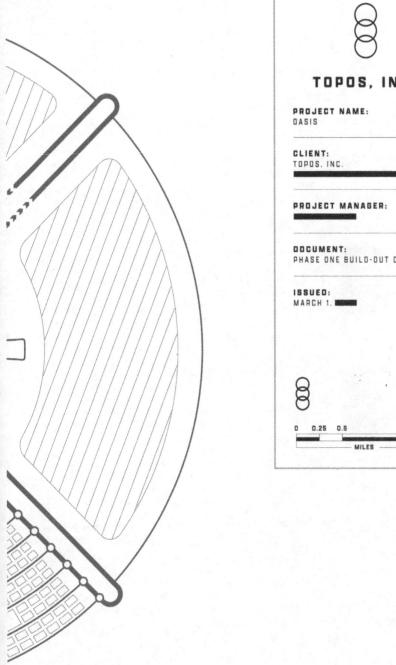

TOPOS, INC.

PROJECT NAME:
OASIS

CLIENT:
TOPOS, INC.
▬▬▬▬▬▬▬▬▬

PROJECT MANAGER:
▬▬▬▬▬▬

DOCUMENT:
PHASE ONE BUILD-OUT OVERVIEW

ISSUED:
MARCH 1, ▬▬▬

N

0	0.25	0.5		1.5

MILES

CHAPTER ONE

CONTRABAND

(Ember)

"**E**mber."

A voice was growling in the darkness, waking me up before it spoke again.

"You're gonna get us killed."

I heard the shuffling of blankets accompanied by a panting sound.

"Let go of the book."

That voice.

Mrs. Grisham.

She was having that same nightmare again, the one that always ended with the sound of her head banging against the wall behind her bed. The one that always seemed to—

And there it is.

As I heard the footsteps outside the bedroom I shared with my little brother, Henry, I could tell Mrs. Grisham was shuffling down the narrow hallway to the kitchen. I wondered if she was still wearing her gaudy silver nightcap. It didn't take long before I heard the familiar sound of a whisk scraping against a metal bowl. I could picture her now, slopping runny lab eggs into a metal pan. No salt, no oil, just eggs. It was only a matter of time until she would be "cleaning" the pan with soap and fork, cussing under her breath.

"She's burning them again," I mumbled to Henry, who was sleeping below me on the bottom "bunk."

Our makeshift bunk bed was an old dining room table that I slept on top of. Like he did every morning, Henry sprang out of bed, salivating at the wafting aroma of burned lab eggs. He tucked a small wooden sword into the back of his pants, the kind he'd use to wage war against his favorite imaginary enemy: the Holdouts.

"Close the—"

Henry disappeared so fast I couldn't finish telling him to close the curtain to our room. The shiny silver curtain had three teal circles stacked on top of one another—the Topos, Inc. logo. It was standard-issue— every caretaker who had taken in the extra children seven years ago had received one to divide their unit. Of course, calling Mrs. Grisham a "care-taker" was a bit of a stretch.

Can you really use the word "care" to describe someone who hates you?

She didn't just hate me and my brother; Mrs. Grisham also hated "mess." She hated risk. Compliance was her way of life. This was, of course, the only reason she had agreed to taking Henry and me in the first place. It's not like she wanted us. Topos just gave us to her because she had the space, and because they probably knew she would do anything to stay in their good graces, even if that meant taking on, as she so lovingly called us, "two hellions."

I reached for my book, which was tucked under the blankets with me. I had taken to sleeping with it since Mrs. Grisham started having her nightmares about it a few years ago. Like clockwork, she would wake up screaming about my book once every few cycles. On those mornings, I knew I needed it to be out of her reach.

Last night I had been reading about a boy who fought a giant using only a few rocks and a slingshot. It only took one shot for the giant to be knocked out—dead. Henry loved this story, so I'd read it to him last night before we went to sleep.

For a moment I studied my beloved book. The leather binding was worn, and there was a tear in the cover from Mrs. Grisham attempting to scratch out the tiny oars engraved on the lower-right corner; it was the only time she'd gotten her hands on the book, when Topos had delivered me to her doorstep seven years before. I had asked her what those oars were, but she'd only given me an exasperated response of, "Why should I know?" Naturally, this meant she *did* know, but I knew better than to ask again.

Even though there was a busy day ahead, I couldn't help opening the book just one more time. I flipped through the pages to the story about two brothers testing their flying machine on a huge stretch of white sand. I loved this page because there was a tiny drawing of the scene scribbled into the bottom corner. I always imagined that my mom had drawn it.

I had been reading the stories in this book for as long as I could remember. I probably had them all memorized. But I still liked to read them because sometimes, if I read long enough, I started to feel like someone was reading to me—my dad, I think. Normally I had a hard time remembering his voice, but sometimes when I read my book, it would come back to me. Flipping those pages was like a magic portal to another world—a forbidden world. But lately, the voice had been fading into a hazy memory, and the portal was getting harder and harder to open.

I could hear Mrs. Grisham making her way down the hallway to the bathroom—the only bathroom in the unit. With the curtain still open, she peered in to see what I was doing. Her wiry brown hair dangled in front of her eyes.

"Reading." She mumbled something else under her breath and yanked the curtain shut.

Oh, yeah, the "care" just oozes out of her.

I knew she couldn't resist saying something else, and sure enough it came.

"You know you have to put that away in the daytime," Mrs. Grisham said in the passive-aggressive and painfully unmotherly tone she normally used to address me.

"Oh, really? I've never been told that."

In the list of everything Mrs. Grisham hated, did I mention she also hated sarcasm?

"One day you'll get caught with that book, and Topos will send you to Sleep Camp. And I'll tell you one thing: I'm not going with you."

With that threat, she slammed the bathroom door.

I couldn't help rolling my eyes as I leapt from the tabletop, thumping my feet to the floor and then slamming to a seat on the ground. I loved making extra noise just to drive Mrs. Grisham batty. After grabbing my green sneakers, I slapped them on the ground, shoved my feet in, and stomped multiple times for good measure. I smirked with self-satisfaction. But I knew that she was right. If I got caught with that book, they would send me to Sleep Camp.

Going over to the dining chairs I had fashioned into shelves for my clothes, I grabbed the pair of tall gray boots I never wore and reached inside the right boot. I pulled out a rusty old butter knife—contraband. All supplies that came in the morning nourishment delivery were to be picked up every evening and taken back to the Midpoint Distribution Center, but I secretly held on to this knife for a very specific reason. I scurried to the vent beside the bed and used the knife to twist the screws at the four corners. Then I slid the vent cover to the side, shimmied my upper body into the vent, and reached for a bundle of dirty rags tucked into the back-right corner—the remnants of Henry's baby blanket.

After climbing back out of the vent, I unwrapped the bundle and found the singular clean rag in the middle. I carefully wrapped my book in the clean rag, reconstructed the bundle, then shimmied back in on my stomach to return the bundle of rags. Soon the cover was back over the vent, with the screws back in place and the contraband knife back in hiding.

Job well done.

As I left my room, I met Mrs. Grisham in the cramped hallway.

"You're all dusty," she said with a look of disgust. "Brush yourself off."

"Good morning to you too."

"Are you hungry?" she asked dutifully, still clearly peeved.

I gave her a grin I knew she detested. "I would like some burned lab eggs, please."

Every morning the clanging sounds of never-ending construction signaled the start of a new day. As I packed my backpack for the special event later at the Pathway, the sounds of whirring and beeping machinery ricocheted through the tiny unit. It was year thirteen of the "three-year construction" of Oasis, the City of the Future. It had grown easy to ignore the noise, and even easier to ignore any hope that this construction would ever be finished. I could barely remember a life without it.

Normally I would've been staying inside that day, since Tenants remained in their units on Day Five, but I had something important to do, something secret. Henry had been begging me to tell him what it was ever since a teacher at Oasis Academy had pulled me aside to invite me. When I had informed Mrs. Grisham I would be leaving the unit on this particular Day Five, she struggled to hide the jealousy and distrust seeping out from her thin, tight, lip liner–lined lips.

"Why would they choose *you*?" she said.

I grinned. "Because I'm so witty."

To be honest, I wasn't exactly sure how I had been chosen, nor did I know exactly what we were going to be doing. The teacher had only told me we were going for "interviews." For what I had no clue. None of that mattered. I was headed outside on a Day Five like the important people in the city.

And I'm actually going to Building One.

Right on schedule, the Administrator's sugary voice rang out across the Oasis-wide speaker system.

"Good morning, Tenants. It's another beautiful day in Oasis. It will be sunny today with a light breeze, a perfect day to enjoy some time on the Fibonacci. I look forward to seeing you soon for the Topping Out Ceremony. Remember—"

His voice stopped and the lights went off. Once again, the power had gone out across all of Oasis. I walked to the kitchen and heard Mrs. Grisham cursing.

"Blast these flickers! Interrupting the best part of the day." She returned to scraping the pan with a fork as she added, "What a good man."

This might be the only thing Mrs. Grisham and I agreed on. The Administrator was definitely a good man. If he hadn't founded Topos, Inc. and moved most of the Tenants of the prewar country into his properties during the war, everyone would probably be dead. It was common knowledge that it was the Administrator who finally negotiated a peace deal that stopped the fighting. Henry and I had a tradition of counting down the days until the Administrator's next arrival in Oasis. He hadn't visited in over a year, but whenever he came, it was like Christmas, summer, and your birthday mixed together. There were parades and SpotStop games; they even swapped out the smell of fresh linen pumping through the air for the scent of a crisp ocean breeze. The arrival of the Administrator meant food deliveries arrived on time and the power never went out. He always made sure to open a new public park or playground for the children, or unveil a new virtual world on the Fibonacci. At the ribbon cutting for Astra Avenue Park, Henry even got his picture taken with him. But since the Administrator hadn't visited for over a year, Oasis was on the fritz.

The lights flickered back on, but the broadcast had already ended.

"Blast it," Henry said as he waged imaginary war with his wooden sword. "Take that, you grubby Holdouts!"

When Henry asked if she wanted to play war, Mrs. Grisham sighed and told him to help her pack up the plates, silverware, and pan to be sent back to the Midpoint Distribution Center. With her hand in a fist, she released one finger at a time and muttered to herself again.

She's counting down the days until Henry and I go back to Oasis Academy.

I knew it was only three hours until the Fibonacci arrived, and our "caretaker" could disappear into the virtual world. Henry was still lost in his own imaginary world, drawing his sword and fencing into the air while singing the all-too-familiar Fibonacci jingle. "Come join me on Fibonacci, where everyone is happy. My friends and me on Fibonacci. Why not just be happy?"

As I swiped my Travel Card and watched the metal bars swing open, I saw a T-Force Agent staring me down. He was lanky and gave me a suspicious leer as he started to approach. I could tell he wanted to know why I was out of my unit and hopping onto the Interlink. The Fat Agent next to him wasn't so ambitious. He grabbed the Lanky Agent by his collar and dragged him the other way, muttering about having bigger fish to fry. Part of me had hoped they would ask me what I was doing. I wanted to prove I belonged out here.

It was roughly a ten-minute ride to the Pathway Station. I wished it were longer. Riding on the Interlink was one of the few chances I had to catch a quick glimpse of the parts of the city I was never able to explore. My Travel Card opened very few doors in Oasis, and anywhere in the city beyond the confined path of my daily routines was a mystery to me.

For the last minute or so of the ride, the Interlink all but grazed the bottom of the scaffolding surrounding the half-built but intricately constructed buildings. The tall ones were my favorites. I had never been in a building higher than three floors.

But one day I will.

"Haven't you ever seen the city before?"

The voice startled me. I turned and noticed a face I had seen many times before. My pulse quickened, and my cheeks flushed. I felt my jaw fall open in amazement.

Pull yourself together, Ember!

"You came out of nowhere," I said.

"That's what happens when you're looking up at the sky. You don't notice anything else around you." Cade Carter grinned with the kind of confidence that said he knew how to get his way. That he was accustomed to being noticed—and admired. I didn't respond as my mind scrambled for a minute, trying to think what he was doing on the Interlink. Then it hit me.

The interview. We're going to the same place.

I couldn't believe I was riding with the SpotStop Champion and Oasis poster boy for the last two years.

Henry would be going out of his mind right now.

Cade took off his circle-rimmed sunglasses and tucked them into the pocket of his unbuttoned blazer. I was suddenly not sure if my overalls and green sneakers had been the right outfit choice for this day.

"It's probably hard to notice things when you're surrounded by a crowd of fans," I said.

"That's why I like Day Fives. I can actually get around the city."

I wanted to say something like, *It's only the important people who are out today,* but I held back. He already knew that.

"Think they'll ever finishing working on all these buildings?" Cade asked.

"I wish I could stay on here and go all the way around Oasis."

He brushed his perfectly cut hair back and looked indifferent. "It all looks pretty much like this."

"No way. You've seen it?" I said before I realized how uncool I sounded. "I mean, you don't like it?"

"No, it's just—I hate waiting. I'm supposed to be getting my own place soon."

I really wanted to ask him where he lived, how much of the city he'd seen, what it's like being out on Day Fives, how many times he'd been to Building One, and so many other questions. But instead, I remained silent.

"So, I assume you're coming to do this interview thing, right?"

Cade seemed to already know the answer, but I nodded anyway.

"I figured this was a SpotStop thing. They're always interviewing me about that," he said. "But you don't play SpotStop. I would know you if you did. Maybe this will actually be about something cool. But it'll probably be boring."

If only you knew how boring it was staying inside all day.

"I want to meet the Administrator," I said.

This seemed to get Cade's attention. He gave me a smug smile.

I cocked an eyebrow. "What?"

"Tell me when that happens."

I wanted to ask him why, but the doors to the Interlink opened. Cade hopped out and hurried away before I could even catch up. As I stepped into the pristine Pathway Station to try to follow him, I bumped into a scraggly and sickly-looking man wearing a worn overcoat. He glanced at me, but I looked away, not wanting this important moment soiled by someone normal. Especially someone who smelled like he hadn't showered in cycles.

The Pathway Station was the meeting point of the four Interlink tracks, which divided the circular city into four quadrants. Two of the four tracks were almost never used because they led to the new and undeveloped portions of Oasis. The circular, covered outdoor station was surrounded by multiple paved pathways that led away from the station to various official buildings. The average Oasis resident could only travel down two or three of those paths to carry out their normal business. That day, I was traveling down my fourth.

As I moved through the station, looking for a sign for Pathway Eleven, I found my eyes returning again and again to the glow of Building One. The simple, teal-tinted building was encircled by the station and was the exact center point of the city. It was also the only building in Oasis taller than seven floors. As I stopped to peek my head over the metal bars of the checkpoint, my eyes went straight to the eighth floor—the

Administrator's office. From that vantage point, he watched the happenings of the whole city. Whenever he visited, people would find the most inventive ways to contort their bodies over those same bars, hoping to see him peeking out the O-shaped windows that lined his floor. I once even saw a young mother holding a baby over the checkpoint to give the newborn an uninhibited view until an Agent made her stop.

When I finally found the sign for Pathway Eleven, I scanned my Travel Card and the metal bars swung open, inviting me in. At the end of this path was a building unlike any I had ever seen. It was shaped like a rainbow meeting the earth, and the entire facade was glass. A sea of unfamiliar faces greeted me, including a slender and striking face that caused me to stop.

Is that really—?

In the distance stood a tall and captivating woman of about forty years. Everything about her was long—her legs, her neck, her nails, even the way her mouth formed words when she spoke. I had seen her before; this was the woman who was always photographed standing near the Administrator. As I started to inch closer to her, my heart raced, and soon I was standing face-to-face with the beautiful woman.

More like face-to-belly button.

"Hello, Ms...."

Blank. Utterly blank. The name—any name—escaped me. If I had been asked her name five minutes earlier, I could have easily said it, but now I had no idea. *I'm blowing this. I'm really blowing it.*

For a moment I considered just turning around and sprinting back down the paved path, then perhaps changing my name and hiding out until this epic embarrassment blew over. But before I could decide if that was a good idea, the woman smiled at me.

"Aylo. Azaz Aylo."

Of course. Azaz Aylo, a name hard to say and harder still to forget. It was the kind of name I had to think about before speaking aloud. Azaz welcomed the mental stuttering in her presence. It suited her demeanor.

She was a woman of great stature, not only physically but in terms of her accomplishments. I knew she had started working for the Administrator before Topos, Inc., was widely popular, nonetheless in charge. Her loyalty had landed her a position in Topos's capital city, where she was given the title of "Administrator of Oasis." But to ensure she was never confused with *the* Administrator, her official title was "the A.O. of Topos, Inc."

I'd heard many descriptions of Azaz Aylo. She had a reputation for being a merciless yet beautiful sphinx. Mrs. Grisham had once said she was unknowable and mysterious. Others said she was highly regulated and unsurprising. Most Tenants respected the way she led Oasis, and all of them pretended to. Seeing her in person, I couldn't help but stare with my mouth wide open, wondering what she was doing there.

"Right this way." Azaz led me to a group of teenagers on the other side of the room, her heels click-clacking on the concrete floor. I remembered that I still hadn't said her name.

"Thank you for being here, Ms. Aylo," I said in a voice that sounded more like a squeak.

"Thank you for being here"? C'mon, Ember. Say something a little less stupid, please.

Plus, I didn't have the slightest idea where "here" really was.

For the rest of the day, I hoped I would have the chance to talk to Azaz Aylo again and redeem myself, but the opportunity never came.

The time passed by smoothly as I was asked the same ten questions by rounds of nice, anonymous adults. Why they cared how many friends I had at Oasis Academy, how well I knew my little corner of the city, or what I wanted to do when I grew up, I had no idea. But I told them I knew everything about my tiny portion of space, had very few friends, and wanted to do anything that got me a better Travel Card, and they seemed pleased. After a few hours, we were given a handful of cell-cultured meat sticks for our trouble and released for the day. After scanning my Travel Card to open the lobby doors and leave the building, I saw the same two Agents I had passed that morning standing right in front of me.

"Out of the way, kid." The Lanky Agent pushed past me. He squiggled over to Azaz, the Fat Agent clomping in his wake, but she ignored them and approached me.

"Excuse them," she said loud enough for the Agents to hear.

The Lanky Agent's tall, gangly body was so deflated in embarrassment that the Fat Agent had no problem reaching the back of Lanky's head and giving it a good smack. I smiled.

"Very good work today," Azaz told me.

I thanked her but didn't say anything else. I didn't want to risk it.

Her words stayed with me as I skipped all the way back to my unit.

Very good work today.

Very *good work today.*

The smell of fresh linen wafted through the air as the LED bulbs lining the street dimmed in conjunction with the sun. As the Administrator was just finishing his evening announcements, I mouthed along with him.

"And remember, the future is a door, and your dreams are the key."

After scanning myself into Mrs. Grisham's unit, I waltzed into the kitchen in such a good mood that I could resist making a snide remark about the smell of burned cricket pasta. When I saw a roach scuttling across the floor, I called out playfully to my brother.

"Henry, a Holdout snuck in! Come quick, and bring your sword."

But he didn't run into the kitchen like he usually did.

"It's time for battle!" I said again.

Still nothing. I called again, but he didn't come, and neither did Mrs. Grisham. I paused, listening for any sound in the unit, but I couldn't hear anything. Not even the sound of the Fibonacci coming from her room.

What are they doing?

I assumed Henry must be asleep, so I came up with a plan to sneak down the hallway and fling open the curtain to startle him. He was my little brother, after all; it was hard to resist a good jump-scare. I tiptoed down the hall, hardly able to conceal my excitement. I edged toward the curtain, then flung it wide open and raised my fist as if I were brandishing a mighty sword.

"To war, my brother!"

Henry was sitting up in bed, hugging his knees with a heart-wrenching look of horror. I rushed to console him, but as I did, I noticed our room. Clothes were strewn about in every corner; pillows were on the floor; chairs were tipped over. I looked at the wall and saw the vent cover lying on the ground, surrounded by screws. My single boot was on its side right next to the contraband butter knife.

No . . . this can't be happening.

I rose slowly and walked over to the vent. My foot slipped on a piece of fabric. I looked down and saw the bundle of rags beneath me. I hesitated in front of the vent. I think I already knew what had happened, but I wasn't ready to face it. When I finally crouched down to look inside, I saw that the book was gone. I rushed back over to Henry.

"Where is it?"

He looked up at me, stunned. I didn't even recognize my own voice as I yelled again.

"Where is it?"

Henry refused to answer me and made a run for it. By the time Mrs. Grisham had come in to see what was going on, Henry was sprinting in circles around the room. It was his only defense. I chased him like a wild animal.

"Where is my book?!"

As I ran, I noticed Mrs. Grisham looked unusually tense. She inspected the corners of the room the way a guard might in a high-security prison. I grabbed Henry by the back of his shirt.

Henry spoke as he gasped for air. "Please. I didn't wanna do it. It was me or the book."

That didn't make sense.

"You're lying!"

"Of course he is," Mrs. Grisham calmly interjected. "He's a kid. But you're not, so you know better than to lie."

The comment felt like a slap on my face.

"What are you talking about? He took my book. I need it back."

"Lying again," Mrs. Grisham said. "That wasn't your book, Ember. We just found it yesterday. Right?"

Henry gave me a look to let me know I wasn't the only one baffled.

What is she talking about?

Mrs. Grisham knew that book and Henry's sword were the only possessions we'd arrived with. There had been an all-out brawl when she had tried to confiscate and dispose of my book all those years ago. For some reason, she'd relented and let me keep it after all, as long as I followed all her rules about when I could read it and when I couldn't, and how it had to be hidden during the day.

But this behavior was a whole other level. Now Mrs. Grisham was just acting insane.

"The nice Agents came to pick it up today," she continued. "I told them you and Henry hadn't read it, because you haven't."

"But you know that I read it. I mean, you were just telling me this morning—"

"No more lies!" Mrs. Grisham boomed. "I told them the truth."

"What 'truth'?"

"How Henry found a book beneath some dirt at the Astra Avenue Park yesterday on one of our outings. He brought it straight to me without even opening it. He's such a good boy. Eager to please. Well ..."

I noticed her wringing her hands together and darting her eyes around the room.

"And of course, since he can't *really* read anyway, it wouldn't have mattered if he did open it. But he didn't. Because he's such a good boy. As soon as he brought it to me, we came straight back so I could call the Agents and let them know. But, as you know, Henry got sick last night and spent the evening throwing up. In the kitchen, the bathroom, right where you're standing."

"No, he didn't—"

Mrs. Grisham interrupted me with a loud, strange giggle. I wondered if I was having a dream.

"That's why I waited until today to tell the Agents. And—*poof*—there they were, showing up just like angels."

"I was sick?" Henry asked, looking almost convinced.

I knew better.

"What happened? Where is my book?"

Mrs. Grisham just dug herself further into the fake story. The more she repeated it, the more she seemed to believe it. When I finally gave up asking her about it, Mrs. Grisham seemed revived—glowing, even. She all but danced out of the room.

Maybe she has gone insane.

After a long silence Henry whispered to me. "I didn't want to. You have to believe me. She said they were going to take me or the book."

I ignored him, shuffled over to the far side of the room, and flipped off the light switch, silently climbing into my bed. Henry handed me one of my blankets. After half an hour of muffled sniffles into his pillow, I heard his breath slow into a steady pace. He had fallen asleep. I knew I wasn't going to be so lucky tonight.

The book was gone.

My parents . . .

I think I had known deep down it was only a matter of time before it was taken. But I'd hoped I would have more time with it. Just a little more.

Will I forget them now?

All I could think about was one of the last things my mother ever said to me. The words echoed in my head.

Never lose this book.

TO "THE OUTPOST"
N
W
E
S
CHERRY HARBOR
THE GROVE
THE STICKING PLACE
GUEST HOUSE

CHAPTER TWO

CHERRY HARBOR

(Sky)

"**L**ies. It's all lies."

I couldn't stop thinking of my mom's words. They had stayed in my head all day, playing on repeat, until they finally brought me to this place.

This place of lies.

It was so dark, but looking up, I saw the brightest stars I'd ever seen. I stared at the set of buildings in front of me. My legs ached, and my back was drenched with sweat. I must have walked for miles. I hadn't thought to bring a flashlight with me. I hadn't brought anything because I never thought I'd actually find anything.

But the Holdouts really do exist.

The city—you couldn't really call it a city. I noticed old doors made into shutters. The shells from broken refrigerators now covered the sides of some buildings. On one sign I saw a name: *Cherry Harbor.*

There were no lights. It was so quiet.

Where are the people?

My heart was beating faster than it ever had. I'd been warned about the Holdouts my whole life. Told they were vicious rebels. That they were merciless killers. But I'd always thought it was just a myth. I'd always doubted they were real. Just like I doubted pretty much everything now.

Lies . . . all lies.

A whistle made me stop. Someone nearby was whistling. I spun around but didn't see anything. Then I took off running.

"Who's there?" a voice called behind me.

I cursed and found a pile of metal tubes to hide behind. As I crouched down, I realized my hiding spot was a mound of AC ducts. I heard footsteps approaching.

"Little late fer a run, don't ya think?"

Wait—what?

The voice. That didn't sound like a killer. He sounded friendly—like a father.

Not that I would know what that sounds like.

"Lincoln, is that you?" the man called out, even closer now.

I bolted and headed for the trees, with the footsteps following me. Trees. So many trees. I tripped over a branch but caught my fall. It was dark, but I could see enough to weave through the forest. The guy kept following me, though, calling out random names like he thought one of them could be mine. I couldn't let him catch me—who knew what he would do? He was a Holdout, a monster. They all were. I needed to get away, to get far away from this—

Something struck me in the head. A rock? A weapon? A human fist? I stumbled but kept running. Something dripped into my mouth. It had a metallic taste. When I pressed both hands on my forehead, they became quickly soaked in blood.

I broke out into the open on some sort of path. Road. Whatever. I didn't care. I was feeling dizzy, my eyes blurry. I gasped for air. I clasped my head—my pounding head—and as I did, I heard more footsteps.

They're going to capture me. They're going to kill me.

I wanted to run faster, but my knees buckled, and I crumpled to the ground. Some figure, massive and muscular, suddenly towered over me.

Then I blacked out.

My throbbing head woke me up. It felt like someone was continually shooting a SpotStop puck against my forehead. When I opened my eyes, it took me a moment to see everything clearly. The room was spinning, or maybe *I* was spinning. I touched my head and found a bandage wrapped around it. I rubbed my eyes and looked around me. Everything slowly came into focus.

What is this place?

On all four sides of the room, books lined the walls. Stacks and stacks of old books on wooden shelves. It was a big room, but no one was in it except me. Metal boxes sat on the floor, some open, some sealed. There was a collection of pill bottles near my head. I looked down and noticed the shirt I was wearing, and it wasn't mine. I knew I hadn't come here wearing a short-sleeved button-up with electric orange flowers.

This has got to be a dream. A really weird dream.

I tried shaking awake, but that only made the throbbing in my head worse. I examined the room, the tattered books, but everything started to get hazy again. The dizziness was pulling me down. I tried to fight it, tried to focus again. Then I noticed a crossed pair of rowing oars mounted above the door, with something etched on one of them. I squinted to read the inscription:

Laid plainly before their eyes in their mother tongue. Or else whatever Truth is taught to them, these enemies of all Truth quench it again.

As I read those words, it felt like a bucket of water had been dumped on my head.

A memory flashed before my eyes. I was a kid sneaking into an underground hideout. There were words written on all the walls, including those same words I was reading on these oars.

I snapped back to the present. I tried to piece together where I was, and why. I had run away from Oasis, that much I knew. And I was looking for . . . what, exactly?

Had I come looking for those words?

The memory flashed again. My mom was yelling at me, telling me I shouldn't have come to the hideout. That I should have never read those words on the walls.

Lies ... all lies.

It had felt necessary to leave Oasis and search for this place. Necessary enough to risk everything. But lying there, my head pounding, seeing the words I thought I'd come for, I wasn't sure it was worth it.

They must have attacked me. Clubbed me down and captured me. That has to be it. They are monsters. Did I really risk everything just to get offed by a bunch of savage Holdouts?

I sat up, feeling woozy again. I knew I had to find a weapon or something. I had to get out of here. In the corner there was something that looked like a spear. Holdouts fought with spears, like barbarians—that's what I'd been taught, anyway. I stood up, but my dizziness forced me right back down again. I tried again and made it to my feet, then walked across the room. When I picked up the spear, I realized it was just a table leg that somehow resembled the weapon I was looking for.

The ground moved, and the room spun again. I leaned against the wall, then heard a noise. I went over to the door and pressed my ear against it. Someone was yelling. There was laughing and gasping. I heard another cry.

They're torturing someone.

There was a loud thud that sounded like a body clunking up against the door.

They shot him. They killed him.

In an instant, everything seemed as if it were moving in slow motion. I saw the doors swinging open. This was it. They were going to kill me too, now. I had to do something. I had to fight! As I lifted the "spear," feeling heavier every second, the doors opened wider. I was so young—too young to die—but that didn't matter. I charged ahead with the fake weapon drawn in front me.

"Everyone back. Get back!"

I was standing on a front porch. That's where the open doors had led. To a group of—*surely, I'm dreaming*—kids. A circle of kids sitting on the grass in front of me, laughing and pointing at me.

Who—what is happening?

"That was a good one, Mr. A," said a guy who sounded about my age. "That even surprised *me*."

I waved my weapon in the air and yelled at them. "Everyone faces on the ground now. Do it now!"

The youngest kids—maybe twelve years old—looked a little scared. One little girl ducked her head under her arm. As if it couldn't have gotten any weirder, I looked around and spotted a man with a shoe on his head, holding the door open. He had a red-and-blue blanket draped across his shoulders and a sword made of clothes hangers. He didn't look afraid of me at all. Ridiculous, but not afraid.

Other kids stood up from where they had been sitting on the grass. Nothing made sense.

I had to get out of there.

"Step back," I told them. "I'm warning you."

The guys my age stood up, looking ready for a fight. There was no way I could take all of them. But there was also no way I could let them take me captive. I heard applause. The man with a shoe on his head approached me. He had a big grin, a huge grin.

"Well done. Bravo! You played your part well. Now let me see my spear."

I tried to spin around to face him and make him back off, but he moved too quickly. Before I could breathe again, I was put in a chokehold. I dropped my weapon and suddenly couldn't breathe. The man leaned in and whispered into my ear.

"In a moment I will let you out. You'll take a bow with me, preferably with a nice smile, and we'll go inside and talk."

I tried to shake his hold from me, but it was hopeless. He was way too strong. Way too strong for a man with a shoe on his head. I choked and nodded so he would release me from his hold. Then he spun me around for a bow. The younger kids applauded like this was some sort of weird play. The older teenagers sat back down. The man signaled to someone in the crowd.

"Rosa, will you take over for a moment? You know this story like the back of your hand."

A young woman stepped forward and started talking about some story that didn't make sense. I didn't pay attention to it. All I could do was stare at her as she brushed a hand through her lush, curly hair. She seemed nervous to stand next to me.

She's beautiful.

"Um … as you can see, there was lots of fighting," she said. "I mean— never like that, but anyway. Uh … may I start over, Mr. A?"

I realized it was "Mr. A" who was pushing me inside.

"Yes, of course you can," he told the beautiful girl. "Here, use my goggles."

"It was an amphibious invasion, which surprisingly has nothing to do with frogs. They had to storm the beaches—"

Her voice trailed off as "Mr. A" led me back inside and shut the door. Just as it closed, I broke free of his grip and took a deep gulp of air, ready to fight him. Ready to be hit by him if I had to be. I tried to look as dangerous as I could.

He seemed unimpressed, like nothing violent was happening. He only turned and walked to a bench on the other side of the room. "If you want to hit me, now's your chance."

I didn't move. I didn't want to hit him. Not really.

He let out a deep sigh and sat down on the bench. He removed the shoe, followed by what turned out to be a curly wig made of who knows what.

Why is he wearing a wig?

Then he reached into a jewelry box on his right and pulled out a few trinkets. One of them was an old coin. He used his wig to polish the pieces.

"What is your name?" he asked.

I'm not telling you anything.

After a moment, he grinned at me again. "Oh. The quiet game, I see. I know it well. I warn you: I always win."

Sure enough, we just stood there in silence, doing nothing. He seemed perfectly content shining each trinket with his wig. I stood and watched him until I couldn't take it anymore.

"I don't like you."

He chuckled. "Well, you're not very charming yourself. But my name is Mr. Amos. Do you have a name?"

I glanced over at the door. I wondered what he would do if I just took off.

"You were talking about William Tyndale in your sleep last night."

"You're lying," I said.

"'Laid plainly before their eyes in their mother tongue' ring a bell? You said that last night, or something that sounded like it. That's Tyndale."

I felt my stomach drop but said nothing.

"Suit yourself," he said. "But it's a True story, one of the most inspiring in the world. He was killed for translating a book. He never got to finish. Luckily, someone else did. It was a pretty big seller, I might add."

No. I don't believe it. Not that story. Not that man.

"Lies...all lies. I know about your kind. You lie to control other people's minds. You Holdouts are like witches or something."

He smirked at me. "You'd speak that way to a witch? That would be ill-advised, my boy. Luckily, you're wrong. I'm not a witch—only women are witches. I'm a warlock."

Mr. Amos rose from his seat, and a ghoulish cackle burst from his lips. I stumbled backward in fear, and the weirdo collapsed into his chair, chuckling.

"No, I'm just a man, like you. Except I'm better looking."

It was all I could do to stare at him. Nothing made sense. All of this must have been some wacky dream. Maybe I really *had* been hit in the head with a SpotStop puck.

"Are you going to tell me your name or not?" Mr. Amos asked.

"I'll tell you my name if you tell me that story."

The man seemed to light up when I said that. Something changed in his eyes. "Then you've come to the right place, my boy." He rushed over to a chest in the corner of the room and began to rummage around. "I know I have that hat in here . . ." He threw wigs and hand-painted masks from the trunk. "Ah! Yes. There it is." He pulled a tight black tube sock onto his head and some papier-mâché around his neck. If I hadn't been convinced he was a lying monster, I'd have laughed when he spun around to face me and began to speak in a completely different voice, a booming one.

"*You stand between the people and their God. You stand between them and knowledge. Between them and Truth itself.*"

Hold on, I thought. *What is he talking about?*

Mr. Amos changed his voice and looked at me. "I'm Tyndale right now. He's the hero."

Real or not, I was sure Tyndale didn't look like *that*.

The man changed positions, lifting his nose like he smelled something awful. I decided to sit to watch this.

"*Oh, pishposh, Tyndale. You don't understand. You want to translate the Bible and give it freely to the commoners. But the Bible is a book of complexities. We can't let just any uncouth plebeian read it. I shudder at the thought. What if they all draw different conclusions? There are very few among us who can handle free thought. Most common people need us to think for them.*"

I sat there, baffled.

"*The people must be free to choose God, or to reject him,*" Mr. Amos said in his booming Tyndale voice. "*They must read it and decide for themselves.*"

His nose went back up to the ceiling as he—I didn't know what to call it—snorted?

"*How naïve. That would uproot our whole society. Peace requires cohesion, and cohesion requires control. If we give them this book, we will never control them again. No, no. That won't do.*"

I wanted to say something, but I was truly speechless.

Mr. Amos was Tyndale again. *"No man should have to go through another to access the Truth. I will get this book to the people, and when I'm finished, the poorest, lowliest man will be more righteous than you."*

The Truth? This book?

No way.

"We will kill you first," he said with his nose up and shoulders hunched over.

Mr. Amos returned to himself. "And they did."

"They did what?"

"Tyndale had to flee his own country to continue his work, but he refused to quit. He was writing and printing and distributing the Bible as widely as he could. He finished a little over half of his translation before they sent a man to trap him—a man who was born wealthy but lost all his money gambling. The only way he could get his status back was to hunt Tyndale like an animal. He befriended Tyndale, pretending to support his work, and once he gained his trust, he betrayed him.

"For the sin of letting the common man read about his own God, Tyndale's enemies strangled him to death. Even after he was dead, they burned him at the stake. That's how much they hated him. But Tyndale didn't hate *them.* You know what his last words were? As they prepared to squeeze the life out of him, he said, 'I pray their eyes will be opened.'"

There's no way. Why would he die for a book? How could anyone care that much about anything?

That's what bothered me most about the story when I first read it on the wall in the hideout. No one would die for nothing. Was I supposed to believe he died for ... what? Paper? I heard my mother's voice in my head again.

Lies ... all lies.

After a few minutes of silence, I couldn't help asking Mr. Amos a question. "What's a Bible?"

"Hmm," Mr. Amos said. "That will be a story for later this week."

"What's a week?"

"Oh my."

I shook my head. "That story was awful."

"Everyone's a critic." Mr. Amos stripped off the tube sock. "But a deal's a deal. What's your name?"

"It's Tr—" I stopped myself. "It's Sky."

"What a good name." He tapped his finger on his head and wandered the room. "You're probably too old to join the lessons. How old are you?"

"Seventeen."

"Ah, a Last-Year. Perfect. Do you have anywhere to stay?"

"I'm not staying here."

"Of course not. This building is for the pupils to study in, and it's also my house. You'll have to get your own."

I hate this guy.

"No. I mean, I'm not staying with *you* people. I know that Holdouts are dangerous, but you, specifically, are crazy."

The man sighed and shook his head. He was doing that a lot. Then he strolled to the door and opened it. The beautiful girl was still talking to the rest of the kids.

"*You are about to embark on a great crusade,*" she said in an enchanting storytelling voice, "*toward which we have striven for many months . . .*"

I noticed every boy my age looking at her—what had Mr. Amos said her name was? Rosa?—the same way I did. What was she talking about? Who cared? She could have recited the ABCs, and I would have listened. Actually, if she'd told me to punch one of those other boys in the face, I would have. I would have seriously considered it, at least.

Mr. Amos gestured for me to join him on the porch. Finally, I was going to leave that place. Not even Rosa could make me stay. But then came a sinking feeling. Doubt.

I had come to prove the story was a lie. It obviously was, just like everyone said. Just like my mom said. So why couldn't I go?

When Rosa finished her story, Mr. Amos congratulated her and sent her back to her seat. All eyes were on me. This was the part where I was supposed to leave.

Go, you idiot. What are you just standing here for?

I looked in the direction of Mr. Amos, but it wasn't him I saw.

Tyndale.

There he was again. I could see him, I swear. It was like he was burning to death right there on the porch in front of me. Was I going crazy? Could someone who never existed make you lose your mind? I had seen him everywhere I had gone for months. He was haunting me. But how could I ever say that out loud without sounding like a lunatic? I couldn't go back yet, not until I proved he was a lie. Not until his ghost let me go.

Once again Mr. Amos gave me that stupid grin and walked over to where I was standing. He leaned in to whisper in my ear.

"If you ask nicely, you can stay in the guesthouse."

I grunted. It was the nicest response I could manage.

He stood up and faced the group. "Early dismissal today. I'll see you all back here tomorrow. Last-Years, don't leave any First-Years to walk home alone. Run along."

The group scattered, and Mr. Amos led me down the porch steps and across the yard to a tiny wooden building. He smiled at me as he thrust his shoulder against a large wooden door. The old door didn't budge. I watched him back up and get a running start, then slam his full body weight against it. This time the door swung open.

"There we go," Mr. Amos said. "Home, sweet home. No electricity in here. We haven't managed to run it through the grove quite yet. You know how to light a match?"

I had no idea what he was talking about, so I acted like the question was so dumb it was offensive. I leaned forward to look inside.

To call it a dingy shack would have been a compliment. It looked more like a garbage dump. As I shuffled in, I had to step over cardboard boxes and wooden chests. A glass display I slid by appeared to be full of trash.

Mr. Amos noticed my reaction.

"Be careful your face doesn't get stuck that way, my boy. Don't worry; this is my storage room. Your room's back here."

The man pushed open a double door, and the whole building was flooded with light. As I stepped inside behind Mr. Amos, the floorboards creaked underneath me. The back wall of the bedroom was lined with glazed glass windows. In the corner, flowers and plants were hanging from the ceiling. Instead of smelling dust and rot, I was surprised to catch a whiff of mint. A little lemon too. I spotted a bed, inches off the ground, on a low wooden frame with a blanket folded neatly under the pillow.

This actually looks ... peaceful.

Mr. Amos turned to leave the room. "I'll let you get settled. They'll be back in the morning around eight o'clock."

"They?"

"Your fellow pupils, of course. It's a Two Tales Day. I have to go prepare my costumes. Oh, and I'd open a window if I were you. It can get pretty toasty in here."

As the door closed, I took one long look around the room and then collapsed onto the bed.

I sighed.

What am I doing here?

Then there was Tyndale, in my imagination, burning to death, smiling, holding a book. I could almost feel the heat of the flames. He was reaching his hand out ...

"Just leave me alone."

CHAPTER THREE

T.R.U.E.

(Ember)

Over half a cycle had passed since the book was taken. Everything at our unit at 1607 Hatcher Avenue still looked the same. The Fibonacci arrived on time. Nourishment deliveries came every morning, as always. But nothing felt the same.

I wished I felt angry; I was used to that. But instead, I felt empty—like there was a gaping hole in the middle of me and everything from the outside world passed through without my even noticing. I wasn't sure what the feeling was, really. I also didn't know exactly how to deal with it, and that eventually made me angry, which was comforting because, like I said, anger was a feeling I understood. Another part of me kept wondering when T-Force Agents would knock on our door and demand to talk to me. I imagined them dragging me to Sleep Camp. I hardly put up a fight, not even in my own imagination.

I had barely said a word to Mrs. Grisham or Henry, not even to tease either of them. Sometimes I walked up and down Hatcher Avenue to avoid going inside the unit, trying to remember the stories in my book and growing more frustrated at the ones I was forgetting. Then I would return to the unit and go straight to bed, popping a meal replacement pill on my way. I didn't play with Henry, and I didn't get on the Fibonacci. The time I used to spend reading my book was now spent staring at the ceiling.

I can't believe I lost the book. I failed my parents.

On Day Three, I woke up in a dark mood. When I rolled over on my bunk, Henry was standing there holding out a cricket cookie he had wrapped in toilet paper—an offering of one of his most prized possessions.

Classic Henry.

Even if I tried to explain everything to him, he wouldn't understand. He was only seven—he didn't remember the night they'd taken our parents, the night when I'd clutched him and the book in my arms, promising I'd never let anybody take either of them.

I walked past him without taking the cookie.

Mrs. Grisham made an attempt to talk in the kitchen, but I ignored her.

"Do you want any eggs?"

I shook my head.

She stared at me, peeved. "Honestly, could you just let it go?" She was clearly talking about my book. It was the first time she had mentioned it since the day it was taken.

I glared at her.

After a few moments of silence, she leaned over and whispered almost inaudibly into my ear. "I didn't have a choice, you know? The Agents just showed up out of nowhere, asking about the book. I didn't tell them. Why would I risk my neck like that? I'm not crazy. A few dreams, and then the T-Force show up like they . . ." Her voice faded away for a second before she launched back into her excuses with even more gusto. "They threatened me! They told me that I had to give it to them, that it was either the book or Henry. They were carrying the Teal Lady on them. They could have injected Henry—*or me.*"

Something about her mentioning the book set me off. I didn't need to be reminded about the Agents taking it, but to hear Mrs. Grisham acknowledge that she had given it away made me want to give her the silent treatment until she died.

As I scanned the kitchen, refusing to look at her, I saw the fancy indoor rocking chair. With its wine-colored wood stain and plush baby blue cushions, it was the nicest piece of furniture in the unit. There was an unspoken rule that no one was allowed to sit on it, not even Mrs. Grisham. A few years ago, Henry had snuck onto it to get a few good rocks in while Mrs. Grisham was getting dressed. When she came back and saw him, she burst into tears and didn't leave her room for the rest of the day, not even to make dinner. Henry hadn't gone near it since.

"What did you want me to do? Give them Henry?" Mrs. Grisham said, a little louder now. "Don't you care about your brother? Or *me*?"

Walking past Mrs. Grisham, I went over and sat on the chair, feeling the comfortable cushions underneath me. Then I began to rock back and forth, and as I did, I glared at the woman. This time she didn't start crying, but I could see her pinched little lips trembling in fury.

By the time we left the unit, Mrs. Grisham's "adults-only" meal replacement pill had set in, and I could tell she was feeling much better. I was the first to step out of the door and couldn't help noticing the row of identical units looked particularly lackluster on that perfectly glorious day. I spotted a lost squirrel who had somehow found his way over the great curved walls that surrounded the city.

You're trapped now, buddy. Just like me. Just like all of us. Trapped forever.

Behind me, Mrs. Grisham began to frantically babble about how much she loved the T-Force. I was going to turn and ask her what she was talking about, but that was when I noticed a female T-force Agent with an oddly sweet face staring directly at me. Henry squealed and gripped the back of my overalls for protection.

She's here to take me away.

"Who doesn't love seeing a T-Force Agent on the job?" I heard Mrs. Grisham say. "Don't you love it, Ember? Henry? It's so nice. So inspiring! They truly are the—"

The Agent ignored Mrs. Grisham and walked right up to me, then handed me a letter without saying a word.

For a moment, I didn't know what to do. No one really knew anything about Sleep Camp or how you got taken there. Not really. But I had never heard about anyone getting a letter. An invitation to Sleep Camp? As I looked at it, I noticed writing on the front. *To Ember Grisham, 1607 Hatcher Avenue, Oasis*

Grisham wasn't really my last name, but Oasis rules insisted the kids without parents adopt the last names of our caretakers. Under different circumstances, I may have said something about the way the letter was addressed. But then the Agent spoke.

"You'll need to come with me."

"Right n-n-now?" I said.

"Right now."

Holy Administrator. This is it. They're taking me. I'm going to Sleep Camp.

Henry tried to drag me backward, toward the unit. "You can't take her!"

"Henry! Henry, stop that right now! Are you crazy?" Mrs. Grisham said, grabbing for him. "There's nothing you can do."

There *was* nothing he could do. No one ever resisted a T-Force Agent. If I complied immediately, maybe I would get a shorter sentence. Maybe they would question me and let me go.

"I'm ready to go," I said. "It's fine, Henry. Don't worry. Just let me go. It's okay."

The Agent turned and walked away. She knew I would follow her, and I did. I turned to look back at Henry. He looked so devasted that I had to lie to him.

"Don't cry. I'll see you later, okay? I'll see you later."

The Interlink was bustling with people, and the Tenants had to cram together shoulder to shoulder to stay away from us. No one ever wanted to sit next to a T-Force Agent, especially not one with a Tenant in her custody. It was a silent ride, and everyone stared at me. I saw one woman shed a tear. Stop after stop, the Agent didn't move until there was only one stop left. My heart skipped a beat when we got off the Interlink and headed straight to the Building One checkpoint.

"Are we—are we going in *there*?" I asked.

Still the Agent didn't speak, but she pulled a sparkling Travel Card from her pocket and raised it to the scanner. The bars swung open.

When I stepped onto the Building One grounds, I felt grass crunch underneath my sneakers. I wanted to bend down and pet it; it was unbelievably green and soft looking. Oak trees lined the wall that separated the grounds of Building One from the Pathway Station. My eyes traveled up the eight teal-tinted stories to the symmetrical line of O-shaped windows that circled the top of the building. I imagined the Administrator poking his head out the window and waving at me.

I wish he were here.

To my utter amazement, the Agent scanned her card and the main doors of the building opened. She led us straight onto an elevator. The doors closed, and I counted the floors as they went past.

One, two, three…four! Five! Six!! Seven!!!

Seven floors! I had gone up *seven* floors. If it hadn't been the worst day of my life, it would've been the best day of my life.

When the doors opened on the seventh floor, I was consumed by the smell of fresh ocean air. I was led into a small waiting area down the hall and to the right of the elevator. Inside the room was a shiny metal door with a plaque over it that read, *A.O. of Topos, Inc.*

"The A.O….," I said under my breath. Then I remembered the letter in my pocket.

"Take a seat," the Agent said. Then she smiled.

Why is she smiling?

I sat down and pulled the letter from my pocket. What could it say?

"Enjoy your last day of consciousness. Sincerely, Topos."

"Hope you like sleeping forever. Love, the A.O."

But I had to know what it said. The Agent had slipped back down the hallway and left me alone. I pulled the letter from my pocket and opened it with shaking hands.

From the Desk of Ms. Azaz Aylo, A.O. of Topos, Inc.

I am pleased to inform you that you have been selected to serve as a Member of the T.R.U.E. (Tenants for the Reduction of Underage Extremism) Youth Task Force. You will report to office number 700, Building One, on Day Three at 11:00.

I stopped reading and looked up, lost in thought.

Today is Day Three.

I looked at the clock on the wall—11:00. I looked at the number on the door to Azaz's office—700.

My meeting is right now.

Right then, Azaz Aylo emerged from the door.

She was wearing a pastel purple top with sensible ruffles around the collar, tucked into a pair of slim gray trousers. Her long black hair was delicately tossed behind her shoulders. I couldn't help but stare at her with my mouth wide open, just like I had when we'd first met.

"Welcome, Ember."

She knows my name. She actually said my name.

"Would you step in, please?" she asked.

As I followed her, I could feel my vision narrowing. Everything around me suddenly seemed blurry, and I had to squint to keep Azaz in focus as she glided around her desk, sat gracefully, and said in her soft yet authoritative manner, "Tell me, Ember, do you like living in Oasis?"

Not at all. I've been stuck here for seven years. I'm desperate to go somewhere— anywhere else.

I gave her an enthusiastic nod.

"My position as A.O. allows me to travel anywhere I please within the city," Azaz said, "as well as to Topos, Inc. properties all over the world. But you wouldn't like that, I suppose, since you like it here."

"Oh. I would. I mean, I do like it. But I would—I would also like to see somewhere else..."

Azaz chuckled at my nervousness and continued speaking. "I didn't begin in this position. No, I had to dedicate years of service first. But I would say it was worth it, wouldn't you?"

"Yes," I said, waiting for an Agent to pop out from a hidden door and drag me away.

Azaz plucked a pastel-colored pen from a glass jar on her desk and twirled it slowly between her fingers.

"Yes, loyalty opens the door to adventure. It awards you special privileges, like the ability to travel on any day you please, even Day Fives." She winked at me. "And I've found that the Tenants reward loyalty as well. Just look at the way they praise the Administrator. Hardly a day passes without someone coming up to him and thanking him profusely for his improvement of their lives. They applaud when he steps into a room. They mourn when he leaves. Yes, they also reward loyalty. Because they know, like I do, that it's very hard to come by. Very hard. It takes someone extra special."

I wanted to look confident, but I couldn't stop fidgeting with the edges of my overalls pockets.

Azaz returned the pen to the jar. "To be loyal also takes someone brave and intelligent who possesses a mature level of discretion." She paused to look me straight in the eyes. "Can you keep a secret, Ember?"

"Yes," I said without hesitation.

That was the Truth. I hadn't told anyone about my book—at least anyone who didn't already know—for years.

Remembering my book made my stomach hurt, but I fought to avoid showing it. I could tell that as she spoke, Azaz was observing every movement I made. She was making note of every fidget, blink, and shift of my weight. At one time there was a long moment of silence where her gaze seemed to intensify. I just kept telling myself to breathe slowly and steadily.

Act natural. She may not even know about the book. And if she does, maybe she doesn't even care.

The examination ended with Azaz pointing her manicured finger toward a sleek faux leather office chair in front of her desk and saying, "Please, sit."

The chair squeaked as I sat, almost as if it were doing it on purpose.

"I have a very serious question for you," Azaz said.

Oh no . . .

"Would you say you are loyal to Oasis?"

Loyal?

My mind flashed with images of adventures in the world beyond Oasis and teary Tenants expressing their gratitude with rapturous applause.

"Yes," I replied.

"Good. I have heard many great reports about you. You're clever, brave, a bit too forceful. I was, too, at your age. I imagine there are many ways we are alike, you and I. In fact, I also lost my parents very young. No need to be surprised or concerned. I know a great deal about all our Tenants. Your parents were Julia and Adam Aaronson. You haven't seen them since you were nine. You have a brother—Henry, I believe. You're very lucky. My parents left me by myself."

I shifted in my chair, suddenly uncomfortable.

"But no matter," she said. "If they hadn't, I never would have met the Administrator. He found me here"—she pointed down at the city—"before there even was a 'here.' So you see, it was all for the best. The people who choose you—those are the people who matter."

She gently cleared her throat and continued to tell me the story of her life with the Administrator. I remained transfixed on her every word. The A.O. had lost her parents too. She was just like me.

During her story, Azaz ushered me around to her side of the desk and showed me a hand-drawn sketch of Oasis done by the Administrator. It was beautiful. Then again, everything in the office was beautiful. There was a mural of the ocean on the wall, and a delicate assortment of pastel-colored glass jars holding her bundles of multicolored pens. There was no Fibonacci in the room, which I would have assumed someone in her position would've been able to access at all times. But Azaz seemed different—like an ornate antique from the past, but also the most sleek and shiny building in Oasis.

Soon we were sitting in front of her desk with me on the floor, reviewing blueprints for future Oasis construction. They really did have plans to finally complete all the work. Who knew? I gazed at the new development plans, full of multistory buildings connected by elevated covered walkways and punctuated by a slew of new SpotStop fields. There was a massive half-dome building dedicated to the virtual world, which blended into the wall of the city, making a grassy hill for Tenants to sit on. The units seemed bigger, and the Interlink track was four stories deep instead of two.

The sketches made me want to jump into them and begin living there right away. I was absorbed by the drawing I held of a brightly colored, bird-shaped delivery drone.

"But there is great trouble in Oasis—resistance to the world we're building," Azaz said in a different tone, holding up a sketch of the renovation plans for Building One. "Shortsighted people always fear the future."

As I glanced at the woman, I noticed the shift in her demeanor. As she stood and walked back behind her desk, I returned to my chair, suddenly embarrassed to have been sitting on the floor. My body felt a chill as if the room had gotten colder. I looked up and noticed my seat was directly under an icy stream of air coming from the ceiling vent.

"There are stories being told by people your age that are disturbing your peers. Agitating them, stirring them toward revolt. And the worst is, they aren't even true. We imagine these stories stem from a few pieces of contraband, most likely from forged written 'records' in the form of books."

My heart felt like it stopped.

She knows. She's known the whole time, and this was just a trick to get me in here.

"These books, we believe, are the reason for a sudden spike in social unrest. We've had more young people carrying out impulsive acts— becoming violent, becoming nasty, even."

Azaz paused and swallowed daintily.

"This is very personal for me, this place," she pointed upwards this time, toward the Administrator's office. "This is my father's dream, and he has entrusted me with it. He's designed a world without chaos, where every person, every idea, is in its proper place, and we don't have to fend against the onslaught of human passion. Have we not had enough turmoil? Can't we let the people rest, Ember?"

I nodded.

Rest...yeah...good idea...

"Every time one of these lies spreads, it erodes our city. It's an attack on our entire way of life. The world beyond our properties...it's unspeakable."

For the first time since seeing Azaz, her cool presence seemed to crack slightly. She pressed her fingertips into the desk until they turned white.

"The Holdouts are vicious," she continued. "They hate everyone who lives here, especially those from Topos, Inc. You've heard of the Holdouts, yes?"

"Like...on the Fibonacci?"

The Holdouts were the villain in every Fibonacci game. They were always sneaking into your virtual city and lighting it on fire. You got extra points if you caught one early and turned it in.

She's talking about them as if they're real.

"These Holdouts are not safely behind the walls of the Fibonacci," Azaz replied. "It's a horrible place where they live. A place full of lies, a place full of hunger, a place full of revolt. They refuse to cut the cord of human mythology and don't realize they're clinging to nothing but pain. There is constant unrest. Nothing is stable. It's nothing like Oasis."

It seemed ridiculous to ask, but I couldn't help myself. "So—they're real?"

"Unfortunately. The stories they tell, they drive people mad. They're like poisons to the brain that stunt evolution and cripple progress. And their stories spread like a sickness. But not here. I won't let the sickness get us here, no matter how hard they try to infect us."

Thoughts moved swift as lightning through my mind. In between images of violent Holdouts and poisoned brains, I wondered if the horrible stories Azaz was talking about could be like the ones from my—

Ember! Forget about the book! But . . . she has to know it was mine. I have to do something, or this meeting ends with me being dragged to Sleep Camp.

"What do we do?" I said, jumping to my feet. "We have to stop them."

I had to prove I was loyal. That was my tactic. That was the only way I saw to survive this.

Azaz looked up at me with a smile. "That is why you're here."

Right.

I had completely forgotten what I had just read in the letter. It hadn't said anything about my book. It was about the T.R.U.E. Youth Task Force, whatever that was.

"Tenants for the Reduction of Underage Extremism," Azaz said. "You will serve as an undercover extension of the T-Force. For the time being, I will not be telling you who your fellow Members are, but know that I hand-selected every single one of you because of your extraordinary potential. You, especially."

There was something about her gentle voice that made me believe her words. That assured me of my potential— my *extraordinary* potential. Suddenly, serving on this Youth Task Force was the only thing I could think of.

"I am giving you six Tracking Tokens." She handed me six rose-gold medallions. "To activate one, you flip it three times and then press your thumb into the face on the center. Only *your* thumbprint will work. Once it's activated, a signal will be sent out to the T-Force and me with its exact location. We will handle the situation from there."

I looked at the tokens and saw an engraving of a man with the face of a panther on them—the T-Force logo.

"Don't you need my thumbprint?" I asked.

"I already have it."

I said nothing but took my seat again. I couldn't help holding the tokens away from my body, as if they were somehow poisonous.

"But what will I use them for?"

The A.O.'s voice was almost trance-inducing as she spoke. "I felt compelled to establish the T.R.U.E. because I cannot stand seeing anyone suffer, especially children. Do you understand the severity of what happens when people your age are told lies? Ember, stories that aren't true are lies. Lies bring danger, even death. They are most fatal for the innocent, the trustworthy, and the unsuspecting. These are the people most likely to suffer. Those who are wiser must protect them." Azaz rose to her feet. "*We* must protect them."

It felt like fire was being kindled in my stomach. I already wanted to make the A.O. proud, but I began to think of Henry as well. Innocent, trustworthy, and unsuspecting Henry.

What if I lose him too? I'd never forgive myself if I did.

"What do I need to do?" I rose to my feet again, ready to get to action right away.

"If you suspect that anyone is sharing, may share, or could share one of these false stories, activate the Tracking Token and slip it somewhere on them. In their pocket, or in their bag. That's all you have to do."

I nodded, wondering what would happen to someone after placing the Tracking Token on them. Before I could ask, Azaz extended her hand to me.

"Ember. The protector of the innocent."

I shook her hand and smiled.

After we said our goodbyes, I headed out the door. As I exited the grounds of Building One back into the Pathway Station, I had a feeling that people were watching me. But it didn't matter. I strode to the Interlink with an air of superiority. A well-dressed young female Envoy offered me a seat on the ride back. We rode next to each other in the respectful silence of equals.

When I was back strolling down Hatcher Avenue, my hand gripped the six Tracking Tokens in my pocket. I took my time walking. After all, it was a glorious day. I stopped on the front stoop of 1607 feeling warm from the inside out.

"Adam and Julia Aaronson," I said out loud.

My parents.

I reflected on the past cycle. Five Paths, six Tracking Tokens, and seven floors.

If they could see me now, they would be proud.

CHAPTER FOUR

TEEK

(Sky)

I must have fallen asleep because I woke to Mr. Amos standing above me, covered in white powder and wearing multiple bows placed throughout his wig. For a moment I thought I was having a terrible nightmare, but I wasn't so lucky.

Before I could protest, I was being dragged out the door of the shack I had slept in and onto the porch of the slightly larger shack next door. There was a sign on the door I hadn't noticed the day before:

The Sticking Place.
What you hold on to, sticks.

The "pupils" were seated in the exact same places as the day before. The littlest kids sat cross-legged in the front, with the prettiest of the older girls spread out among them, keeping them quiet. The older boys were gathered toward the back, leaning on the trees or standing tall with their hands in their pockets.

Mr. Amos raised his fist. *"Liberty! Equality! Fraternity!"* Then he lowered it and said with a wink, *"Or else death."*

As the pupils cheered, I looked around to see which direction provided the best escape if I suddenly bolted. Mr. Amos continued.

"Before we begin our sordid tale, I have a special guest to introduce to you." He waved me over to join him. "Come on; don't be nervous.

Pupils, this is Sky. He will be joining us from now on. Sky, welcome to the Sticking Place." He made a grand sweeping motion as if he were unveiling a skyscraper instead of an ugly wooden cabin surrounded by patches of uneven grass.

The younger kids looked confused, the older ones looked defensive, and no one looked happy. A few of them whispered to one another. One of the kids in the front who had been scribbling away in a notebook raised his hand.

"Mr. Amos, pupils begin studying at the Sticking Place at twelve. He looks much older than that. Which group will he join?"

The boy speaking was like a full-grown man trapped in the body of a scrawny child. His short-sleeve checkered dress shirt was tucked perfectly into jeans. His dark brown eyes looked like they belonged to someone old and wise, but his spaghetti arms gave away that he was just a dorky kid waiting to get punched.

I glared at him, but he avoided looking my way.

Mr. Amos replied, "He's seventeen. But since he's new, he'll be joining the First-Years."

Wait, what?

Everyone started squirming in their seats, but most especially the little dork who had asked about my age. Once again, his hand shot up.

"Mr. Amos, given that he's the wrong age, I don't think it's right for him to join the First-Years or the Last-Years."

Well, I don't think it's right that you're a twerp.

"What do you suggest, Lincoln?" Mr. Amos asked him.

"Well, uh...," the boy named Lincoln said, appearing to think it over. "I don't think he can join us at all. Not without breaking the rules."

All the pupils began to talk, some agreeing and others disagreeing with Lincoln. I could see the fear in the boy's eyes as he struggled to keep eye contact with Mr. Amos. I wanted to tell him off, but Mr. Amos was right next to me, and I hadn't forgotten the chokehold from the day before.

Mr. Amos addressed the group. "I have talked with the leaders of Cherry Harbor, and we've agreed this is a very unique situation. We've never had a young guest before, and we want to make sure he has the same opportunities as every other pupil."

"But—" Lincoln said in protest.

"That's our decision." Mr. Amos said, cutting him off.

First-Years and Last-Years... Sticking Place... I had no clue what they were talking about. But the very fact that some little twerp was suggesting that I shouldn't be there only made me *want* to stay.

I can break rules. I'm very good at breaking them.

After I took my seat, Mr. Amos began acting out the character of some girly dude he called a "Frenchman," dancing around the porch and singing about "brotherhood" and "guillotines." I didn't really listen to much of what he said. Instead, I kept thinking of the boy who wanted me gone. I could feel the glares of the rest of the students on the back of my head. I felt stupid being there, listening to Mr. Amos talk about something called the "French Revolution."

I planned to have a little chat with Lincoln as soon as I could.

After Mr. Amos finally finished his story, he announced a fifteen-minute snack break so he could change costumes and the pupils could "have a little munch" on pecans. I casually walked over to the scrawny kid, who was sitting by himself.

"Can I talk to you?" I asked.

Lincoln nodded. He scrambled to his feet, and I led him around to the back of the Sticking Place, out of sight of the other pupils. As soon as no one could see, I shoved him against the wall. Then I leaned down so my eyes could meet his.

"Listen, you stupid teek! If you do that again, I'm going to shove your face into the ground until you cry. You got it?"

He gave me a look of horror, and I knew why.

"What, never been called a teek before? Well, get used to it. Because you are one."

I pushed him into the wall one more time; then I stepped away, pretending to zip my lips. I walked off and fought the urge to look back and see if he was crying.

It was Two Tales Day—or whatever Mr. Amos called it—which just meant I had to spend more of my life watching Mr. Amos dance around the front porch while I was being eaten alive by mosquitoes. Beautiful Rosa was already sitting on the grass in front of the porch. She was braiding her thick, soft hair. Another guy, the tallest and strongest guy there, was across the lawn, gawking at her. I could tell he was waiting to make a move. But she wasn't looking at him.

Is she looking at me?

She got up and walked in my direction. She was coming straight toward me.

Get wrecked, big guy. She's coming for me.

She was just a few feet away. What was she going to say? What was *I* going to say?

She tossed her braided hair behind her shoulders and opened her lips.

"Lincoln?"

Lincoln?

She walked right past me.

"Rosa?" Lincoln squeaked back.

"Where are you, Lincoln? We're about to start again."

"Oh. I'm coming."

I could hear him wiping his little nose. He was going to tell her I called him a teek; I just knew he was. I made sure I was standing right behind Rosa. He noticed me as he turned the corner to find her.

"Are you okay?" she asked him, kneeling down to his level.

I looked him straight in the eyes and slowly nodded my head.

So help me, kid, if you blow this for me . . .

Lincoln opened his mouth to speak, "The new—"

"It was the war that covered the whole world!" Mr. Amos proclaimed, cutting Lincoln off.

"Oh, he's starting." Rosa grabbed Lincoln by the hand. "We'll talk after, okay? You don't want to miss this one. Come on. We can sit together."

The two came jogging past me.

"Come on, Sky," Rosa said. "It's starting."

I followed behind them. Most of the spots on the grass in front of the porch were already filled. Rosa brought Lincoln to the front row and sat down. Then she gestured to me.

"There's a spot here, Sky."

What was I supposed to do? Not sit with her? No way. I went straight to the front row. There was a little girl on her right, Lincoln on her left, and an open space next to him.

"Move," I said to Lincoln under my breath.

He didn't hear me, or at least pretended not to.

"Sit." Rosa smiled and pointed to the seat next to Lincoln.

I could hear the kid gulp when I sat down next to him. He pulled out his little notebook and pencil from his back pocket. His hand was shaking as he started to take notes.

"Listen carefully, my pupils. This tale takes place across an ocean. There was a man who was really a beast. An evil force that took the shape of a tiny, ugly little man named Hitler," Mr. Amos said.

He was leaning over the front porch railing, wearing a dusty trench coat. He hadn't managed to scrub all the white powder off his face during the break.

"Hitler was consumed by hate. That's what you need to know about him. He hated God; he hated humanity; he even hated himself. But he channeled that hate onto one group of people—the Jews."

Lincoln was writing so fast.

What in the world is he writing?

"Hitler wanted them all dead. Every single one. We couldn't have that, could we?"

"No!" the pupils chanted in unison.

"Of course not! We needed someone who could stop him. Someone who could infiltrate his inner circle—a spy. This spy had to meet multiple qualifications. He had to be smart, brave, and speak multiple languages. He had to be an effective communicator, someone clever who could think on his feet. There was only one man for the job."

"One man for the job," Lincoln mumbled under his breath as he wrote. He was writing everything, word for word.

Next it was Rosa who spoke under her breath. She said the name at the exact same time as Mr. Amos.

"Wallenberg."

Mr. Amos came and sat on the middle of the porch with his hands clasped in front of him. "Wallenberg went to Hitler's territory as a diplomat. But he wasn't really there for diplomacy. No, he was on a secret mission to rescue as many Jews as he could. And at times, he had to lie to do that."

Lincoln stopped writing suddenly. I saw his hand go up. "Did you say 'lie'?"

"I did," Mr. Amos replied.

"He was a bad guy, then?"

"No, a good guy. A hero."

"But heroes don't lie."

"Just keep listening, Lincoln. I'll explain."

"But—"

"He said *wait*," I said.

What's wrong with this kid? Does he want this to go on forever?

The scribbling in his notebook started again, and Mr. Amos picked up where he'd left off.

"Wallenberg was deployed to a nation that was in the business of loading all their Jewish citizens onto trains and shipping them to their deaths at the hands of Hitler. This didn't sit well with Wallenberg, so he created protection passes which said anyone in possession of the pass was a citizen of a different country—a better country that doesn't want to have all their Jews shipped away. This pass would save their lives. Of course, not everyone holding the pass was, in fact, a citizen of a better country."

Lincoln's hand shot up again.

"Yes, Lincoln?"

"So, Wallenberg lied?"

"Yes."

"That's not right, then. That's not the right thing to do."

I heard Rosa chuckle quietly to herself.

"That is an interesting point, Lincoln. Let's take it to the group. Is lying wrong?"

Everyone said yes so fast, it made my skin crawl.

"Is saving lives right?"

Again, a collective yes.

"Now, here's the kicker: Is lying to save lives right?"

Finally, it got interesting. Everyone was yelling. It was hard to make out what everyone was saying, but they seemed to be split right down the middle.

I personally didn't care what the answer was. It seemed like a dumb question. But it was nice to see the perfect pupils live a little.

Mr. Amos didn't seem eager to get control of the group. Honestly, he looked like he was enjoying it as much as I was.

"What's the answer, Mr. Amos?" Lincoln's voice cut out over the crowd.

Mr. Amos tapped his head. "The answer. Hmm."

Even I wanted to know the answer at this point. I hoped it was the opposite of whatever Lincoln wanted it to be. That kid really got under my skin.

"The answer is that sometimes in life, the bad things are all mixed up with the good things, and it's very hard to separate them out. But we must try. Wallenberg wasn't lying for his own gain; he was lying to save lives. Heaven knows that's different, and heaven knows why. That's where I would direct this question if I were you."

Lincoln's face looked like a Fibonacci with a bad glitch. He hated that answer, so I loved it. I was the first to start what became a round of applause. But I had to stop clapping when Mr. Amos sprang to his feet and did a little girly twirl before saying in a deep voice, "Tomorrow: *Enigma: the greatest code ever cracked.*"

Another applause. I didn't start or join that one.

When everyone began to leave, I tried to talk to Rosa, but she took off with several other girls, walking down a dirt path that led through a grove of huge trees. It was a strange sight. There weren't that many large batches of old trees, at least not anywhere around Oasis. The grove was set on top of a short, red cliff overlooking a lake. I had never seen that much open water before. I have to say, I kind of liked it. I enjoyed a few minutes of watching the water and thinking about nothing before heading back to my cabin. As I walked back, I noticed the little teek on the porch of the Sticking Place, talking to Mr. Amos. I assumed he was telling him about me, about what had happened. But I didn't care. What was the old man going to do to me? Send me back to Oasis?

I walked back to my shack and headed to my room. I tried to convince myself that I had all the proof I needed that these stories were bogus. Everything in this place sounded made-up. *Sticking Place. Cherry Harbor.* No serious people would use those names. This whole place was just some kind of weird fantasyland where, sure, the people seemed happy, but they were still crazy. And crazy is just one step away from dangerous, so, basically everything I was told about these people was true. The Holdouts' whole existence was based on lies. All lies. Still, I couldn't help thinking about the story Mr. Amos had told.

Or more like made up.

There was one part of the Wallenberg story that made sense to me: he was a spy.

I could be a spy.

I told myself that was why I was sticking around, to spy. Not because of some made-up guy dying for a book. Not because I couldn't stop dreaming about the moment he died.

I was looking through all the old books in my room when I heard the front door open. Soon I heard someone knocking on and opening the door to my room.

"I need to talk to you," Mr. Amos said.

He looked so serious compared to how he had appeared around all the pupils. He looked bigger too. I noticed his arms for the first time. They were huge.

"I heard what happened with Lincoln today."

I rolled my eyes. "I barely touched him."

"He's very excited to finally be in the Sticking Place. This is his first year," Mr. Amos said, his expression still serious.

"Good for him."

"He's *twelve*."

"He's a brat."

Mr. Amos came closer to me. I tried not to look afraid.

"A seventeen-year-old shouldn't be bullying someone who is twelve. Seems a bit unfair, doesn't it?"

Now he really towered over me. I had to lean back to look at him.

"One other thing, Sky. What you said to him today, you should never say that again."

"Oh? And what did I say?"

Mr. Amos shot me a testy look.

Oh, that.

"You mean *teek*?"

Mr. Amos leaned over and faced me, eye to eye and nose to nose. A lot like I'd done with Lincoln. I stumbled into the wall.

"*Never* say it again."

Something seemed to burn in his eyes. I wanted to sink into the ground.

He turned and walked away.

Maybe I'll be leaving this place sooner than I thought.

A short while after our nice chat, I watched Mr. Amos take the trail through the woods that Rosa and her friends had taken, and a few moments later I decided to do the same. The sun was starting to disappear, but I could still make out where to go.

As I wound my way through the trees, I contemplated taking off. Just going back to Oasis, or even somewhere else. But there was something about this place. It was so simple. But it was also something more.

Surprising.

I'd always heard the Holdouts were most cruel to children. But all the kids I met looked fine. Actually, they looked better than fine. They looked happy.

The buildings of Cherry Harbor didn't seem to follow any kind of pattern, with shacks spread out randomly, connected by narrow dirt streets. I followed one dirt path until I came to a building that seemed to be in the front and center of the town. *The Building One of Cherry Harbor*, I thought. It was another mismatched hut with a sign staked into the dirt out front that read, "Town Meeting: 6:00 p.m."

I peeked in and saw a bunch of people sitting around a long wooden table in the middle of the room. Men and women of all ages. I didn't see any of the pupils or anyone I recognized. They were arguing. I ducked back down so I could listen to their conversation.

"*¡Ay, Dios mío!*" a woman yelled. "We put our own children at risk. For what?"

At risk? What risk?

"We all know the trouble that can come from this," a man said.

I wondered what they might be talking about. A food shortage? An illness? Maybe another war?

An older man spoke. "We don't know this youth is a risk. We must treat the sojourner like a native."

Wait—what? Are they talking about—

"He called Lincoln a 'stupid teek'!" a younger woman snapped. "He's not a sojourner. He's a snake in the garden."

"He can't stay!" the first woman I'd heard thundered again.

I knew exactly what they were talking about.

Or, rather, *who* they were talking about.

The older man spoke again. "Where will he go?"

"Back where he came from," the younger woman said.

"Where he will only learn to hate us more," I heard another voice mumble.

For the next twenty minutes, I heard all sorts of people talking and arguing—about me. It felt strange. Alarming. But also, kind of funny.

Me? They were worried about me?

A few times I had to let out a quiet chuckle at something they said. Soon the disagreement became unbearable as everyone kept trying to talk over each other until the sound of iron pans banging together made everyone silent.

"You're harboring a spy," the younger woman said. "Oasis is a day's walk from here. Your new guest is *clearly* one of *them.* He's probably *working* with them."

Mr. Amos must be in the room.

"Anna, that's enough," a man said.

I made a mental note to definitely avoid a lady named Anna.

"She's right! You let a spy into our home!"

"Please, Mrs. Hernandez."

Another mental note to avoid Mrs. Hernandez.

"Since the founding of this town, we have always had an understanding with the people in Oasis. They assured us they would leave us alone."

"Well, obviously they've changed their minds," the woman named Anna said. "They aren't leaving anyone alone anymore, and now they've sent someone to stake us out."

The arguing continued until I heard the voice I had heard all day speak. "I know the boy is from Oasis," Mr. Amos said.

The crowd erupted again, but Mr. Amos yelled over them.

"But I don't believe he's a spy."

Is he defending me?

"Then what *is* he?" Anna asked.

I heard something slide across the floor, so I peeked in again to see Mr. Amos walking toward all the people at the table.

"A runaway."

"I don't want to send the boy back, Amos, but things just aren't like they used to be. Topos is expanding all over the country; soon there won't be any Holdout territories," a woman said. "Oasis is their capital city; agreement or no agreement, they won't leave us alone much longer."

Anna spoke again. "I know not everyone supports our work with the Oarsmen—"

"There are no Oarsmen," Mrs. Hernandez said.

Oarsmen?

"Like I said," Anna continued, raising her voice. "Whether you support us or not, they see us all as the same. Open your eyes, people. Topos never intended to leave the Holdout territories alone. They lied. They know the Holdouts will be the people who finish the work the Oarsmen started, so they want to snuff us out. I'm getting word about new Oarsmen outposts all over the country that are just forming and already have members disappearing. We're lucky they haven't found our outpost yet, but that didn't stop them from attacking one of us on the path to Oasis. They won't stop until we all pledge allegiance to the Administrator. Whether you like it or not, they're coming for all of us."

For once everybody in the room fell silent.

"They may come," Mr. Amos said. "They may be on their way now. It's only a matter of time before they start taking Holdout territories all over the country by force. There are more of them than us, and they take in more every day. So, we have options. We can wall ourselves off from everyone and wait to be sieged. Or we can grow our numbers—starting with this young man."

More discussion. Lots of people asked the same sort of question: "What if it doesn't work?"

Mr. Amos was blunt in his answer.

"Then he'll turn us all in, and Cherry Harbor will be destroyed. Or it *will* work, and we'll learn how to teach the Truth to people who have never heard it before. And then we'll do it again and again and again and again, until *we* outnumber *them*."

"You're talking about revolution?" a man asked.

"No," Mr. Amos said. "I'm talking about restoration."

CHAPTER FIVE
PROTECTOR OF THE INNOCENT
(Ember)

Lily Smogg caught my attention. I was doing my usual beat at Astra Park when I caught her mindlessly writing something in the dirt with a stick: *Mr. Gorbachev.*

A lightbulb went off in my head.

I know that name. I read it in my book.

I would never have suspected Lily Smogg. She lived just a few units down, and Henry was friends with her brother. I'd played with her growing up. But there she was, a threat, an agent of chaos. What choice did I have? Typically, I liked to small talk my suspects before slipping a Tracking Token on them, to give me time to decide where to plant the Token without getting caught. But it was so obvious with Lily. She was wearing a chunky headband that only barely tamed her frizzy hair. I could slip the token into her headband without her even noticing, so that's what I did. I flipped the Tracking Token three times, pressed my thumb on the panther-man's face, and presto. It worked like a charm.

This was my fourth catch so far.

My second and probably most victorious catch was when I'd heard a new boy at the Oasis Academy orientation openly admit he was sketching a comic book series based on a story his parents had told him about a minister who'd walked to a place called "Selma." The first and third had been less victorious, but regardless, after each catch, I was invited to Azaz's office, where I told her all about who I had turned in. She always showered me with warm praise. That afternoon, after explaining I had turned in a childhood friend, Azaz appeared overjoyed.

"You have used more of your Tracking Tokens than any other Member," she told me with a spark in her eyes. "Keep this up, and I'll be promoting you to *leader* of the T.R.U.E."

Walking back to the unit, I vowed to spend every waking moment I had at the parks, the Pathway Station, or riding the Interlink, waiting for someone to mention something that they shouldn't. I would even keep an eye on the virtual worlds on the Fibonacci, although those were so highly monitored, I doubted anyone would say anything there.

I had two Tracking Tokens left. But I didn't plan on having them much longer.

A few days later I entered the unit after patrolling, and I was surprised to see all the lights were on. It was late like always. I had grown accustomed to arriving after Henry and Mrs. Grisham were asleep. I heard Henry crying in the bathroom and ran to him.

"Henry, what's wrong?"

I found him crouched on the ground next to the sink, with Mrs. Grisham holding an ice pack to his eye. There was a line of dried blood trailing down his lip, and his knees were bleeding as well.

"What... who? Who did this?" I asked Mrs. Grisham.

"Killian Smogg," she replied. She removed her wedding band and handed it to me to place on the counter before scrubbing the blood off Henry's knee. Both Henry and Mrs. Grisham were wincing as she added, "I called the medical line, and no one could see him. But I told them what happened, and they think he'll be fine."

"The medical line? The people on the medical line wouldn't care if we all died because it would mean less work for them."

Mrs. Grisham not only didn't scold me; she nodded in agreement. Her mood had changed ever since I had joined T.R.U.E. She didn't know exactly what I was doing, but she knew it had to be important since we were now getting two nourishment deliveries every day instead of only one. Ever since she had spotted me walking with the A.O. herself, she had been sickeningly agreeable.

Henry, on the other hand, was grumpy. I had to go everywhere by myself, so he could never tag along with me. By the time I got back, if he was still awake, I was too tired to play. Then I would be gone in the morning before he woke up. Even though I was basically ignoring him all the time, Henry was always sure to leave a meal replacement pill and a cell-cultured meat stick on my bed every evening for me to eat once I got back.

Sometimes after coming into our room at night, I would spend a few minutes just looking at him. It was only a year ago that he had stopped climbing into my bed when he had bad dreams. Even though I wouldn't admit it to Henry, I missed him doing that now.

I helped Mrs. Grisham clean him up and get him into his bed. After Mrs. Grisham turned off the lights and left us alone, Henry whispered, "It's all my fault."

Of course he'd say that.

I highly doubted it was his fault. Henry had a nasty habit of taking the blame for things he didn't do.

"Why were you playing so late?" I asked.

"I wasn't breaking any rules. The sun hadn't set, and Killian lives two units away. I don't have to scan to play with him."

"Well, I don't think you should play with him again."

"He doesn't want to play with me anyways. He doesn't want to play with anyone. Not since they took Lily."

Lily Smogg. They had taken Lily Smogg, and now her brother was beating up my brother. I had never felt anything like I felt in that moment. It was like embarrassment, but so much worse.

"We don't need them anyway," I said.

For a few moments, he was quiet before responding. "I guess not. But he was my friend."

I heard him trying to roll onto his side.

"Ow."

The next morning, I went straight to the Smoggs' unit. I was tempted to just walk right in—my new sparkling gold Travel Card would allow me to scan into any unit I pleased. But Azaz had made me promise to only use it in emergencies, so I rang the buzzer instead.

As fate would have it, Killian opened the door.

He was about half my age, but unlike most eight-year-old boys, he was already quite large. I only caught a quick glance inside his unit before he stepped out and slammed the door behind him. The smell of dirty diapers was forming a cloud of stench. Chairs had been turned over. Meat stick wrappers littered the floor, and there wasn't a caretaker to be seen. Killian also seemed to have a bruise on his face, but it seemed too big to have come from Henry. It was a sad sight, but I hardly noticed it.

"What do you want?" Killian said.

"You hurt my brother very badly, which is an idiotic thing for you to do. But for some reason, he still wants to be your friend, because *he's* an idiot too. But he's also nice and, clearly, you're not. But if you apologize to him, I'll let you two play together."

I paused for a moment, then moved closer to him, my eyes boring into him.

"But if it happens again, you will regret it."

I left the pale-faced kid without saying goodbye.

That night, when I arrived back at the unit, Henry was in the bathroom, bleeding again and insisting that he was fine.

"Blast it!" I shouted. "I warned him."

"He's not like this. He's just mad, and almost everyone in his unit got taken. He's just mad."

He begged me not to be angry, but I ignored him.

All night I sat in bed, plotting and spinning the fifth Tracking Token between my fingers. Killian hadn't said anything about fake stories, but surely, he knew some. I bet he was the ringleader for some kind of underground lie-peddling society. He probably wrote the lies himself; after all, his sister was involved.

I put a token on her. Now you're next.

It was probably *his* fault she was gone now. I would catch him at something. I knew I would.

The next morning, I went straight to Azaz's office, where I was given written permission to skip my Academy lessons that were beginning again that day. Instead of going to my own classes, I followed Killian Smogg everywhere he went, but I found nothing. Not one mention of anything except his incessant hunger and occasionally the new war game on the Fibonacci. I did see the little punk pummel at least three more of his friends. Oddly enough, each time it was right after they asked him about the whereabouts of his sister. I wouldn't let myself make the connection.

Since it was Day Two, almost every young boy in Oasis attended the SpotStop game at Oasis Academy. Henry and Killian were among them. Cade Carter—the best player in Oasis—was competing that night, so the stadium was packed with young people, and it was easy for me to attend without being noticed.

As I shuffled into a seat four rows behind my brother, a gaggle of older girls shoved past me, squawking about how they couldn't miss Cade's warm-up throws. I had just spotted Henry for half a second before the whole stadium stood to their feet and was overcome by a wave of girlish shrieks. Cade Carter had taken the field, along with his opponent, who was looking extremely insignificant. I could only chuckle.

He's not that big of a deal.

They both approached the great metal wave-shaped board and peeled a magnetic puck from the prearranged stack. The goal was to slide the magnetic puck up the wall of the metal wave with just the right amount of force that it would stop, facing upside down, at the end of the board. The closer you got to the edge without the puck flying off, the more points you received. Cade was evidently doing very well in his warm-up throws because the crowd was jumping up and down with enough force to rock the bleachers.

Looking between the shoulders of two older boys who were critiquing Cade's form *very* loudly to the pretty girl next to them, I caught a glimpse of Killian navigating through the crowd. Henry was waving his arms at him and smiling. Telling Killian to come over by him, that he had saved his friend a seat. A moment after Killian reached Henry, I saw the big kid grab my brother by the collar.

I burst through the boys in front of me and climbed over another gaggle of giggling girls. I reached Henry just in time to grab Killian's fist, which was winding up for the first strike.

"Stop it!" I yelled at Killian.

Suddenly, every head in the entire stadium seemed to turn to us. Even Cade Carter, who was mid-throw, turned his head to see what was happening, his puck flying off the top rim of the board and hitting his opponent in the face. As I looked down onto the field, I saw Azaz sitting in a special seat, watching me. I was surprised that she didn't look mad.

She looks proud.

As I looked back at Killian, he appeared as if he'd just woken up from a trance. With all eyes on him, his own eyes welled up with tears. His apish posture softened into that of a scared little boy.

You're not fooling me.

Before he darted away with his hands over his face, I slipped a Tracking Token into his pocket. It didn't matter that the boy had never mentioned one word about a fake story. He deserved it.

"Let's go," I told Henry as I grabbed his hand to lead him out of the stadium.

"It's all my fault," Henry said, tears filling his eyes. "I know it."

A crowd of T-Force Agents rushed past us toward Killian.

Are they going to take him right now?

Henry saw it too.

"Ember, wait! They're going for Killian. He didn't do anything. He didn't hurt me!"

I grabbed Henry by the shoulders, "Forget about him. He's a filthy, mean teek."

He flinched. "Ember..."

"Let's go."

The ride back on the Interlink was unbearable. Henry cried the entire time. I couldn't stop him. We were walking silently down Hatcher Avenue until Henry finally said, "Do you think you'll ever get your book back?"

The question felt like ice being injected into my veins.

"No." I glanced around us to make sure no one could hear us. "You shouldn't talk about it."

"Remember that story about the man holding on to the boat?"

"Henry, I told you not to—"

"I love that one," Henry continued with a sniffle. "It was that flower boat with the pilgrims. He was awesome." He smiled and his puffy, watery eyes lit up.

"I don't remember it," I said. "They were all lies anyway. No good for anyone."

"But you loved that story. Remember?"

Before I could tell him to be quiet, he was talking a mile a minute about deadly storms, broken ships, and miracles. I used to love to hear Henry tell stories, but tonight it was making me sick. I looked around us in every direction, terrified of who might be watching. Then I saw her.

Oh no.

It was worse than a nightmare.

"Henry. STOP!"

Azaz had just turned the corner and was walking down Hatcher Avenue.

"Stop?" Henry asked. "This is the best part."

"I said *stop.*"

The clicking of Azaz's heels on the pavement was getting closer, but this didn't stop Henry.

"Remember when they pulled him back onto the boat, and what's crazy is that he ended up being the great-great-great-great-great-great-great grandpa of, like, a million people—"

"HENRY!"

"Ember?" Azaz said as she approached us and stood right behind Henry.

I tried not to show my panic as I gave her my sweetest smile. "Yes, ma'am. This is my brother, Henry."

"I was just talking about—"

"Nothing," I said, interrupting Henry. "Just talking about the Fibonacci."

Azaz looked around and gestured at the door. "Isn't this your unit?"

"Um, yes. Yes, ma'am."

"Well, I just came to introduce myself to your caretaker. Is she in?"

"She's—"

I looked over to see Mrs. Grisham peeking through the front blinds.

"Uh, yes, she's in."

"Good," Azaz said. "I'll be one moment."

Henry and I waited on the front stoop while Mrs. Grisham made a complete and utter fool of herself. I had never seen her look so animated.

"Holy Administrator! Welcome. Can I get you some cricket pasta? Goodness, I haven't cleaned yet today. Oh my. I can't believe it—the A.O."

As we waited for a few moments, I felt beads of sweat on my forehead. I couldn't stop thinking about that book again. That stupid book.

Does she have it? Is she asking Mrs. Grisham about it?

When Azaz walked back out of the unit a few minutes later, she dusted herself off and gave me a curious look. It was almost an affectionate look.

"I believe that went quite well," Azaz said with a look of accomplishment.

She reminded me of our outing tomorrow, then said goodbye to Henry and me and walked briskly back down Hatcher Avenue.

"Wow ... the A.O.," Mrs. Grisham gushed, watching her leave.

"Wow," Henry repeated.

After we had walked back into the unit, Mrs. Grisham kept talking about the surprise visit.

"That A.O. is really something, isn't she?"

I just nodded and mumbled something in agreement.

"She thinks you're pretty special," Mrs. Grisham added.

"What did she want?" I asked.

Mrs. Grisham smirked. "Let's just say that between you and me, *if* you stay on her good side, I think we're both going to be pretty happy. So, I suggest you stay on her good side. Also"—she pulled a sparkling gold envelope from her robe pocket—"this is for you."

Another letter. This one with a giant letter *A* on the seal. I opened it slowly. Inside was a note that read:

Ember,

I want to personally thank you for your commitment to the T.R.U.E. Youth Task Force. I've been following your work. You have a talent for protecting the innocent. I know that if you stay the course, you will make

*a lasting impression on our wonderful City of the Future. Azaz has told
me so much about you. I look forward to meeting you soon.*

    Sincerely,

    The Administrator

    P.S. Good work this evening.

I was flabbergasted.

"The Administrator wants to meet me," I mumbled in shock.

Henry squealed. "Holy Administrator! *The* Administrator wants to
meet you?"

"He *what*?!" Mrs. Grisham screamed.

We spent that whole evening celebrating. Mrs. Grisham danced
around the kitchen, cooking cricket pasta while I read the letter aloud to
Henry over and over (skipping the P.S. section). By the time I crawled into
bed that night, I felt as if I were glowing from the inside out.

Protector of the innocent.

For the first time in a long time, I went to sleep without thinking
about the book.

CHAPTER SIX

SKY'S TUTOR

(Sky)

"Mr. Sky!"
I saw Mr. Amadi rushing across the lawn to me. I was leaning up against the wall beside the front door of the Sticking Place, surrounded by Last-Year girls.

One girl, whose name was either Mary or Shelby—I couldn't remember—whispered, "Uh-oh. Somebody must have told him about last night."

"Last night?" Lincoln said, coming out of the door of the Sticking Place and onto the porch.

Mary or Shelby said, "Yeah . . . some of us may have broken curfew a little bit and—"

"Don't tell *him*. He's a snitch." I looked down at Lincoln. "What were you doing in the Sticking Place?"

"I had a meeting with Mr. Amos. Why did you break curfew?"

The girl replied, "Sky asked us to go to the lake."

"Mary!" I said, trying to stop her.

"It's Shelby."

"Right. Sorry."

At this point, Mr. Amadi was already walking up the porch steps. He bumped his head on a hanging plant on his way up.

"Who hung that there? Mr. Sky, I have heard a bad report about you. Is it true you encouraged a group of our young ladies to break curfew and go with you to the lake last night?"

"No," I said.

"Is that true?" Mr. Amadi said, opening up the question to the group surrounding me. I could see Lincoln's mouth starting to stretch open. I knew he was about to rat me out.

"No sir, that's not True."

Ugh. I hate that kid.

Mr. Amadi crossed his arms over his dress shirt. He was always more dressed up than anyone else because he was the "mayor" of the town. I hadn't been here that long, and I had already heard him give his "My family helped found Cherry Harbor, blah blah blah" speech way too many times.

"Mr. Sky, my family helped found Cherry Harbor—"

Here we go.

"And we did so at great personal risk. The rules we have here are in place to keep us all safe. Swimming in the lake at night without telling anyone—"

"We didn't even swim," I said.

Then the girl jumped in. "Yeah, Sky can't even swim. He said—"

"Shut up, Mary."

"It's Shelby!"

I saw Rosa watching us from the lawn. She hadn't come with us last night, even though I'd asked her to. I spoke loud enough for her to hear me.

"Look, no one was going to get hurt. I'm a good protector."

"That may be true, but you're a bad influence," Mr. Amadi said. "There will be no more excursions after dark. Do you understand?"

I nodded, but I wasn't listening to him. My spy work had turned out to be way less exciting than I'd expected, and I needed some way to fill the time that wasn't just listening to Mr. Amos's endless ranting. Like hanging out at the lake with the ladies.

The doors to the Sticking Place burst open, and Mr. Amos came out of the door "riding" a "horse" made from a broom.

"Oh, hello, Mayor. Good to have you. Are you staying for today's story? Or, even better, perhaps you could tell the pupils the story of how your family founded Cherry Harbor? No better history to preserve than our own."

"Amos, you flatter me. Of course I will."

You've got to be kidding me.

Mr. Amos yelled over the crowd of pupils. "Everyone, take your seats. We have a very special lesson today."

I reluctantly took a seat at the back of the group. It was going to take a lot of my focus to drown this story out.

"You may or may not know this, but my family helped found Cherry Harbor..."

I thought Mr. Amadi's story would never end, but finally it did. Before we could leave, Mr. Amos said he had a "big announcement."

"Remember, the Cherry Games are in just over two weeks. First-Years are not required to compete, but they are welcome to join us. To participate in the competition, you must find a partner and sign up together on the sign-up sheet, which our very own Rosa Hernandez has graciously volunteered to manage for us."

I looked across the yard and smiled at Rosa. Her cheeks turned hot pink as she smiled and looked away. Mr. Amos told me I'd been here a "week," which seemed a little longer than a cycle but felt like forever. I still didn't really *like* Cherry Harbor or the Sticking Place, but every time I tried to leave, I got this weird feeling that I shouldn't. That there was something here I needed to find out. Besides, I didn't know how to go back to Oasis now. Not without a way to explain why I had left—which

I could barely explain to myself. How could I tell people I'd left because of a feeling? Because of a nightmare brought on by a made-up story? Because the word "lie" was said so much that I'd started to wonder what it really meant. I didn't want to think about any of that. It was far easier to just pay attention to Rosa. Far more fun to see her blushing.

As always, at the end of every lesson, everyone except the Last-Years went home. But even though I was technically their same age, I always had to go back to the guesthouse. I was determined to get to Rosa before I had to leave. I wanted to ask if she would be my partner for the games.

I dodged and swerved around multiple hungry children running home for lunch. When I saw Rosa turn the other way, I had to pick up a particularly small First-Year and fling him out of my way. Luckily, the kid loved it.

"Do it again! Do it again!"

I ignored him and finally reached Rosa. She had been swarmed by Last-Years discussing their reading from the night before. Last-Years had extra reading every night, which seemed like a nightmare to me. Just as I approached, everybody suddenly stopped talking.

"Need something?" Bradford asked as the girls around him giggled. "We're talking about Last-Year stuff. You wouldn't get it."

He was one of the largest male Last-Years. The only times he ever talked to me were to remind me I was an outsider.

"I wouldn't want to get it," I said.

He pointed at my chest. "Nice shirt."

For a moment, I wasn't sure what the guy was talking about. Then I looked down and remembered.

The T-shirt.

Mr. Amos always laid out embarrassing outfits for me to borrow, but this was by far the worst. I'd gotten used to the patterned button-ups he seemed to have an endless supply of. But he'd only had a T-shirt to lend me today. A T-shirt that read *Who's Your Daddy?* I had told him I wasn't going to wear it, but Mr. Amos just snorted and told me to put it on.

"Nothing is wasted in Cherry Harbor," he had told me.

Now, as everybody laughed about my shirt, I felt my entire face feel burning hot.

"Who *is* your daddy, Sky?" Bradford said.

I wanted to punch him in the jaw for that. But the truth was, I had never hit anyone my own size, and I wasn't going to start with this gorilla. I turned around and walked away. Just as I did, I could hear Rosa calling out to me.

"Sky. Sky, wait."

As I turned around, I saw her approaching. Bradford followed just steps behind her.

"What did you need?" she asked.

Bradford puffed out his chest. I was sure the color in my face hadn't disappeared.

"Nothing," I said, turning to leave again.

Bradford's probably going to ask her himself.

As I made my way into the guesthouse, I decided I hated the stupid special Last-Year hour.

I slammed the bedroom door and flopped onto the bed. Just as I crashed down, I felt something jab me between the ribs. Right away I knew what it was.

Another book.

I peeled it out from underneath me and then chucked it against the wall. Every day, Mr. Amos put a different handwritten book filled with stories in my room like this. And every day, I *never* read it.

I get enough stupid stories all day long. Why would I want more?

As I looked at the book on the floor, I was hit with a wave of inspiration. I scrambled across the room to pick it up and then lay back down on my bed. I held the book in my hand and couldn't help the smile on my lips.

I knew exactly how to get to Rosa before Bradford did.

About an hour and a half later, I staged myself on a metal box in the storage room with a different book. One of the many in the room. I held it in my hands and waited, and waited, and waited until Mr. Amos came through the door, de-wigging. I snapped the book up over my eyes. Then I nodded and said, "Uh-huh," as if I'd never read something so amazing.

Mr. Amos stopped what he was doing and gave me a curious look. Then he stripped off his costume and tucked it away in one of his chests.

"Fascinating one, huh?" Mr. Amos finally asked.

"What? Oh. I didn't see you come in. Yes—it's incredible. Best yet."

Mr. Amos laughed. "I didn't expect you to find *The Exhaustive List of Memorable Dates* so gripping."

I didn't get it until I looked at the cover of the book I was holding.

"You know, Mr. A, I think I'm starting to see why you like these stories so much. I just wish I could hear more."

I'd never called him *Mr. A* in my life.

Mr. Amos grinned. "Like an extra hour a day?"

Exactly.

"Do you mean it?"

I didn't have to fake my enthusiasm now.

"I think extra study would be good for you, my boy. I'm happy to see you taking initiative. You'll begin tomorrow."

With that, Mr. Amos left for his bedroom in the Sticking Place. I couldn't believe it had been that easy.

Stupid teeks.

The next day, at the end of the lesson, I walked—more like strutted—over to the group of Last-Years. I couldn't wait to see Bradford's dumb face when I told him I was joining them. But before I reached them, Mr. Amos caught me and said, "This way, my boy."

I assumed this was some kind of quick orientation, so I prepared to smile through another pointless story. It was worth it to stick it to Bradford. And to see Rosa. Mr. Amos and I both sat down inside the Sticking Place. Even though I'd been living right next door, this was my first time inside since the morning I'd woken up there.

That's a whole lot of books.

I noticed that the wooden horizontal slats on all four walls were arranged in an upward moving pattern from dark to light. The bookshelves were arranged by size. Large books on the bottom, smaller books on the top. Leaning against the right side of the room was a metal stepladder, with more books filling up the left side of each step. Lining the base of the walls were metal boxes and aluminum briefcases, some open, some closed. The door to Mr. Amos's bedroom was cracked open just enough for me to see his nightstand, also covered with books. And mounted over the door was the same pair of crossed oars I had seen on my first day. I shuddered while another vision of the Tyndale story passed through my mind. The part where his friend betrays him. I remembered Mr. Amos saying, "And once he gained his trust, he betrayed him." That part made sense to me. That guy was living in the real world. But then, that same image came again. Tyndale, burning alive with a peaceful look on his face, reaching out to me.

I noticed a small, shiny container about the size of a Topos, Inc. lapel pin in a glass showcase. Before I could ask Mr. Amos what it was, he spoke.

"Sky, I'm very proud that you want to dedicate extra time outside of your lessons to learning these stories," he said as he threw open the front window curtains.

"I can't wait to get started with my fellow Last-Years, Mr. A."

And I really can't wait to ask Rosa to be my partner for the games before Bradford does.

Mr. Amos cocked his head to the side. "Oh no. You aren't ready to join them yet. They are far past you. That's why I got you a tutor."

"But—"

"And as soon as your tutor tells me you're ready, and I confirm that, then you'll join your fellow Last-Years."

This isn't good.

There was a knock at the door, and Mr. Amos called, "Yes, come in, Rosa."

As she opened the door, Rosa's silhouette glowed with the light of the sun from behind her.

No, wait. This is very good.

"What a great idea, Mr. A. Brilliant. Just brilliant!"

"I'm glad you think so," he said, "because you'll be spending an extra thirty minutes a day with your tutor. Then you'll walk your tutor back home."

I couldn't believe it. Somehow my plan had suddenly become so much better. What luck! A part of me wanted to hug Mr. Amos. Of course, I didn't.

"Do you agree to these terms?" Mr. Amos asked.

"Absolutely," I said right away. "Good. Let me introduce you to your tutor."

I grinned at Rosa. "No need, Mr. A. I already know her."

She laughed at me.

"Her?" Mr. Amos chuckled.

At that exact moment, another tiny silhouette peeked out from behind Rosa. When he emerged into full view, I shook my head. "No. Nu-uh. *No way.*"

Standing before me was Lincoln, trembling and looking pale.

Mr. Amos continued. "Lincoln is one of our brightest First-Years, and his father has agreed to let him lend his services to you for the time being, given that you walk him home afterwards. He's too young to be in the grove alone. He will go over the stories I've already told and make sure you've understood them. He takes very thorough notes. That's why I picked him to be your tutor."

My tutor.

Within seconds my plan had exploded in my face. As I glared at the boy, his eyes dashed around the room at everything except me.

Rosa beamed. "You're lucky, Sky. Lincoln is my favorite First-Year." She winked at Lincoln. "But don't tell the others."

Lincoln looked down at the floor and grinned like an idiot.

I forced a smile at Rosa. "I. Can't. Wait."

Mr. Amos appeared to be pleased with himself as he headed out the door.

"Rosa and I are off. You and Lincoln may use the Sticking Place for now until the weather gets cooler; then we'll have to share."

The door closed and we were alone. I could see Lincoln gulp before he began to speak in a trembling voice.

"Our-our-our first lesson today is the Space Race. You may"—he swallowed again and checked his notes—"remember this story from our previous lesson. It started many years ago during a world war and—"

I walked toward him, wanting to him stop. But he kept going.

"Uh, it was, um, about space. But also about life on Earth...yes. There were two powers who opposed each other—"

"Shut up." I closed the window curtains. "This is how this is going to go, you stupid—"

Then I stopped myself and remembered what Mr. Amos had warned me about.

"Listen, you stupid *kid*. You and I are stuck here every day for thirty minutes, but you are *not* my tutor. You're going to sit there silently every day, and in a few...'weeks' or whatever, you're going to tell Mr. Amos that I'm ready to join the Last-Years."

Lincoln's whole body was frozen in fear, but apparently his mouth still worked because he said quietly, "I can't do that. That would be a lie."

"Then lie."

"No," Lincoln said. Then he began, with even greater determination, to tell the story again. "There were two powers, and we were one of them.

The other ones were called communists. They didn't like us, and we didn't like them."

I tried to shove Lincoln against the wall again; then I plugged my ears and yelled. I even threw books at him. But the kid would not relent. Despite it all, Lincoln kept telling his story as best he could. His first tactic was speaking as quickly as possible.

"Duringthewaracrossthewholeworldweworkedwiththesepeople-called—" But that tactic didn't work because he ended up needing to breathe.

This was when I tried pushing him.

He gulped a huge breath of air and continued. "—communists. Who were actually pretty bad, but not really as bad as the guys we were fighting called Nazis, who were really, really, really bad. *HEY! No pushing!* There was a man who worked for the really, really, really bad Nazis named von Braun. He invented these extremely deadly—but also awesome—missiles, which he turned into rockets for space travel—*I mean it. No pushing.* The Nazis lost, and von Braun ended up coming here and working for us. When the war ended, the communists said they were going to space and—"

This was when I tried plugging my ears.

"—WE COULDN'T LET THEM BEAT US TO SPACE BECAUSE THEY HATED FREEDOM AND THOUGHT THE GOVERNMENT SHOULD CONTROL EVERYBODY. WE RACED THEM TO SPACE. THE SPACE RACE, GET IT? BUT THE COMMUNISTS WERE WINNING EVERYTHING. THEY HAD THE FIRST PERSON, FIRST ANIMAL, FIRST WOMAN, FIRST … I DON'T KNOW WHAT IT'S CALLED, BUT IT FLOATS IN SPACE AND IS A BIG PIECE OF EQUIPMENT."

This was when I started throwing books.

"So, we started a new competition to the moon. The problem was—*ow!*—we didn't know how we were going to do that, but luckily von Braun, the guy from the really, really bad guys, said that he knew how. So, we put him in charge—*c'mon, Sky, cut it out!*—and we won. Did you hear that? We won! It was really a big deal because we put our flag on the moon, which meant that space would be free, like we were. So, it *was* about space and inventing and being bold—*don't throw those; they're important.* It was about *space*, but it was also about how we should live on *Earth.* We represented freedom. That's why we had to win."

By the end of the story, we both had completely exhausted ourselves and were sitting on opposite sides of the room.

Despite how annoyed I was, I couldn't shake a nagging question. "Was that all a lie?"

"No," Lincoln said.

"Mm-hmm. Yeah, it was."

Lincoln cautiously got up from his seat, worried that I would throw something else at him. He shuffled over to the glass showcase and pointed inside to the shiny trinket that had caught my eye.

"Do you see this? It's from the moon."

I pretended not to care. "No, it's not."

"Yes, it is. It's moon dust. An old, rich person dropped it off here. It's from the moon."

"No one's ever been to the moon."

Lincoln gently insisted, "Yes, we have."

All I could do was shake my head and think, *Stupid teek.* Maybe—hopefully—the kid could read my mind.

"It's time to walk me home," Lincoln said.

"Walk yourself home."

"I'm not allowed to."

"Says who?"

"Mr. Amos. And my dad."

"You always listen to your dad, huh?"

I thought that would embarrass him, but he wasn't embarrassed at all.

"Yes," he said as he made his way to the door. "Don't you always listen to *your* dad?"

If he had been as big as Bradford, he couldn't have knocked the wind out of me better than with that question. I ignored him and looked away.

We ended up passing Rosa on our way to the grove. She snuck over to give Lincoln a hug. It took every ounce of control for me not to roll my eyes while she was looking.

Lincoln's voice raised a nervous octave. "Um, Rosa? Um, I was, um, wondering if you, um, would like to be my partner for the Cherry Games?"

Are you kidding me?

I grabbed Lincoln's arm and began to drag him away. But Rosa followed us.

"Hold on one second, Sky."

I'll kill him, I swear.

"I would've loved to be your partner, Lincoln," she said. "I'm sure we would have won, but I already have a partner."

Rosa looked at me and smiled. "It's Bradford."

Of course it's Bradford.

Lincoln bowed his little head with an annoying level of dignity. "I wish you both the best."

"Let's go." I pulled him into the trees and out of earshot from Rosa. "He probably asked her today. And instead of being there, I was wasting my life away locked in a room with *you*."

"You wanted to ask Rosa to be your partner?" Lincoln asked.

"Just shut up."

Lincoln chuckled softly.

"What is it?" I said.

"I like Rosa too. We have something in common."

"I said shut up!"

TOPOS, INC.

CHAPTER SEVEN
THE ASSIGNMENT
(Ember)

As I passed a trio of Agents through the now-familiar Building One checkpoint, I could hear them whispering something as they looked at me. Someone mentioned Azaz's name. I ignored them as I scanned into the building and again onto the elevator. After heading up to the seventh floor and then being redirected to the meeting room on the sixth, I was happy to see I was the first person to arrive.

I was finally meeting the rest of the Members of the T.R.U.E. Youth Task Force. Even though I had no idea who my fellow Members were, I was confident that they would all be exemplary. Azaz had personally selected every Member, and she only picked the best of the best.

The meeting room was bright teal and had fifteen faux leather chairs lining each side of a long rectangular table. The sixteenth chair, presumably Azaz's, was situated at the head. After a few moments, a girl around my age with curly black hair slicked into a high ponytail at the top of her head arrived. I knew the girl couldn't stand me even before we spoke.

"Hi. I'm Ember," I said with a polite smile.

"Chloe Kelly," she said, nodding professionally.

I had seen her before. She was in a class one year above me at Oasis Academy. I often saw her riding the same route as me on the Interlink. Chloe didn't appear interested in chatting as she looked for her name plaque on the table, so I decided to do the same thing. I was pleasantly surprised to see my plaque next to the seat that was probably reserved for Azaz. Chloe's plaque was nowhere near as close.

A boy and a girl shuffled in, presumably siblings, since they were both rather fat, with piglike features and sweaty foreheads. They found their names—Lawrence and Poppy—and sat down without saying a word to anyone but each other. As the room filled with more and more young Members who greeted each other distantly, I could tell that everybody knew the level of dignity demanded by our mutual, honorable occupation.

Everyone was successfully playing it cool until the last Member to arrive strutted into the room. It was Cade Carter. The girl named Poppy squealed with glee when she realized the only seat left open was the one next to her, right across from me. As Cade sat down, he seemed completely unaware that everyone was staring at him.

He's obviously used to the attention.

As he looked up and noticed me, Cade flashed his charming smile. I nodded at him. I wasn't about to let Oasis's poster boy distract me today. I might be his leader one day. Soon after all fifteen seats had been filled, the Members began swapping stories about their latest catch.

A young, devilish boy named Reggie Stonebridge spoke over the group.

"I stuck my Tracking Token on my kid brother just for fun so I could see what happens when it goes off."

Everybody stopped talking and stared at Reggie. Even Chloe, who had kept her air of indifference even after Cade walked in, now appeared interested in what this Member was about to say. Reggie stood up, knowing he had our attention. He circled the room like a drone.

"It was the middle of the night. *Dead* middle. My kid brother was sleeping. *Dead* asleep. I heard someone scan into the unit—a fat guy and a skinny guy. It was so dark I could only see their syringes glowing with a teal liquid."

"The Teal Lady," Poppy, the pig-faced sister, said in astonishment.

Reggie gave a slow and showy nod. "Yeah."

He sure likes being dramatic, doesn't he?

"They both had a Teal Lady in their hand, and three more on their belts. I followed them to the bedroom. They already knew who I was. Pretty cool, right? I had them sneak up on my brother while he was sleeping. You should have seen his face when they injected him. He sat up and screamed. Must have really hurt. Then his body twitched like a zombie. Then he froze. I thought he was dead, but his eyes were still moving. Then his whole body went soft, and they carried him off. My caretakers didn't even leave their room. They were too scared of the Teal Lady. It was amazing."

As everybody looked on, some appeared half-terrified while others seemed half-delighted. Some were a mix of both. But I didn't believe him.

There is no way that's what my Tracking Tokens are for.

Before I could think about it much further, Azaz Aylo floated into the room like a mermaid with legs. As soon as she entered, everyone sat up straight in their seats.

"My dedicated T.R.U.E. Members," she said as she arrived at the front of the room. "I'm very proud."

She invited all of us to stand up and say our names and our reason for being here. Since I was sitting closest to Azaz, I was last to go.

"I'm Ember and I'm here for my brother."

The words seemed to leave my mouth before I even thought about them. Maybe because I wanted to distance myself from Reggie's cruel comments about his own brother. I wasn't there to hurt anyone; I was there to help—to protect the innocent, like Henry. I wanted him to grow up in a place that was safe. That's what my parents would have wanted for him.

For the most part, the "meeting" was a party. There were fruity candies and fizzy drinks, and, of course, cell-cultured meat sticks. We all ate and talked and even laughed together. Cade talked about himself, naturally, and Chloe kept to herself. But everybody got along well. Azaz eventually had to regain our attention by gently clearing her throat. We all rushed back to our chairs.

"There is another reason we have gathered today," Azaz said. "An assignment straight from the Administrator himself."

You could smell the ambition in that room after she said that.

Azaz continued. "Both the Administrator and I will be forever indebted to whoever accomplishes this task. And as an extra special reward, you will be personally thanked by the Administrator himself *in his office.*"

The members were panting like hungry dogs now.

I bet I'm the only person here who's had personal contact with the Administrator.

Yes, that had only been a letter. But now I had the opportunity to win a personal meeting—*in his office.*

"You may work alone, or you may work together," Azaz told us. "But only one of you will meet the Administrator. Are you ready for the assignment?"

She pulled out a bulletproof briefcase and opened it, revealing a rectangular metal box. Then she clicked open the latches and removed a sealed plastic bag from inside. I stopped breathing for a moment as I kept blinking, thinking I was seeing the wrong thing.

Is that what I think it is? It can't be. No, no, no. It can't be.

Azaz held the familiar leather-bound notebook to the room as if it were some kind of cursed object.

"We confiscated this contraband. After reviewing its contents, we have determined it's the vilest collection of lies we have ever come across."

My book? The vilest collection of lies?

I felt like I'd been punched in the gut. Was everyone looking at me?

Do they know?

But as I looked around the room, no one was staring at me. All eyes were fixed on Azaz.

"The contents of this book could endanger us all. We are so relieved it's in our possession. But we must know where it came from. This is your assignment."

I felt immobile in my seat, too surprised to say anything, too stunned to even think. I had been taking my cues from Chloe. When she snarled,

I snarled. When Chloe smirked, I smirked. That seemed to be working, so I kept doing this as Azaz continued speaking.

"You will each be given ten minutes alone with the book, monitored by me. I warn you: do not linger on any particular story. You are only being given this level of access to aid in your search. After today, you will never see this book again."

I never thought I'd ever see it again.

I tried to piece together this horrible bundling of my past and present. *What are they going to do with it?*

Azaz must have told a joke because everyone laughed, so I joined them, snickering. I realized my best way forward—the *safest* way forward, for Henry *and* for me—was to be a clear enemy of the book and all its contents. I would hate the book the most. I would look the hardest for its owner. Zeal to curb suspicion. That was my plan.

"As usual, if you find the culprit or someone who even gives a *hint* of being the culprit, plant the Tracking Token on them. We will handle the rest," Azaz said. "If we conclude that you've found the true guilty party, you will be elevated to a position of leadership and inducted by the Administrator himself."

The sweet-looking T-Force Agent who always accompanied Azaz entered the room, resealed and relocked the contraband, and carried it back through the door she had entered.

"We will begin your individual ten minutes of study with Members on this side of the table," Azaz waved her pointer finger from one end of the table to the other, ending with me, "and end on this side. Cade, you will be first."

Cade Carter rose to follow Azaz into the next room. I could have sworn that Poppy tried to reach for the back of his blazer as he walked past, just to say she'd touched him. All of us waited in silence until he came back out. It was clear no one wanted to work together, not even the siblings.

One by one the Members entered the room and exited ten minutes later, most with a smug grin on their faces as if they already knew who was guilty.

I was last to enter. My feet felt like lead as I walked into the room. Azaz and the Agent were both sitting at the end of a long table opposite the book, which was lying in front of an empty chair. As soon as I sat down and touched it, I felt like I might burst into tears, but I was able to hold them back.

As I opened the front cover, I remembered the tear Mrs. Grisham had made. Scribbled on the inside was a sketch of a man rowing a rowboat with the words, *For our children. May the past guide you into the future.*

My hand rubbed across the page as if I could read the words I knew so well just by touching them. I swallowed as I flipped through the book, acting like I'd never seen something so hideous before, making sure to display the appropriate faces of disgust and resentment every few moments.

As I got near the end of the book, I saw the name of the flower boat Henry had been talking about.

The Mayflower.

I could feel my eyes burning with tears.

There was a hand-drawn sketch of the boat. I swallowed again and then slid the book across the table as if it meant nothing to me.

"Are you finished?" Azaz asked. "You still have two minutes."

"I'm finished."

I turned to leave the room, but before I could, Azaz stopped me. "The Administrator told me about his letter. Keep up the good work."

I nodded and told her thanks.

"Oh, and Ember?" she said, stopping me again. "I shouldn't say this, but I'm confident *you* will be the one to meet the Administrator."

As I looked at Azaz, I felt my fear evaporating. The same warm feeling I'd had the first time I'd met her washed over me. I knew she cared about me, that she had complete confidence in me. I wanted to tell her the Truth—that the book was mine, but she didn't need to worry about my spreading any of its contents, because it would never hurt anyone. I wanted to display my complete loyalty to her and to Oasis.

She will understand. She won't let that come between us.

Suddenly I stopped—I'd had a realization.

It was clear that Azaz believed in me, maybe more than I even realized.

But she could *never* know the Truth about my book.

CHAPTER EIGHT
CHERRY GAMES
(Sky)

When I arrived at the open field at the entrance to the grove, I couldn't believe what I saw.

When they say the Cherry Games are a big deal, they mean it.

It looked like everyone from the town—adults, pupils, and children—were gathered for this event. There were more people in Cherry Harbor than I'd realized.

I spotted Lincoln with his family spread out on a bunch of large blankets. There were so many of them, they could have an entire town themselves. His mom was handing out sandwiches and glass jars to all the kids. I wondered why Lincoln was sitting there munching on a sandwich instead of getting ready for the games.

Guess I'm not the only one sitting out.

As I scanned the field, I could see Mr. Amos dashing across the lawn, carrying massive stones as if they were as light as pebbles. He always had to show off and perform in front of a crowd. He was wearing some kind of one-shouldered dress made of bath towels. I was sure it had some made-up "historical" meaning. Mr. Amadi was walking around in a suit. On a scorching day like this one, I knew he had to be soaked in sweat.

As Mr. Amos ran by Mr. Amadi, he gave him a signal to start. The crowd roared.

"The Cherry Games will begin in five minutes!" Mr. Amadi yelled.

I found a seat in the field by myself. Moments after I sat down, Rosa was standing next to me.

"You should be warming up. It's a long day."

I shook my head. "Nah, I'm not competing."

"Of course you are. You have to," she said in her soft, pretty voice.

This time I just shrugged as I told her I didn't have a partner.

Rosa gasped. "Oh no. I didn't even notice you weren't on the sign-up sheet. This is all my fault. I'm so sorry, Sky."

"It's not your fault."

It might be a little bit your fault.

She gave me a sweet look, and I swear it looked like she was blushing again. Or maybe it was just the hot sun turning her pink. Rosa was about to say something, but her mother's panicked voice cut through the moment.

"Rosa! Come here now!"

"*Ay, voy, Mamá,*" Rosa yelled back, looking again at me before she left. "I'll talk to Mr. Amos. Don't worry. Just start warming up."

As she returned to her family, Rosa gave Lincoln a pat on his head. The way a big sister might do with her younger brother. I looked around at all the families everywhere. Big, booming, rowdy, and loving families. Smiling and laughing and talking. It was such a strange sight. An annoying sight. A sight I had never experienced in my life.

Maybe I can pretend to be sick. I can act like something's wrong and get out of—

It was too late. Mr. Amos was already running through the field with a burning torch.

Why is he carrying that? Is he going to burn something?

The crowd was excited to see Mr. Amos hand off the torch to Mr. Amadi. The mayor stood far away from the crowd in a large circle made of rocks. When Mr. Amos handed him the torch, Mr. Amadi dipped it to the ground, and suddenly flames encircled him. For a moment I thought this might have been an accident, that Mr. Amadi might have accidentally torched himself. But no. Around him was a perfect ring of fire. Wiping the sweat off his forehead, Mr. Amadi faced the crowd, ready to make a big announcement.

"Let the Cherry Ga—"

Rosa and Mr. Amos rushed in front of everybody to interrupt him.

Oh no.

"Excuse me! Excuse me, everyone. One moment," Mr. Amos said. "It has come to my attention that there is a pupil without a partner."

The crowd all started to talk. They all said things like, "Oh no" and "Poor child" and "Get that kid a partner."

I should've pretended like I was sick. Now I'm stuck.

"It's all my—" Rosa began to say.

"My fault," Mr. Amos said, cutting her off. "It was an oversight. And of my own guest, even."

I saw him cupping his hand above his eyes as he looked around the crowd, shouting, "Sky, where are you? Come up here, my boy."

I seriously considered just running away. Somewhere. Anywhere. But instead, I slowly approached Mr. Amos and then stood by him. It was a mixed reaction from the crowd. I don't think many of them expected me to be the "poor child" without a partner. Now they looked nervous, even angry. Especially Rosa's mom, Mrs. Hernandez.

Having no idea where to look, I locked eyes with Mrs. Freeman, Lincoln's mom. At least she had a face that was friendly and easy to look at.

Mr. Amos spoke to the crowd. "We need one brave volunteer. I believe all the pupils that aren't First-Years are accounted for, so it will have to be a First-Year."

Silence. Total silence. Nobody moved and no one raised their hand to volunteer. I wasn't exactly shocked. I knew the pupils thought of me as a bully, especially the First-Years. But with each passing moment, my heart sank a little more. I felt like I was shrinking before everybody's eyes.

Then I saw I hand pop up. I couldn't believe it.

Lincoln was volunteering.

I saw his family applauding and congratulating him. For a moment I didn't see him as an irritating little dork. Or at least now he was an irritating little dork that had just saved me from feeling like a real idiot.

"Uh, may we perhaps put this out?" a voice called out beside us.

Mr. Amadi was still inside the ring of fire. Mr. Amos jumped.

"Oh my, Mr. Amadi. You're cooked! Yes. Put this out and let the—"

"—games begin!" Mr. Amadi cheered.

I stood next to the net above my head and tried to catch my breath. It was game point in our partner volleyball match. Lincoln and I were tied with the other team. It didn't matter that they were two Second-Year girls. They were two *really good* Second-Year girls, and we were about to beat them.

I needed a win after the first few events.

From the first event, it became obvious that everybody around me was in good shape. Great shape, actually. We started with a partner relay, and all the pupils were fast. Especially Lincoln. He ran ahead of everybody and then kept running, never tiring. Then I started to run. Then everybody caught up to me. Then everybody passed me. Then I started seeing stars and my legs turned to jelly.

Yeesh. The outside time must be good for these kids.

The second event was even worse. It was a diving competition, and I had to tell Lincoln I couldn't swim. He didn't tease me about it. Instead, he took my place and ended up pulling off incredible dives. His body hit the water without one single splash. Everyone was shocked, even his parents. I was able to redeem myself a bit when we did balance walks next. Lincoln and I both struggled, but I was able to last longer than Bradford. This gave me a little extra spark of energy heading into the volleyball match.

As one of the girls lined up to serve, I shook out my shoulders. I had seen the best SpotStop players do that, so I thought it might help.

As the ball soared to us, Lincoln rushed across the grass like a squirrel to hit it back. We volleyed back and forth for what felt like ten minutes. He jumped, I dived. I jumped, he dived. We just kept hitting the ball back over the net. After a particularly strong hit from one of the girls, I ran to the ball, but it zipped right past me.

"Blast it!" I cried.

But Lincoln was right behind me, sprinting and diving.

Holy Administrator.

He actually hit the ball back over the net, and the girls missed it! The pair of Second-Years looked like they had no idea how Lincoln even managed to touch the ball.

"Heck, now we're cookin' with gas!" Lincoln's dad said from nearby.

Before Lincoln could stand, I scooped him up in a hug.

"What a hit," I told him.

As I put him down, I noticed his knee was bleeding.

"You alright?"

Lincoln looked at me in pure shock. "Uh-huh."

For the next competition, each of us was handed a jump rope.

"What am I supposed to do with this?" I asked Mr. Amos.

"It's called a *jump rope* for a reason," he said with a grin.

"So that's all we do?"

Surely there was more to this event. But no. Whoever made it the longest without missing a jump, or quitting, won.

It took me maybe thirty seconds, maybe less, before I wanted to quit. I could barely breathe. But I would have sucked air for as long as it took to beat Bradford jumping next to me. Of course, I didn't have the chance because my left foot got tangled in the rope, and I fell down face-first. I could have lived with the pain, but then a bunch of moms ran over, acting like I had probably died. They were saying, "Are you alright, sweetie? That was some fall."

4CHASING EMBERS

"I'm fine," I said. But they would not stop talking about "how much that fall must have hurt," like I needed them to tell me it hurt. I knew it hurt. I just didn't want them to tell everyone else. Especially not Bradford.

I couldn't even resist them; I didn't have the breath. I just lay on the ground, watching the action. Lincoln was our only hope. By some incredible miracle, our team was not only not last; we were in fourth place. If Lincoln could just hold out, we had a shot.

The pupils were dropping like flies. It was down to players from four teams—Lincoln, Bradford, a stupidly fit Last-Year guy, and one of the Barlow twins—the boy.

There was a chant coming from the Freeman family. Mr. Freeman was so excited he was jumping with Lincoln but without a rope.

"Lincoln! Lincoln! Linc—"

"Lincoln!" Mrs. Freeman yelled. "You alright?"

Lincoln had fallen.

That was it. That was game for us. Bradford would win, take home the prize and the girl. That's what winners did.

I rolled over onto my hands and knees and pressed myself up to standing. Lincoln was fine; he was coming to me with his hand out for a handshake, bruised and sweaty. But before he reached me, there was another yell from the moms in the crowd.

On his highest jump yet, Bradford landed down on the side of his foot and crumpled to the ground. I had to hold back a cheer. The boy twin stopped jumping to help him up. So did the fit Last-Year.

What are they doing?

When Bradford tried to stand, he winced in pain. His parents ran onto the field and his father examined him.

"It's swelling up pretty bad," I heard his dad say. "Let's get you over to our blanket."

But Bradford resisted. "No, I have to finish the Cherry Games. There's only one event left. We could win."

But as he tried to take a step, his ankle collapsed underneath him. He looked at Rosa and dropped his head. Rosa helped Bradford back to his family's blanket, where Mrs. Hernandez was waiting to take care of his ankle. Rosa sat down next to her dad.

"So, what happens now?" I asked Lincoln, who was standing beside me.

"Their team is disqualified. It's too bad. Only the top three teams compete in the final event. Rosa would have loved that."

I watched Rosa delicately wrapping a bandage on Bradford's ankle.

Poor guy. No way she stays with him now.

That's how life worked. The winner takes it all. Loser takes nothing. He was a loser now. A loser like . . .

Wait a minute.

I turned back to Lincoln. "Wait. If they're out, that means—"

"Whoa!" Lincoln said. "That means we're in the top three! Of course, it hardly feels right under these conditions—"

"Shut up! We're in. Let's go!"

I dragged Lincoln over to Mr. Amos.

"They're out, so it's us, right? We're in the top three?"

Mr. Amos readjusted his towel dress and put his finger to his head to think. "Well, we haven't had to do this in years, but yes. I believe you are."

"Sweet!"

"But you will have to get the other team's blessing to compete in their place."

"That can't be a real rule."

"Ah, but it is." Mr. Amos pointed at Bradford. "Off you go."

I was dragging Lincoln by the wrist again back toward Bradford and Rosa. There was no way he would give us his blessing. No way he would give me a shot to be a winner. Not while he was a loser.

"I, for one, feel much better about this," Lincoln said, jogging beside me.

I just rolled my eyes.

Rosa was still focused on Bradford's swollen ankle when we got to them. She pulled back his foot, and he winced.

"Oh, Sky. What is it?" Rosa said with a smile.

I can't do it.

"I …" I made eye contact with Bradford. "Never mind."

I turned to leave, but then Lincoln said, "We need your blessing to compete in your place. Would that be alright?"

Bradford forced himself up to a seated position.

Here it comes.

Bradford reached out his hand. Was he going to hit him? No, that wasn't it.

"You want me to …," I said.

"Shake it," he said. "Good luck. I hope you guys win. Seriously."

"Uh, okay. Yeah. Yeah, me too." I shook his hand. "I hope you … your ankle … feels better, I guess."

"Thanks," he said, smiling.

"Thanks." I turned away.

Bradford had really surprised me, just like Lincoln had earlier. Just like this entire town.

Lincoln jogged behind me.

"Nice," he said.

"What? Oh yeah. No big deal. Let's win this thing, okay?" Out of the corner of my eye, I saw Mr. Amos watching me, grinning.

Everyone was moving their blankets back to a spot near the lake, which made me uneasy. Lincoln said exactly what I was afraid of.

"The last event is always a water event."

"Okay," I said, trying to keep it cool. But on the inside, I was panicking.

"As in, swimming. Which you can't—"

"For once in your life, please shut up."

There were three logs tied to the shore, each with a number, one through three. Team One was the stupidly fit Last-Year guy, with his partner, another stupidly fit Last-Year guy. Team Two was the Barlow twins, and Team Three was us.

Mrs. Amadi finally let Mr. Amadi change into shorts, which he wore with his blazer. He spoke over the crowd.

"Welcome to our final event. The previous scores of the three qualifying teams no longer matter. The first-, second-, and third-place winners will be decided by this event. These are the rules. Each team will be given one log, which they must use as a raft to get to Mr. Amos, who is already floating many yards away in the lake."

I looked out and there he was, sitting on a chair on a pile of floating wood, sipping an iced tea.

"The players may not swim, but only paddle with their arms and legs. If either team member loses their balance and falls into the water, they must return to the shore and pick up one of these smooth stones, which they now must carry with them as they journey across the lake."

I thought my heart might explode out of my chest.

A water event. Why does it have to be a water event?

"When they reach Mr. Amos, they must answer his question. Every team will be given the same question. If they solve it correctly, he will give them one fresh flower. If they can make it back to shore without getting the flower wet, then—and only then—they will be declared the winners of the Cherry Games."

All of us lined up at the start line. I just had to stay on the log. If I could do that, I never had to swim. Lincoln was taking very slow, very loud breaths in through his nose.

"Is that really necessary?" I said.

He only pointed two fingers at his eyes and then at the water, breathing just as loud.

The mother of the Barlow twins was shrieking in my ear about how nervous she was.

Mr. Amadi announced, "Ready, steady—"

Just don't fall. Just don't fall.

"GO!"

I knew I was supposed to spring into action. But I couldn't move.

Mr. Amadi took on the role of announcer, shouting, "Team One is off in a flash. But Team Two is pushing their log in right behind them. Team Three seems to be having some trouble on the shore. Oh. Here they go. Team Three has pushed their log in and—oh! A member of Team Three has already hit the water."

I'm drowning! I'm drowning!

I could hear Lincoln yelling as my life flashed before my eyes.

"Stand up! Just stand up, Sky!"

Oh . . .

When I stood, my head was out of the water.

"I'm good. I'm good."

"I know. C'mon!"

We dragged the log back to the start and Lincoln picked up a stone, which he held under his stomach.

"Team Two seems to be rocking a bit, but they are making good headway. Oh. And there goes Team Three—in the water again. They're really going to have to make up some time."

"Reach for my hand," I heard Lincoln say. "It's okay. Grab my hand. There you go. Now grab the log. Grab it and pull yourself up. You can do it."

We went back to the shore again. I wanted to quit, but then I saw Rosa, standing with Bradford, cheering for me.

Winner takes it all.

I grabbed a stone and jumped back onto the log.

Mr. Amadi was having the time of his life.

"Team One has just about made it to Mr. Amos. Hold your breath, folks. This dismount is quite tricky. Oh no! And Team One is in the water."

I could hear Mrs. Barlow screeching with excitement.

"Team Two is now in the lead, but Team Three is right on their tails. It looks like Team Two has successfully made it onto the barge."

"Get 'em, Barlows!" I heard Mrs. Barlow scream over the sound of the crowd.

"Team Two made light work of Mr. Amos's question. They are already back in the water with their flower. An interesting strategy—one of the players is holding the flower between his teeth. Team One seems to be struggling to disembark. Oh. In the water again. But Team Three, with our last-minute addition, Sky—uh, what's his last name?"

No one knew, so he pressed on. "Team Three is on the barge."

I crashed onto the barge, and Lincoln landed right on top of me. I was trying not to hyperventilate, but I was smiling. Mr. Amos had a stupid voice, of course, to match his towel dress.

"Team Three, an ancient query for you," he said in a slow, drawn-out tone. "There is a place one enters blind and comes out seeing. What is it?"

Lincoln rattled off answers. "A womb? An egg? The world? A doctor?"

I tried to jump in.

"A tunnel?"

"A cave? Is it a cave?"

Mr. Amos shook his head.

Lincoln looked like a man about to flip an Interlink using only pure will. His face was turning purple as he spoke without stopping for a breath. "Okay, so it's not literal. It's a metaphor, then? Is it a metaphor? Right. You can't say. It must be a metaphor. Seeing. Seeing . . . so it's like seeing, but not, like, learning something? Oh wait. Yes! Like enlightenment. Like, um . . . books? No. A place for books—a bookshelf. No, of course not. A place for learning with books. Um . . . oh! Oh, oh!" He was jumping up and down. "The Sticking Place! It's the Sticking Place."

I corrected him. "No. He said blind and then seeing. That's not—"

But before I could finish, Mr. Amos presented him with a dainty purple flower.

Lincoln finally took a breath, then shouted, "Let's go, let's go, let's go!"

I did not want to get back on that log, but I had to. We had a real chance of winning, and I *needed* a win. I could see Team Two not too far ahead of us. I could just make out Mr. Amadi's voice over the sound of the water slapping against our log and Lincoln's now insanely loud nose breathing as he paddled his arms at light speed.

That kid is a machine.

"What a show! Team Three is moving at bullet speed toward Team Two."

Lincoln held the flower high above his head in his right hand, and I was holding the two stones on the log with my stomach.

"How did you know that?" I yelled to Lincoln.

"What?" he yelled back breathlessly.

"How did you know that answer? It made no sense."

"It was a metaphor. Like seeing with your mind. That's what happens when we go to the Sticking Place."

"I still don't get it."

Gulping for air and trying to paddle with one hand, Lincoln said, "I would love if we talked about this later."

Then I heard Mrs. Barlow crying out from the shore, "AGHH!"

Mr. Amadi was squealing more than announcing at this point as he shouted, "I can't believe it, I can't believe it! Team Two is in the water! What an upset. If Team Three can hold their balance, they just might win this!"

I could see Lincoln's family lined up at the shore, cheering—even the baby, who actually may have been crying, but it blended in with the cheering.

"Now for the dismount. Lincoln Freeman seems a bit shaky, but he's scooting forward off the log onto the shore. What a dive. He's back on the sand, and the flower is safe."

I was edging forward with both stones in my hands. All I had to do was not fall, but I was sure I was going to. But then I heard people chanting my name. Lots of people. I looked up for just a moment, and there they were, the people of Cherry Harbor, and they were chanting my name. Even Bradford.

I rocked a bit and Lincoln reached out his hand. "You can do it. Just a little farther."

And in the next second, everything exploded.

"AND... HE... MADE IT!" Mr. Amadi shouted.

We were swarmed by families whooping, hollering, and shaking our hands. Lincoln insisted that we wait at the shore to cheer the other two teams in, which I thought was stupid but did anyway.

Once everyone, including Mr. Amos, reached the shore, there was a closing ceremony where—you guessed it—Mr. Amadi talked about how his family had founded Cherry Harbor. I didn't listen to any of it. I just watched Rosa listen, and she was fully absorbed in every word.

Guess she's mine now. Poor Bradford.

I didn't make the rules. That's just how power worked. Winners have power, and power wins. As the crowd cleared, I made my way to Rosa. Bradford was sitting on the grass, out of earshot of us. But I didn't think he would do anything. He knew the rules, too, I was sure.

"So, you want to hang back and sit by the lake?"

Rosa looked surprised. "Just us?"

I grinned. "Yeah, sure."

This is totally working.

I reached for her hand because I had earned it. But she pulled it away.

"I'm sorry, Sky. Um ..."

"What?"

"It's just, I'm not interested in you that way."

"But I *won*." Hadn't she seen my win?

"Um. Yeah, you did."

"So?"

"So ... I'm going to dinner with Bradford's family."

Bradford? That loser?

Rosa spoke again. "Congratulations though, Sky. Great job today."

Then she left.

She *left*!

To be with the guy with a swollen ankle instead of the Cherry Games champion.

I stood there like an idiot while everyone left, family by family, to go home for dinner. I figured it would be another night of Mr. Amos's "cooking," which was always just a bunch of cold vegetables and a piece of meat. I told myself that it was better this way and that I could ask him about his question on the barge, but I couldn't help feeling lonely.

I sighed and turned to walk back to my place, but then I felt a little hand tap my shoulder, and there was Lincoln.

"My parents said you can have dinner with us tonight. This way," he said.

And without giving it a second thought, I followed him.

Dinner at the Freeman household was nuts—two adults versus seven kids. Mrs. Freeman didn't sit for more than thirty seconds at a time before she had to pull something off the stove, clean a spill, or burp baby Harriet.

Mr. Freeman was trying to convince the six- and seven-year-olds— Will and Martin—to stop feeding bugs to four-year-old Frederick. Then there was Harper and Benjamin, who were a couple of years younger than Lincoln, who ran around serving the food to everyone. It was delicious food, the best I had ever eaten. Lincoln and I were so hungry we ate it like wild animals.

The dinner table really was nuts, with the scraping forks and Mrs. Freeman yelling, "Don't throw things at your brother!" every other minute. But it was fun, too, and everyone was laughing so much I almost choked on my food.

I had almost eaten myself into a coma when Mrs. Freeman came around filling our glasses with freshly made tea. She met Mr. Freeman at the head of the table, and they raised their glasses. Everyone rose to join them.

"A toast ta family," said Mr. Freeman.

They all drank.

"Then," Mrs. Freeman said, "to Cherry Harbor."

Everyone drank and began to sit back in their chairs, but Mr. Freeman interrupted them by adding, "And to this year's Cherry Games co-champ'yun and our guest—Sky."

"To Sky," they said.

I raised my glass and drank with them.

Then Benjamin and Harper ran me over with endless questions.

"Where are you from?"

"Do you have brothers?"

"Is there no water where you're from? Is that why you can't swim?"

"How old are you?"

"Why is your hair like that?"

"What's the best color?" Frederick added.

"Reckon that's too many questions to answer at once," Mr. Freeman said. "Let's start with best color."

"But I want to know where he's from," Harper whined.

I saw Mr. and Mrs. Freeman exchange a nervous look.

"Who wants dessert?" Mrs. Freeman said.

Everyone all at once cried, "Me!" and she brought the sweet-est-smelling food I had ever smelled to the table, something she called "cobbler." If I could have bottled it up, I could have made a killing selling that smell in Oasis.

Benjamin and Harper were giggling and whispering into each other's ears while they ate. Then Benjamin said, "I think we should go around the table and say where we're from."

Mr. Freeman gave him a stern look, but Mrs. Freeman jumped in again as a distraction, saying, "Well, I'm from a place that doesn't exist anymore."

"Why doesn't it exist?" I asked.

She seemed unsure how to respond, as if the answer were just too obvious.

"Hmm. Well, the place is still there, but it's a new name now."

"What is it?"

"I'm not sure," she said. "But it's ... not really the same place at all."

I decided not to press it any further.

After dinner we went out into the yard, where Benjamin taught me a stick game he'd made up called "Stooks." The basic rules were that you had to stack sticks from all over the yard into a tower and whoever made the tallest tower won. The trick was you could only use your feet.

I was way too tired to play that game, and luckily, after a few rounds, Mr. Freeman offered to take my place. I leaned up against the house and watched the family as I ate another bowl of Mrs. Freeman's cobbler.

The sun was dropping behind the clouds, and the wind carried the smell of everyone's homemade desserts on it. Harper was singing to baby Harriet and rocking her back and forth. Mrs. Freeman and Frederick were deeply engaged in a conversation about a bug he had found. Will and Martin were scaring the chickens by sneaking up on the coop and then popping out and screaming, and despite the best efforts of Lincoln and Mr. Freeman, Benjamin was winning yet another game of Stooks.

Something about a happy family was unsettling for me. But even more than the smell of the dessert, I wished that I could bottle up this moment and take it with me everywhere I went. I was so wrapped in feeling both happier and sadder than I had ever felt that I didn't notice Lincoln had come to stand next to me.

"Rosa likes Bradford because of the handshake."

"What?"

"Yeah, the handshake, He may have lost, but shaking your hand was something a winner would do. So, he's the one who really won."

I thought this over.

"But I shook his hand too."

Lincoln leaned up against the house just like me. "Women are complicated."

I couldn't help but laugh. When he wasn't annoying, he was actually a pretty cute kid.

"I liked playing with you today," Lincoln said.

"Yeah, me too."

Then we stood together for a few minutes until it was time for me to go.

Every Freeman kid insisted on hugging me before I left, which I normally wouldn't have agreed to, but the exhaustion had worn out my defenses. So, I hugged through a line of sweaty kids, then met Lincoln at the end, with his hand out for a handshake, just like his father, who stood next to him. I shook both their hands and was out the door.

No one else was walking home that night because home is where everyone already was. I walked through the grove toward the guesthouse feeling warm, full, but also empty. I saw the Sticking Place glowing by the light of the moon. Mr. Amos had fallen asleep waiting up for me and was snoring in a rocking chair on the front porch.

I took a long look at the scene—Mr. Amos in his chair, the bright moon reflecting off the lake, the trees moving in the wind. It was perfect. It was all perfect. The whole night had been perfect.

It was at that moment that I realized why I had *really* come to Cherry Harbor in the first place. For the feeling I'd had today. For the way that big family had looked spread out across the yard. For the moment when Lincoln had raised his hand to be my partner.

Then there was Tyndale in my imagination again, smiling as he died, forgiving everyone who had hurt him. Lincoln, the Freemans, Tyndale—they all had one very important quality in common, something that made sense of why I had abandoned everything I had ever known to find this crazy place.

I finally understood. I thought I had come to Cherry Harbor to look for lies. But I had actually come to look for love.

That's when I knew I couldn't stay.

CHAPTER NINE

SCAPEGOAT

(Ember)

"**O**utside of Oasis, are people the same as us?"

The man's gentle rasp made me stop and turn around slowly. I had seen him on and off for the past cycle. I wouldn't have thought anything of it since there were new people in Oasis all the time. But on more than one occasion I had overheard him asking multiple different people that same question.

"Outside of Oasis … are people the same as us?"

The occasional polite person would pretend to ponder the question, but most just said no outright.

Astra Park was mostly deserted except for a few children who had clearly been sent to run out their excitement while their caretakers got ready for the big day, a sparse assortment of grown-ups seeking breathing room, and a single Agent, looking lifeless. I didn't want to waste my time on this man, especially since his only crime was being contemplative. But more important than that, it was the day of the Topping Out Ceremony, so everyone was out of their units to celebrate.

In the past, a Topping Out Ceremony celebrated the completion of a new structure, but since Oasis construction was so radically behind schedule, this year's ceremony was not so much about what they *had* completed but what they *planned* to complete in the future. The event itself wouldn't have drawn a crowd except for the fact that the Administrator himself was coming to speak. Not on a Fibonacci screen, but in real life—in the flesh. The whole city was buzzing with excitement, and since it would be quite impressive to hand the contraband to the Administrator himself, every Member was desperate to snag the owner of my book before he arrived. So, I *had* to appear suspicious of everybody and constantly on the hunt to make sure nobody became suspicious of me.

This time the man was asking his question to an elderly woman. Even though the cool morning winds clipped apart their conversation, I could still make out what they were saying.

"Outside of Oasis . . . are people the same as us?"

The old woman replied without pausing to think. "Regardless, we are the same as them." She laughed and then added, "Silly question."

I noticed the man's eyes light up.

"Men . . . are all the same, I think," he said.

"Equal, yes."

"Naturally."

The man suddenly had the strangest look in his eyes.

Like he's about to cry.

After this, the pair struck up a lively and hushed conversation that I couldn't quite make out. The man was ragged looking and seemed plagued by an incessant itch in his right arm. Watching him scratch at his scabby skin while the old woman drooled down her chin, seemingly without noticing, was becoming too disgusting for me to bear. I was about to leave when I heard the man say "leather notebook."

This made me stop once again and watch him even more intently. Sure enough, he seemed to be indicating the size of the notebook with his hands.

"Holy Administrator . . . ," I said under my breath, my heart racing with excitement.

What a brilliant twist of fate. I don't know why I had felt compelled to watch this man—maybe because he was new and unorthodox—but my instincts had been right on. He knew about my book. If I turned *him* in, I would be free of any suspicions about me. I'd also be free to meet the Administrator and take my rightful place as leader of the T.R.U.E.

It was, after all, a position promised to me.

Of course, the man might have been talking about a different leather notebook, but even so, he was an excellent scapegoat. And it was the perfect day for a sacrifice.

I skipped toward the pair, trying not to appear as gleeful as I felt. This was such an unbelievable stroke of good luck. I reached them just as the old woman was scuttling away, but before she could speak, the man locked eyes with me and became suddenly pale. Then he did something quite disturbing.

"Ember," he said.

I froze.

Before I could question him—before I could even utter a word—this stranger was hugging me.

I was repulsed, but then I realized the opportunity I suddenly had before pulling away. My fingers found my last Tracking Token, which I activated and slipped into the pocket of his jacket. By now I had become skilled at this; all my practice planting random objects on people just for fun was paying off. So far, I had never been caught.

The man recoiled seconds after I'd placed the Tracking Token on him, causing me to stumble backward and almost fall.

"Hey!" I called out as I caught myself.

The man was more clever than he looked. He inhaled sharply as he pulled the rose-gold medallion from his pocket; then he stumbled backward in horror, shaking his head in disbelief. The few parkgoers stopped to watch the scene. The lone Agent on patrol walked toward us.

"What's going on here?" the Agent asked.

The stranger who had hugged me sprinted away, throwing the Tracking Token on the ground.

"Stop!" the Agent called out as he began to chase him. "I said stop!"

I scooped up the Token and shoved it into my jacket pocket as I took off in pursuit as well. The man's overcoat flapped behind him as he headed toward the Interlink Station. Alarm bells ricocheted through the street as I saw him dive underneath some metal bars at the travel checkpoint. He was fast for his age; I was sprinting as fast as I could but wasn't making much progress.

The man wildly burst through a crowd of passengers, weaving between the nourishment boxes being unloaded off the bottom level of the Interlink. As I followed him, I noticed several T-Force Agents were just strides behind me, following as if I were their pack leader. Soon we were flanked by an increasing number of my fellow T.R.U.E. Members.

They must have been following me.

It didn't matter. I remained laser focused and ran faster than I ever had in my life. I arrived in the station just in time to see him bound inside the northbound Interlink.

"This way!" I called.

A few T-force Agents and the fastest of my fellow Members—among them Cade Carter and Chloe Kelly—slid in right before the doors closed. The Interlink shot out of the station.

I caught sight of the back of the man's head as he pushed his way through the crowd swarming Cade Carter and ran toward the sealed hatch at the end of the compartment. I reached him just as he unsealed it, but the rush of air shot me onto my back, taking Chloe with me.

"Stop the Interlink!" we both yelled to the Agents.

The shrieks of Cade's entourage drowned out our voices. The man climbed down to the underbelly, where shipments were transported. He was shoving, kicking, and flinging his frail body at the door, but he couldn't get it open. He slammed into the ladder and clung to it as the Interlink came to a sudden, violent halt. Chloe and I rushed through the open hatch. There was blood streaming down the man's face as he groaned and swayed. He looked up at us and saw he was surrounded by angry Agents. So, he did something completely unexpected.

The stranger leapt up, grabbed the concrete platform, and pulled himself out of the track. But instead of running, he jumped into the neighboring track and jogged the length of it, running his hands against the wall. The Southbound was approaching at bullet speed.

I couldn't help but let out a piercing scream.

A crowd gathered around, reaching out their hands to him and begging him to get out. But he didn't listen, and the Interlink came barreling through.

He was gone.

For a long time I waited in the station, staring blankly and replaying the scene over and over in my mind. Chloe and Cade had returned to their separate hunts. The Agents had left to attend to the crowd assembling at the SpotStop station to hear the Administrator. But I no longer felt like going, not now.

I almost had him. I was almost free.

It occurred to me that there was no blood on the ground. Maybe the man's body had been carried away with the Interlink and the carnage was farther down the track. But there was nothing at all where he had been standing.

Where did he go?

Unable to escape my curiosity and feeling desperate, I took one more look around to make sure I was alone and then jumped into the track myself. It was a deep jump—about seven feet. I landed awkwardly on my ankle, wanting to scream but forcing myself not to. I didn't want anyone to come rescue me yet. I limped around the bottom of the track. I could feel my ankle swelling, but it didn't seem broken.

For a few moments I examined the spot where the man had been standing before the Interlink came. There was nothing there—not one drop of blood. I grazed my hands against the wall like I had seen him doing. At one point I pressed it, hoping it might move.

This is stupid. I know he's—

I couldn't even think the word.

"It's his own fault anyway," I mumbled unconvincingly to myself.

As I leaned against the wall, I heard a clicking sound coming from inside it that made me jump. Then another click, and another.

The wall creaked open, as if it were an automatic doorway that I had scanned into. But I hadn't scanned it. It didn't matter—I was too exhilarated to think that through.

In front of me, where the wall had been, was a narrow, round corridor with insulated tubes bundled together and running along both sides. After I entered, the door behind me snapped closed as if it were angry. I was seconds away from having been flattened, but luckily it was only the back of my jacket that was caught in the slamming. I slowly removed my jacket and left it with the door, so as to not upset it again.

I walked down the corridor and turned right. The path in front of me was sloped downwards and dimly lit with a thin strip of light running along the floor as far as I could see. I stepped slowly forward, conscious of every sound my feet made hitting the ground. Even my breath seemed to echo off the walls. About fifteen minutes into my walk, I stopped to rest my ankle and noticed strange scribbling on the wall.

Outside of Oasis

Are people the same as us?

Regardless, we are the same as them.

Silly question.

Men are all the same, I think.

Equal, yes.

Naturally.

A spark of hope soared through me. That was exactly what I had heard that morning.

I may turn this man in after all.

My mind started to wander as I limped down the corridor. I could see my induction. The Administrator pinning the Topos, Inc. emblem on my lapel and presenting me to the city as the new leader of the T.R.U.E. Henry standing there cheering while Mrs. Grisham looked awestruck. All my friends there to watch, my parents telling me how proud they are of me.

My parents . . .

Thinking of them made the pleasant daydream abruptly end.

What am I thinking? They won't be there.

When I came back to reality, I noticed to my right was another, even smaller, corridor. This door was already open, making me hopeful that the man was inside. I was just the right height not to have to crouch as I entered. I snuck forward and found myself in what looked like the inside of a madman's brain. The walls were rounded like the rest of the tunnel, but these had been painted white so the scribbles of fractured sentences and strange drawings could be seen more clearly.

It was as if I had somehow stepped inside the book my parents had given me. I was surrounded by every story I had ever read, and by some I wasn't familiar with. There was a drawing of a man standing in a small box with wings, running down a beach. I could make out the phrases "of human events" and "the right of the people" and "sweet the sound." On the ceiling was a map of what looked like the world, with names of places I'd never heard of before. I could make out the tiniest sketches of a man and a whale and a man and a giant, and people with stars on their sleeves. This room had everything—except for the man I was looking for.

A list of names on the bottom of the wall caught my attention. Right at the top was "A & J Aaronson." I rushed to touch the inscription.

My parents had been in this very room.

I imagined my dad had written the words and my mom had made the drawings. Of course, there were hundreds of other names signed on the wall. For a moment I fought the urge to review every corner, looking for clues about who they were and why they had been there. Feeling overwhelmed, my ankle throbbing, I sat down on the floor and closed my eyes for a moment, hoping to hear them.

"Ah, so you've found it," a voice spoke from the darkness.

A figure crouched through the doorway.

"Ms. Aylo? What are you doing here?"

"I would ask you the same. I had a seat for you at the ceremony today."

"How did you know I was here?" I asked.

"You activated the Tracking Token hours ago."

I had completely forgotten. I reached into my pocket and then remembered I had left the Tracking Token in my jacket.

"I told the Commander that it was past time we covered these walls, but he refuses. He wants to *study* them." Azaz added under her breath, "I hate this place."

Looking at Azaz's bitter expression, I realized I had to explain myself and fast. "There was a man. He was talking about a leather notebook. I followed him, but then he jumped into the track, and the Interlink came and he . . . But I don't think he died. I think he came here. And look— these are words from that *book*."

As I pointed to the walls, I made sure to say *book* with appropriate disgust.

"I think he's the one we're looking for."

Azaz, seemingly having heard nothing I had said, sighed while her palm grazed the list of names inscribed on the wall. "You saw their names. I suppose it was just a matter of time."

Before I could stop it, my eyes welled with tears. I pushed them down.

"Did you hear me? I said I think I found him—the one who wrote that book."

"Hmm," Azaz said. "Do you recognize these?"

She pointed to *A & J Aaronson*. I felt dazed.

"Yes."

"Hmm," Azaz said again, staring at the names. "It's a shame. It would be better to forget. Missing them . . . it's a weakness. Trust me, I know."

"What do you mean?"

Azaz looked at me with a sad grin. "I understand how you feel. Remember, my parents left me too."

It was as if Azaz had just ripped off a layer of my skin.

"They didn't leave me—" I started to say.

"They did."

Azaz was wrong. I remembered my parents struggling and the man's voice as he dragged them away.

"They left you," Azaz said.

No.

But the memory was so foggy, and Azaz sounded so sure.

"Did you know them?" I asked.

"Yes, everyone knew them. And everyone loved them. Your father was brilliant. He was developing technology that would have ended the war, but—"

"What?"

"He chose not to complete it."

"Why would he do that?"

Azaz seemed like she didn't want to say, but then cleared her throat and began again anyway.

"Your mother became involved in some dangerous business involving a secret society of Holdouts and their allies. She had always been kind, but after meeting them, she was different. She was angry, violent, cruel... I wish I didn't have to tell you this."

"And my dad?"

Azaz stared into my eyes. "Your father loved your mother so much that he would believe whatever she said. Her lies got him, too, and we couldn't bring them back to reality. We tried. Please believe me. But it was too late. They were too far gone."

I could feel myself shaking. "What... did the Holdouts... tell them?"

Azaz pointed around the room. "These stories."

I felt like I was falling into a pit with no bottom, or that all the air was being sucked from my lungs. The very stories that I thought connected me to my parents had actually taken them away. I couldn't hate my parents, but I hated the Holdouts so much I could feel it in my bones.

"You were saved just in time," Azaz said. "They were planning to leave and take you and Henry with them. I doubt either of you would have survived. The Holdouts are the cruelest to children. We tried to explain that to your parents, but they were bewitched by those stories. Even though they're all lies."

As I turned in all directions, the words on the walls seemed to be growing bigger and more menacing. They were closing in on me from all sides.

"Don't lose this book," I heard my mother say.

"By order of who?" my father yelled.

I could remember flashes of my parents fighting at the dinner table, and Henry suffocating in my arms. I had lived for seven years without parents to love me, to guide me, all because of these stories. I was abandoned and forced to take care of my baby brother alone because of these stories.

These stupid, horrible, evil stories.

A rage like I had never felt before took me over. I threw myself at the wall and swung at it with my fists.

"I hate them! I hate them! I hate these stories! I wish they had never existed! I hate them! I hate them!"

I took one final blow at the wall, but it held its ground. Then I collapsed on the floor, burying my face in my knees and grabbing my hurt ankle.

Azaz kneeled beside me and wrapped her arms around me in a motherly way. I had always secretly imagined this happening, but not like this.

"You are the only one who can make this right," Azaz said quietly. "No one else has to suffer like your parents. Or like the young Tenants you've turned in."

The young Tenants you've turned in.

I had a terrible feeling that I had done something unforgivable.

I panicked. "What do I do? Holy Administrator. What do I do?"

Azaz took a deep breath, stood to her feet, and then spoke with resolve. "I know where the book is from."

My whole body tensed. My stomach clenched; my ears were ringing. It was like a bomb had gone off right there inside that tiny room.

I have to confess now. I have no other choice.

"I'm so sorry," I said, unable to look Azaz in the eyes. "I never should have . . . I should have told you sooner. I didn't mean . . . I-I just thought you—"

"I understand. It's very personal. It's no easy choice, but the truth *must* come out. Are you ready to tell me now?"

I gritted my teeth and nodded before confessing. Any dream I had of ever leaving the city, of meeting the Administrator, of living anything other than a miserable, boring life was slipping away before my eyes. I would confess and, at best, life would be miserable. At worst, my life would end.

"The book is—"

"Henry's," Azaz said, cutting me off. "I know."

My head was spinning as she continued speaking. She said she'd known since the day we met that the book was my brother's and that I had nothing to do with it. It made no sense. But the more Azaz said it, the more she seemed to believe it. Which was maybe the point. Azaz was sewing a tapestry of falsehoods exactly as Mrs. Grisham had done. And just like Mrs. Grisham, once she was finished, she seemed relieved. Happy, even.

Finally, Azaz held out my final Tracking Token.

"You left this in your jacket. Only you can use it. You know what to do."

I wanted to ask her what she was saying, but the words were stuck in my throat. I couldn't imagine Azaz was implying that I turn in my own brother. For the first time, I had to disagree.

"Henry is innocent. He would never hurt anyone."

Azaz looked punctured, but she pressed on in her usual manner. "Someone must pay the price for hiding this book. It has cost too many lives already."

"No one has died."

"Are you sure?" Azaz said in a snakelike hiss.

I wasn't sure. But I would have never imagined...

But where else would those Tenants be?

What have I done?

Azaz tried to console me again.

"It isn't your fault. You did what was right. You saved more than you hurt. But your brother *is* guilty. Do what you know is right, and this will all end. You can start over. I've already spoken with the Administrator and your caretaker."

She paused for a moment, studying me.

"This is a strange time to tell you ... but I've arranged for you to be under my care, if you would like that."

I remembered what Mrs. Grisham had said the day Azaz visited. "*If you stay on her good side, I think we're both going to be pretty happy.*"

Azaz wrung her hands as a nervous grin crept across her face. "You are the child of two incredibly gifted parents who should have changed the world. You have every spark of their intellect. Every ounce of the potential they wasted is alive in you. I can help you become who they could have been. We can travel together, beyond Oasis. I'll show you places so far away and so different from here. You'll feel like you've left this planet. I want to do this for you, but first you must do this for *me*."

She held out the Tracking Token again.

"But it wasn't Henry," I said once again.

"Then it was you!" Azaz closed her fist and raised her voice in a way I had never heard before. "Do you not understand what I'm offering you? Do you want it or not?'

"Holy Administrator, I'm sorry. I want it. I *really* want it. Please forgive me. I want it!"

"Then it was *Henry*, not you. Do you understand me?

I understood her. I took the Tracking Token from her hand and put it in my pocket. There were tears in Azaz's eyes as she hugged me again, this time for much longer. She pulled away, dabbing her eyes and returning to her normal self.

"Activate the Token tomorrow night," she said.

Then she readjusted her skirt, tossed her long hair behind her shoulders, and turned to go. "I will leave first. You will come after. There will be an Agent who will assist you in getting out of the track. This never happened. Do you understand me?"

I nodded and then watched her duck through the entrance. The click of her heels grew softer and softer and softer. Then it was silent.

As I leaned against the place on the wall where my parents had signed, I noticed that etched above the list of names was a crude drawing of the oars that used to be engraved on the corner of my book. I recognized it but didn't know what it was. When it was time to leave, I pressed my hand against the drawing and took one final, long look at my parents' names, remembering Azaz's words.

I can help you become who they could have been.

"Goodbye," I whispered.

And then I was gone.

When I finally lay in bed after what felt like a never-ending day, I saw Henry popping his head up from under the table. "I missed you."

I was surprised to find him awake. For a moment I thought of my conversation with Azaz and felt a knot tying in my stomach.

"I did," he said.

Since Henry hadn't been able to talk to me all day, he seemed determined to catch me up on *everything*. It turned out that the Administrator hadn't shown up for the Topping Out Ceremony after all.

"A video! It was a stinking video."

Henry talked and talked until he sounded out of breath.

"And then they're gonna build a new SpotStop field, and a huge Fibonacci place, and another Interlink track, and these cool floating paths, and—"

Soon he drifted off to sleep, muttering incoherently in his dreams as I twirled the last Tracking Token between my fingers.

In my peripheral vision, I caught Mrs. Grisham's eyeball peeking in from behind the curtain. She quickly pulled her eyeball back and stepped away. A few minutes later, the eyeball was there again. I shot her a sideways glance, and the eyeball sharply and repeatedly looked left as if it were gesturing for me to come out.

What does she want?

I stepped into the kitchen, yawning and fiddling with the Tracking Token in my pocket.

"Are you hungry?" Mrs. Grisham asked.

I didn't even bother to answer. We both knew the nourishment delivery wouldn't arrive until morning. She paced around the room erratically.

"It's just that, well . . . I don't ask about your . . . *work*. Whatever the A.O. wants, I mean . . . is best. But I—well, I—"

"What is it?" I asked, not making sense of any of her blabbering.

"I didn't do anything wrong," Mrs. Grisham blurted out. "You have to believe me."

She reached for my hand, which I promptly pulled away. Shaking, Mrs. Grisham shuffled to the table, popping a meal replacement pill on her way. "So it's true. The Agents are after me."

"The Agents?"

"I saw them again today. They've been following me. I know it. They've been watching Henry and me. I know it. I know it!"

They've been following Henry . . .

"Calm down," I said.

"I follow all the rules," she cried. "Why me? I follow them all. You know. I swear." She bowed to her knees before me and begged. "For the love of the Administrator, spare me. Spare me, please. I know you can. The A.O. loves you. I know she does. Please. I'm begging you."

There was something greatly disturbing about this scene, about how pathetic Mrs. Grisham looked, crumpled on the floor and sniffling.

"Mrs. Grisham, you're not in trouble."

"W-wh . . . what? But th-the Agents–"

"I'll talk to them."

Mrs. Grisham stayed on her knees, groveling and thanking me, but I couldn't take it anymore.

"Please get up. C'mon. Get up."

Mrs. Grisham sniveled, "You're such a good girl. Such a good girl."

"I'm not."

I sat down at the table.

Mrs. Grisham grabbed a tissue and joined me. Her sentences were punctuated by loud blows every few seconds as she said, "You are. Just . . . keep doing . . . whatever . . . the A.O. asks. Promise me."

I dropped my head on the table, realizing that I had no one else to confide in but Mrs. Grisham. I let out a deep sigh.

"I don't think I can."

Mrs. Grisham crouched beside me, shakily taking my hand. "You can. You have to."

I shook my head. "I can't. I'm sorry. I can't."

Mrs. Grisham became very somber. She began to stare at the chair we weren't allowed to sit in as she twisted her wedding band around her finger. "I used to have a husband."

Why is she bringing this up now of all times?

"He was a lot like you," Mrs. Grisham continued. "He was on his way up . . . but he felt guilty . . . He didn't listen and he . . . well, he . . ."

"He what?"

"Just do what they ask. Trust me."

"And if I can't?"

Mrs. Grisham drifted toward the chair, her eyes wide and unmoving, mumbling. "You would have to get out of here . . . as fast as you could. There is a way—" She touched the chair. "No! Forget what I said; there is no way. The only way is to do what they ask. No way . . . no way . . ."

With this, Mrs. Grisham tottered to her room like a ghost—like a woman who'd died a long time ago. I felt myself doing the same, shuffling back to the bedroom to find Henry still sleeping. He had always been able to sleep through anything. Living in Oasis since birth had trained him for that. His sword was curled up under his arm.

I closed my eyes and took multiple deep breaths. It was now or never. I could hear Mrs. Grisham and Azaz in my head: *You know what to do . . . Do whatever she asks . . .*

The voices grew louder as I snuck toward the bed and removed the Tracking Token from my pocket. Flip one, flip two, flip three . . . press. I quietly knelt beside Henry and slipped it into the pocket of his pajamas. He stirred just a bit, which caused me to stumble backward, but he did not wake.

I was wide awake for an hour before hearing someone barge through the front door. The Fat Agent was brandishing a luminescent syringe and the lanky one seemed to be salivating. I burst out of my room at the same time as Mrs. Grisham, but Henry remained fast asleep. He only awoke when the Fat Agent shouted at us.

"Nobody move. We are Agents of the T-Force. We are carrying H233. There is someone in this unit named Henry. We are only here for him— unless you get in our way."

Mrs. Grisham gasped in horror but stayed out of their way. Henry ran out to me, trying to get away from the men heading toward him with glowing syringes.

"Out of the way," the Lanky Agent told me.

I obeyed and moved while he seized Henry and bound his arms behind his back. Henry shrieked and wailed in terror. It was one of the most horrific things I had ever heard. I plugged my ears to muffle his cries.

"It's almost over," I muttered. "It's almost over."

The Fat Agent raised his syringe, grinning.

Like a little boy crying for his mom, Henry cried for me. "Ember! Help me. Please!

Please help me!"

"It's almost over. It's almost—"

"Help me!"

"—over … It's—"

"Ember! Please—"

"—almost—"

"Oh no. No. no. no. No! Please! Pl—"

"STOP! Stop it! Stop!" I finally screamed. "I made a mistake. It's not him. It's not!"

I tried to run to Henry but was restrained by Mrs. Grisham, who was yelling, "Don't resist. You're gonna get us all killed!"

I was able to escape her grasp just as the Fat Agent's syringe pierced Henry's skin. His body froze up as he wailed in pain and horror. Lunging for the Agents' belts, I yanked out two syringes, and before they could stop me, I jabbed the syringes into their backs. They, too, became paralyzed and screamed. I had to wait about thirty seconds for the teal liquid to empty out into their bloodstreams. Then they collapsed onto the ground.

Mrs. Grisham stood in wide-eyed horror, her hands covering her mouth. "What have you done?" she cried.

I dropped to my knees to reach for the syringe they had used on Henry. It was still three-quarters full. I ripped one more syringe off the Fat Agent's belt and pointed it at Mrs. Grisham. "Don't move," I warned.

Mrs. Grisham gasped and put her hands in the air.

"Help me pick him up," I said, but Mrs. Grisham didn't move.

I thrust the syringe toward her. "Do it now!"

Mrs. Grisham scrambled to Henry and struggled to cradle his limp body in her arms like a baby.

I kept the syringe aimed at her. "How do you get out of here?"

"Well, I-I don't *really* know. Well, I mean. I-I-I—"

"You said you did. Tell me."

"W-w-well, we would have to g-get to the Interlink station and, well, we c-c-can't, so, well, I—"

"*I* can," I corrected her. "Let's go."

"Ember, if they find us, they'll—"

I ignored her as I ran into the bedroom to grab my backpack and pack it as quickly as I could.

I almost tripped over Henry's sword on the way.

"We better go now." I shoved the sword into my backpack and rushed out of the room, the syringe still pointed at Mrs. Grisham, who had edged suspiciously close to the door. "And if you run, I'll tell them it was you."

We scrambled out the door and down Hatcher Avenue, carrying Henry. Mrs. Grisham was crumpling under his weight, but I knew she would rather have died from exhaustion than from my syringe. At the travel checkpoint, my card opened the bars, but the alarm sounded when three bodies passed through instead of one.

"Blast it," I said. "Follow me."

I made Mrs. Grisham, who was still holding Henry, hide behind a large digital display sign that brightly flashed the words "Oasis Topping Out Ceremony Today."

Night shift Agents soon appeared, reluctantly trudging out of the station to respond to the alarm. I heard one mumbling.

"If this is that stupid squirrel again, I swear I'm going to inject it."

I rushed toward them. "You have to help me. I'm a member of the T.R.U.E. Two Agents have been attacked. 1607 Hatcher Avenue. I think they're ... they're ..."

The Agents woke suddenly from the stupor of the night shift.

"1607 Hatcher, you said?"

"Yes. Please hurry."

As they sprinted away, they called for reinforcements. "No. It's not the squirrel! Two Agents down. I repeat, two Agents down."

Once they had cleared, I gave Mrs. Grisham the signal. She rushed over, her knees giving out.

"He may not even be alive," she said, looking at Henry.

I pointed the syringe at her again. "Where now?"

Mrs. Grisham laid Henry's body down and hustled to the far end of the station. She looked into the track, shook her head in despair, and scrambled to the opposite end.

"It's over here," she said in a fluster as she picked up Henry and led me to a small metal ladder on the interior of the track. Mrs. Grisham climbed down gracelessly with Henry hanging over her shoulder, losing her footing on the bottom step and stumbling onto the track, nearly dropping him. I followed close behind them.

As Mrs. Grisham led us, I found myself in disbelief. This was the same path I had been down earlier, but this time from almost two stations away. The time it was taking to walk wherever we were going was making me nervous.

The Agents have to be on to me by now.

"How much farther?" I asked with a scowl.

"I-I can't … r-r-remember. Oh. Oh. I can't remember."

Eventually I recognized the tracks, so I ran ahead to the place the wall had opened for me and pressed on the same spot on the wall.

"Is this where we're going? I know this place. Is this it?" I pressed harder still. "It won't open."

Mrs. Grisham hobbled over and took a deep breath, then laid Henry down beside her. She slid her iron wedding band off her finger and grazed it over the wall until it suddenly stopped as if it had clicked into place. Moving with more effort, she drew a straight line from right to left. At the end of the line, a clicking sound came from inside the wall, like the turning of a deadbolt.

Click.

"Oh my," Mrs. Grisham sighed.

Then she lowered her ring to the middle of the wall and did it again, then again at the bottom of the wall.

Click. Click.

Mrs. Grisham groaned as the door slid open.

"But it opened for me earlier," I said in disbelief.

Mrs. Grisham was stunned. "If it opened, someone opened it for you." She slid her ring back on her finger and picked up Henry again.

When we entered the corridor, Mrs. Grisham led me in the opposite direction I had been down before.

"Stay close to the wall," she warned me.

We walked on an incline up the dim path, turning onto yet another tunnel, this one buzzing with an ominous electronic whine. The farther we ventured into the tunnel, the louder the whine became, escalating into a high-pitched squeal that drilled into my head like a million tiny screws. Mrs. Grisham stopped in front of a seemingly normal piece of wall.

"What is it?" I whispered.

Mrs. Grisham just stared at the wall in horror.

"What?"

"It's still here ...," she replied. "How is it still here?"

"What's still here?"

"This is ... the way out. Topos must still not know ... How could they not know ... ?"

Mrs. Grisham laid Henry down and removed her wedding band again. This time she drew a circle at the bottom of the wall. The circle slid into the wall like a stone being rolled away. A fresh gust of night air streamed in.

"Holy Administrator ..." Mrs. Grisham stumbled away from the wall. "No ... no, I can't. Please, no ..."

I was already crawling out onto the hard clay, my first steps beyond the city walls.

As far as I could see, the ground before me was desolate and obscure. I turned back to look at Oasis; I had never seen it from the outside before. The city was surrounded by tall steel walls, arced at the top like a wave about to crash.

A single beam of light emanating from Building One in the perfect center of the city penetrated the night sky.

I can never go back there. Not now.

As I looked up, I couldn't believe what stars looked like uninhibited by LEDs. They seemed too bright—too powerful. Yet they twinkled invitingly, beckoning me on. They seemed to be promising something beautiful on the other side of the unknown.

The peaceful moment was interrupted by Mrs. Grisham's whimpering and begging. "Let me go back. I'll tell no one. I swear. Just don't make me leave Oasis. They won't let me back."

There was no reason to drag Mrs. Grisham any farther. "Okay—you can go back."

"No one will ever know," Mrs. Grisham promised. Then she passed Henry through the gap and rushed away in a panic before I could change my mind.

The small, circular door closed, leaving no indication that it had ever been anything other than an ordinary piece of wall. The electronic whine was replaced by an almost equally distressing silence. I could feel my panic rising, but the stars beckoned me on again.

We needed to get far away from Oasis.

Henry was too heavy for me to carry in my arms, so I dragged him slowly through the dirt. Every few minutes I would stop, hover over him, and beg him to wake up. But he didn't, so I kept dragging and dragging and dragging.

Soon my vision blurred with the pounding of my heartbeat. My own breath sounded hollow in my ears. I pushed as hard as I could for as long as I could until I finally collapsed over Henry's body. As I landed, I began to cry out like a wounded animal.

I didn't know how long I lay there, screaming, but when I eventually looked up, I could see a figure approaching in the darkness.

T-Force?

I tried to get up, but there was no fight left in me. As I felt myself going in and out of consciousness, I decided to simply stay there in the dirt and wait for whoever this was to come and do whatever it was he was going to do. The darkness captured me for a moment. When I felt myself come back around, a man was looming over me.

"Who are you?" he asked.

"You first," I said, feeling barely conscious.

The stranger shook his head and walked away, saying, "Forget it. I don't care."

"No, wait," I called as I forced myself to sit up. "My brother. I need help for my brother."

The stranger was dragging his hands down his face. "Leave. Just leave."

Is he talking to me or himself?

"Please," my voice barely made out. "I think he's … dying."

The man paced back and forth, slapping his head before finally groaning and picking up Henry's body. He marched toward Oasis.

"No," I said. "They can't help at Oasis."

"Why not? What's wrong with him?"

It took me a minute to finally stand. "It was the Teal Lady. They gave him the Teal Lady."

Shaking, the stranger roared, "AGHHH!"

I watched as he dropped Henry's body on the ground and stomped away in the direction of Oasis, then turned and stomped back, then changed his mind and turned again. He stopped moving and stared at Oasis while repeatedly smacking his own head with both of his hands. He threw down his hands, clenched his fists, leaned back until his chest was facing the sky, and wailed again, "AGHHHH!"

Holy Administrator. He's insane.

He turned back once more, stomping toward me and Henry.

"Please don't hurt us. Please," I cried as I scrambled backward through the dirt. But the young man marched on. He scooped up Henry's lifeless body as I continued to plead with him.

"Please, no. Don't hurt him."

With Henry in his arms, he stood above me and growled, "Follow me."

As I stood to follow, I noticed he wasn't going toward Oasis anymore. He was marching us into the darkness.

"Please don't hurt him," I begged once again.

The man looked back at me. "I'm not going to hurt anyone. I know people who can help. Now, just shut up."

"Who are you?" I asked as I struggled to keep pace with him.

"You first."

"I'm Ember."

He stopped for a moment without turning to face me.

"I'm Sky."

CHAPTER TEN
NO ONE AND NOWHERE
(Sky)

I wasn't sure if the kid was still alive. We'd walked all night, the boy in my arms and his sister following me. We finally reached Cherry Harbor just as the sun started to rise. That was when I was able to get a good look at him. And the kid didn't look good. Not at all.

"Watch out for those," I warned Ember as I ducked under a low-hanging tree limb.

I got a good look at her too. She looked pale and exhausted. Her brown hair was sticking to her neck, and her overalls were covered with dirt. But it was her eyes I noticed. Her eyes weren't tired. They were determined.

When I finally knocked on the door to the Sticking Place, Mr. Amos answered.

"It's open, Jay."

He assumed I was Mr. Freeman. I stepped inside to see Mr. Amos cramming his foot into a boot and rushing around, throwing clothes and bottles of medicines into a bag. He spoke to me with his back turned.

"I don't know how long ago he left, but it's a dangerous walk and—"

"Mr. Amos...," I said.

Turning around, he saw me and dropped his half-packed bag.

"Sky! Where did you—"

His eyes shifted to the lifeless boy in my arms and then to Ember standing in the doorway. This made him snap into action.

"Lay him down on my bed. This way."

Mr. Amos flung open the door to his bedroom and moved the blanket aside so I could lay the kid down on the sheets. He checked the boy's pulse, then looked at me and asked what happened.

"Is he ..." Ember said, her nose stuffy and her voice shot. "Is he ..."

She can't say it. She can't even ask if he's dead.

Mr. Amos answered with a reassuring tone. "No, he's alive. Very alive. What's your name?"

"It's Ember," I told him.

"And this friend of yours, what's his name?" Mr. Amos asked, gesturing to the kid.

I hadn't even asked her for a name.

"M-my ... brother ... Henry," she responded in between deep breaths.

"What happened to him?"

She kept her eyes locked on Mr. Amos as she rummaged through her backpack.

"Holy Administrator," I whispered.

Ember held up a syringe with her hand shaking. "They gave him this. But we got away before they could give him all of it."

I had never seen Mr. Amos look so serious. He stood there, almost hypnotized by the syringe. In the morning light it seemed to glow.

"I need you to get the Freemans and Hernandezes right now," Mr. Amos told me. "Tell them what she has. They'll know what to do."

For a moment I just stood there, looking at him. I didn't want to ask him how these families could know what to do. They were in the middle of nowhere. How could they help, anyway? But I knew Mr. Amos wasn't lying. I had to trust him.

I almost said something to Ember, but she was focused on her brother. She probably didn't even notice me disappear.

NO ONE AND NOWHERE *153*

I was wrong. The Freemans and the Hernandezes knew *exactly* what to do.

They didn't hesitate to drop everything and run to Mr. Amos's cabin with me. As soon as we got there, Rosa went straight to taking care of the Freeman children on the porch while Mrs. Hernandez and Mrs. Freeman raced around Henry. They had all sorts of things—glass bottles of what looked like dried leaves, pills, and steaming liquids. Mr. Amos and the two fathers spoke in hushed tones in the corner of the bedroom. I noticed Mrs. Freeman whisper something in her husband's ear; then he walked over to pull me aside.

"They think it'd be best fer her to not see what they's about to do," Mr. Freeman said under his breath. "You arta take her to the main room fer a while."

I nodded. I had been feeling helpless watching everything, so I was glad to have something to do. I walked toward Ember to guide her out of the bedroom, but the girl screeched at me.

"No! I won't leave him!"

"Whoa. Okay. Calm down."

I stopped, wondering if the girl was going to hit me. Mrs. Freeman handed the warm rag in her hand to her husband and took Ember aside. I watched their conversation. At first Ember was defiant and angry. But she slowly melted into tears. After a long moment with Ember's head buried in her chest, Mrs. Freeman guided her back to me.

"She's ready to go now."

I couldn't help being impressed. But I was slightly irritated as well. I bet I could have calmed her down if she had given me the chance.

As soon as Ember and I were alone in the main room, she became defensive again. But I could tell she was almost too tired to keep it up. I watched as she wandered around the room without speaking. She stopped in the very same place I had when I'd first arrived.

The oars caught her attention, just like they'd caught mine.

"What are those?" she asked.

I shrugged. "I don't know."

She stared at them for a long time, as if she recognized them from something. When she finally glanced back at me, her eyes looked suspicious.

"Where *are* we?"

"The Sticking Place."

"What?"

"That's the building we're in. It's kind of like a school, but also that guy who was here when we got here—Mr. Amos—he lives here. This place, this city, whatever it is—it's called Cherry Harbor."

"Where's that?"

"It's Holdout territory," I said.

"Wh-what? This is—these are—you are—"

"Whoa, whoa. *I'm* not."

She didn't seem to hear me. Whatever calming effect she had gotten from Mrs. Freeman was gone. She hurled out expletives in every direction.

"Holdouts? You brought me to Holdouts? Teeks! You think *teeks* can help him? They want to kill him!"

Before I could say a word, she rushed to the bedroom door to rescue her brother. I ran after her and grabbed her before she could reach the knob.

"Let me go," she demanded. "Holdouts—they could kill him! He could die!"

"If you take him now, he will *definitely* die," I yelled, holding her back.

She slapped at my head and stomped my feet. I could tell she was strong. But I was stronger. I lifted her off the ground and moved her away from the door.

"You don't have a choice. You can't go back to Oasis. No one there will even *try* to help him."

"You don't know that."

"I do. Trust me."

If only you knew.

"You don't know anything," she said back. "You're a teek!"

"No, I'm not."

"You are."

Just tell her the Truth.

"I'm from Oasis!"

She stopped swinging at me, but just to be safe, I didn't put her down. I needed to talk a little sense into her.

"You go back to Oasis, and they'll come after him and you, and no one will help. These people are at least going to try."

When I felt her body go limp, I knew she had stopped resisting, so I let her go. Ember moved into the opposite corner of the room and sat down. She glared at me.

"You really shouldn't say *teek*," I said.

Ember rolled her eyes. I couldn't help but chuckle at the irony.

"You shouldn't," I told her. "They don't like it."

"I don't care what they like," she said, and I could tell she meant it.

I sighed. "Look. I know how you feel—"

"You absolutely *do not know* how I feel! You may be from Oasis, but you've obviously left. You're a teek now too."

"I hate to be the one to say this, but *you* also left. So, I guess we're both teeks."

She gave me a fiery look, a kind that amused me a bit since I understood it. I totally understood it.

"Not me," she said. "I'm not staying here. These people are evil. The second Henry wakes up, we're leaving. You should too. Or you can stay here with the teeks since you like them so much."

I wanted to say that I didn't like them either, but at that exact moment Lincoln peeked his head in through the door.

"It's starting to rain. Can you ask Mr. Amos if we can come inside?"

I couldn't help letting out another long sigh. "You can all come into my place."

Lincoln smiled, and I couldn't resist grinning back. I turned to see Ember scowling at both of us.

"Can you wait here one minute?" I asked her.

She gave me a very cold nod.

After bringing everyone to my place, I arrived back to all of them standing in the main room except Mrs. Hernandez. She was still tending to Henry in the bedroom.

"He's going to need more time," Mrs. Freeman said. "At least a week."

Mr. Amos was pacing the room. "They'll stay with me, then. I'll bunk in the guesthouse with Sky. We'll make a bed for her in here for now."

I could see the disgust on Ember's face. Mrs. Freeman mistook it for fear, so she tried to console her.

"You'll never be alone. We'll have someone watching Henry every minute. Mrs. Hernandez and I will take shifts giving him the antidote."

"Does it work?" Mr. Amos asked.

Mrs. Freeman shuddered. "I pray so. We weren't sure what was in these syringes before. We were only guessing. Now we have one to study, but it just takes time. He's stable, but he's not awake."

She paused and gave Ember a comforting smile.

"Yet. He's not awake *yet*." She opened the bedroom door and gestured for Ember to step in. "Would you like to see him? It may be good for him to hear your voice."

Ember walked into the room with Mrs. and Mr. Freeman, and Mr. Hernandez. I was left in the main room with Mr. Amos. It didn't take him long before he was busy doing what he always did— dusting off his trinkets. His question came out of nowhere.

"Why did you go?"

"What?"

I'd half forgotten that I had tried running away last night.

"You don't have to tell me," Mr. Amos said. "You did the right thing bringing them here. Heaven knows what they would've done to them in Oasis. Children... I can't believe it's gone so far."

"He might have deserved it," I mumbled as I crossed my arms and walked away from him.

"What's that?" Mr. Amos asked. He didn't pursue it further. "So why *did* you leave? What were you looking for?"

"I wasn't looking for anything, I just—I couldn't—It's stupid."

Mr. Amos returned to dusting. "Well, I just want you to know that you're welcome *here*."

It sounded as if he had put a special emphasis on the word *here*.

"Well, I'm welcome in O—"

I stopped myself before I said the name. Mr. Amos did it for me.

"In Oasis. I know. It's hardly a secret, my boy. Cherry Harbor has very few visitors, and only someone from Oasis could make it here on foot. Besides, you gave yourself away by calling Lincoln, well, what you called him. You must not be well-known since Ember doesn't recognize you. Must not get around much."

I decided I wouldn't respond to those last couple of statements.

"Do the pupils know?" I asked.

"We've never told them, but they're very bright, especially Lincoln. It would be best if you told him the Truth about where you're from yourself."

"Why him?"

"Lincoln is a walking lie detector, but even more than that, because he cares for you like a brother. I can tell."

I didn't believe him, but it didn't matter in the first place.

"You'll be important to that girl," Mr. Amos continued, speaking of Ember. "You can relate to her. She'll need that. It's a hard adjustment, living here."

"I don't live here."

"Where do you live then?"

"I..."

I clenched my jaw, unsure what to say.

"Nowhere," I blurted out. "All right? I live nowhere."

"Maybe you should live here, then. It beats *nowhere* any day."

"You don't understand. I can't live here. I'm not like you people."

"Of course you are," Mr. Amos insisted. "People are all the same."

"We're not," I said, turning away from him again and running my hands over my face. "And you know what the worst part is? I wish we were. Yesterday, I had a moment where I imagined what it would be like to be like you. To have family dinners, and games, and stories. To have seven kids like the Freemans. To have a house. But I can't. I'm not made for houses and families and ... and these *stories*." I pointed to all the books surrounding us.

"Honestly, I just don't get you guys. Like, why do you even care about me? What do you get out of it? I'll always think I'm better than you, or that you're all lying or just pretending to like me." I lowered my voice as I sat down on the small stepladder. "I've hated people like you for so long, and now I can't. But I'm still not one of you, and I never will be."

There was a moment of stillness. Mr. Amos had sat down to listen to me. He was tapping his head, which I had figured out meant that he was thinking. Then he rose to his feet and announced, "I have a story for you."

"Please, no."

"Yes. A very good one. You'll like it."

"Okay, just no—"

"There it is!" Mr. Amos cheered as he pulled a single feather and a wide-brimmed black hat from his chest.

"—costumes."

Mr. Amos clipped the feather in his hair, opened his arms, and began another over-the-top narration.

"Our story begins a long time ago."

"Of course it does," I said.

"All over the world, people were being captured and sold into slavery. A ship captain had just landed on our shores. He was a greedy, cunning little snake."

Mr. Amos put on the wide-brimmed hat. "Gentlemen, gentlemen. Would you like a private tour of my ship? How about stepping into this room below deck?"

I sat in place as Mr. Amos appeared to be watching the imaginary men enter the imaginary room below, then dropped to the floor and pretended to lock them in.

"Say goodbye to your home, boys."

As he rose to "steer the ship away," I interrupted him. I couldn't take any more of this.

"*Please* just get to the point."

Mr. Amos sighed. "Still no fun at all."

He removed the hat to reveal the single feather in his hair and finally spoke in his normal voice.

"The captain lured in a dozen or so men—they called them Indians—and captured them. He wanted to sail them to a country across the sea and sell them into slavery, but a group of monks rescued as many of them as they could by buying them and setting them free. Including a man named Squanto. You're sure you don't want me to act it out?"

"I'm literally begging you not to."

"Fine, fine. Squanto lived across the world with complete strangers for many years. And even though he *wasn't one of them,* he lived among them and learned English. But he missed his family, so he decided to go home."

"I just don't understand what this has to do with anything," I said.

"Would you just let me finish?"

"Fine."

"He didn't know it, but while he was gone, a horrible disease came and killed everyone. Everyone he knew was dead when he got back—he *had no one* and he *belonged nowhere.* Are you following me?"

I rolled my eyes. "Is this supposed to be me?"

Mr. Amos winked.

"Years later, new people arrived. They wanted to live on the land Squanto was raised on. But it was winter, and they were starving, and they had no homes yet. Half of them died. Probably they all would have died if it weren't for Squanto."

None of this made sense. If he had been telling me a story where I was being compared to the villain, I would have been fine with that. But somehow insinuating that I was a hero? It made me feel nervous for some reason. As Mr. Amos continued, he became increasingly passionate.

"Other people wanted to help the newcomers, but they didn't speak the same language. No one spoke English *except* for Squanto. And Squanto knew the land. He'd been raised on it. He told the new people where to plant food and where to fish. Without him they all would have died."

"This has nothing to do with me," I said, interrupting again. "Can we be done, please?"

"You don't see it?" There was a tinge of irritation in his voice. "No one else could have helped *but* Squanto. He had to speak English, which he only knew because he had been sold into slavery. He had to know the land, which he only knew because he had been raised on it. But he also had to be alive! Which he wouldn't have been if he hadn't been taken from his people. Squanto could've seen his whole life as a tragedy. He had every reason to quit, to despair, but he didn't. He took his struggles and did something *good* with it! He saved all those people."

I stood up. "What's your point?"

"Think!" Mr. Amos said, grabbing my shoulders. "A special life prepares you for something special. That's *your* life, Sky. That's the point."

Just then, Ember burst out from behind the bedroom doors.

"Stop it! Don't tell those stories to him! Don't tell those while I'm here."

She had obviously been overhearing some of our conversation.

"It's already finished!" I yelled over her.

Ember wiped away a line of tears from her cheek. "No one can say any of those stories! Especially not around Henry."

"Why not?" Mr. Amos asked.

"Because they're dangerous," she said, her voice cracking.

I could see her hands shaking. Her eyes darting around the room. Each new person who followed her from the bedroom only made the shaking worse. She was afraid of them, I could tell. Mr. Freeman tried to say something to calm her down.

"They ain't one bit dangerous. You can bet on that."

That only made things worse.

Ember stumbled away from him. "They are. They kill people."

I knew exactly what she meant, but it sounded crazy when she said it. Ember looked at us like an animal surrounded by bloodthirsty hunters. She inched toward the door and looked like she might run if anyone made any sudden moves.

Mrs. Freeman came no closer but asked, "Who? Who did they kill?"

"My … my …," she said.

"It's all right. *Your* what?"

"My … my parents!"

Mrs. Freeman couldn't help herself. She tried to go to Ember, and Ember made a run for it. She sprinted through the rain toward the grove as all of us ran onto the porch. They all called after her.

"Ember!"

"Come back, dear."

"We won't hurt ya."

Mr. Amos started to rush off the porch to follow her, but I stopped him.

"Let me talk to her."

He gave me a nod of approval, and I took off after her.

She was fast, faster than I expected. I yelled at her in between gulping breaths.

"Come back!"

She kept running.

"Please. I just want to talk to you."

She still ran.

"What about your brother!"

She stopped.

Ember put her hands on her knees and gagged a little, then stood to face me. She was on the verge of collapse.

"Don't talk about my brother."

"I'm just saying, you can't just leave him here. You think these people are murderers."

"They *are* murderers," she said, turning away from me.

I took one step closer to her, reaching my hand out to touch her shoulder.

"These people didn't kill your parents."

"Don't touch me," she said, jumping away like I was poisonous.

I needed a new tactic. I remembered what Mr. Amos had told me.

"It's hard to adjust to living here. But these people aren't evil. I mean, they're weird. They're *really* weird. Honestly, I usually can't stand them. And their stories."

She slowly began to turn to face me.

"Sometimes I miss Oasis," I continued. "I miss my friends, and the street I lived on. I don't miss the food. The food is terrible. I didn't realize that until I came here."

I thought I heard her laugh, just a little.

"Seriously, you'll never eat cell-cultured meat again. Have you ever heard of cobbler?"

She finally faced me. "No."

"Mrs. Freeman, the one who talked to you, she makes this thing called cobbler. You'll forget about Oasis the second you taste it."

She laughed again.

"It does smell better in Oasis, though. It always smells the same everywhere. Here, everywhere you go smells different. It changes all the time. And sometimes it's awful..."

This is working. What else can I say?

"But sometimes, it smells really good. Like cobbler. Besides, you're probably tired. I don't know why you were running away from Oasis, but I ran away, too, and I know that's not easy. They have good beds here. And it's so quiet at night. You've never heard a quiet like it in your whole life."

I waited a moment.

"And I promise you they would never kill anyone."

"How do you know that?"

"Because they haven't killed me."

That seemed to make sense to her, in her own exhausted way.

She sat down in the leaves and covered her face with her hands.

"I think I'm going to be sick."

I knelt beside her, but far enough away that if she did throw up, it wouldn't splash on me.

"You need to sleep."

She dug her head deeper into her hands and sniffled a little. "What am I doing here?"

It was the exact question I had asked myself when I'd gotten here. I reached out my hand to her.

"Let's go back."

She took my hand. I could tell she didn't want to, but she was almost too exhausted to do it on her own. The second she was on her feet, she let go and made a point of stepping away from me.

On our way back to the Sticking Place, we passed Rosa leading the Freeman children the opposite direction through the grove. Lincoln came straight to us and reached out his hand to Ember for a handshake.

"Welcome to Cherry Harbor. My name is Lincoln Freeman. These are my brothers and sisters—Harper, Ben, Martin, Will, Fred, and that's Harriet," he said, nodding to the baby in Rosa's arms.

I whispered to Ember. "Yeah, there's seven of them. It takes some getting used to."

Lincoln gently cleared his throat to remind Ember that his hand was still out for a handshake. Ember didn't move.

I intercepted the handshake. "Okay. Thanks, Lincoln. She's pretty tired, so we'll have to pick this up another time."

I led Ember away from the group.

"Not big on the handshakes, huh? That'll be hard for you here."

As we walked away, I heard Harper saying, "Two new people in one year? This is the best year ever!"

Mr. Amos was asleep in the rocking chair on the front porch, waiting for us.

"Mr. A," I shouted from a distance, waking him up.

He gave me a firm slap on the back as we came onto the porch.

Ow.

"Good man," he said.

Mr. Amos had made Ember a bed out of pillows on the floor of the main room in the Sticking Place. He had made a nightstand out of a metal briefcase and laid a book on it for Ember to read, just like he always did for me.

I said good night, and as I turned around to look at Ember one more time, she was throwing the book on the floor, just like I had.

I like this girl.

CHAPTER ELEVEN
A SICKLY STRANGER
(Ember)

I stood in front of our unit at 1607 Hatcher Avenue, banging on a door that refused to open. I kept calling out Mrs. Grisham's name, but I never seemed to hear my voice shouting. It sounded strange, as if it were an echo in the distance. A panic filled me.

What if Mrs. Grisham never made it back?

Then again, if she *had* made it back, what if she no longer wanted me? What if she refused to take me back now? I knew I couldn't go back to Azaz. She definitely wouldn't take me back.

I have no one.

I pounded at the door, crying for Mrs. Grisham, begging her to take me back, until I heard a strange sound. A soothing voice came out of nowhere. Someone was singing.

I woke up in a cold sweat in a dark room.

Where am I?

But as the fog in my head faded and I remembered everything that had happened, I almost wished I could go back to my nightmare. The woman singing was Mrs. Hernandez; she had not left Henry's side one time all night. At least, for most of the night that I was awake. I had been fighting sleep all night; keeping my eyelids open had been an act of sheer will. But sleep won over in the end.

When I first heard Mrs. Hernandez, I almost ran over to her, worried she was telling Henry a story, but I soon realized she was singing in a different language.

It was a glorious sound.

Unable to sleep in a bed that was more comfortable than my own back at the unit, I decided I couldn't lie there any longer being tormented by my thoughts. I slid out from under the covers and crept to the front door, opening it without Mrs. Hernandez noticing. I sat down in Mr. Amos's chair and closed my eyes, gently rocking back and forth. The morning air rushed over the porch, raising every hair on my arms. When I heard my stomach rumble, I remembered that I hadn't eaten in a very long time.

When I finally opened my eyes after rocking for a while, I noticed a journal next to the chair, presumably Mr. Amos's. I didn't care at all what was in it—I didn't want to know. But there was a pencil next to it, so I opened the journal to a spare page and began to draw mindlessly. I sketched a Tracking Token, and the "Teal Lady," and the strange hideout I had found under the Interlink. Remembering my parents' names written on the wall, I doodled "A&J Aaronson" over and over until the repetition put me in a kind of trance.

Mr. Amos's cheery voice brought me back to reality.

"Good morning. You found the best seat in the house."

I quickly and incompletely ripped out the page I had been drawing on and then slid the journal back where I'd found it.

"It's alright." He gestured to the journal as he stepped onto the porch. "Nothing private in there."

Mr. Amos had the most disarming smile I had ever seen, but I still didn't trust him. As he came to stand next to me, I gripped the arms of the chair.

The tops of the trees sparkled as the sun rose behind them. I couldn't help but gaze at the glowing branches in total wonder. Mr. Amos noticed this and grinned.

"I said this is the best seat, but you know, there may be one even better. Would you like to see it?"

I nodded, temporarily ignoring my distrust of this man in exchange for the clearest view of the sun I had ever seen, and followed him around to the back side of the building, where he had a small wooden barge tied up to the shore, with a single chair smack-dab in the middle of it.

"I keep this one to myself, usually," Mr. Amos said.

The sun was hovering over the lake and kissing it with its light. The water glistened as the morning wind tossed it gently from side to side. Across the lake were nothing but short red cliffs. I had never seen so much wide-open space before.

Mr. Amos pointed across the water. "If you look closely, you can still see some rubble from the war. But the most amazing thing is that plants have begun to grow over it. From sorrows to flowers." He paused to breathe in the morning air. "It's magnificent."

I turned to watch Mr. Amos, who was fully immersed in the beauty of the morning; then I turned back and squinted to search for the flowers he was talking about. It only felt like a few moments before the sun was above us and Mr. Amos was leading me back to the front porch.

"Are you hungry?" he asked. "Mrs. Freeman is bringing her biscuits, and it's not an exaggeration to say they are, without a doubt, the best in the entire world."

"I've never had a biscuit before."

Mr. Amos looked at me as if he couldn't believe this; then he just smiled and nodded. "Your life is about to change."

When Mrs. Freeman arrived, I followed the scent of her fresh biscuits inside and ate until I felt sick. They were, undoubtedly, the best in the entire world.

Since it was only Mrs. Freeman, who seemed harmless, and Mr. Amos, who would have had plenty of chances to hurt me this morning if he had wanted to, and me around, I let myself get lost in the fluffy goodness of warm biscuits the same way I had gotten lost in the sunshine. So much so that I didn't notice Mr. Amos disappear for a moment. When he showed up again, he was rushing into the main room where Mrs. Freeman and I sat in opposite corners eating.

"I know this'll seem like a strange time, but I have to go for the day. Emma," he said to Mrs. Freeman, "tell the parents I need a few more days and that lessons will begin again Monday. I'll be back before sunset."

Mrs. Freeman looked perplexed. "Of course. I'll be here. Jay is coming soon with the kids. We'll watch over things until you're back."

Mr. Amos left without another word. I found this strange because he had not even grabbed one biscuit for himself.

After a busy and noisy day surrounded by people constantly coming in and out to check on Henry, I made my way back to the barge around five o'clock, hoping to see the sun set. I had no idea if that was the right time, and, when I looked at the sun, it seemed like it was going to descend in a different place. I knew that about the sun, I think. But in Oasis, with all the lights mimicking the sun, it wasn't so easy to tell.

After fifteen minutes, it was evident that the sun didn't want to go anywhere, but the lake still looked beautiful, and I hated to go back inside. Just as Mrs. Freeman had promised, I hadn't had one moment alone all day until now. If teeks carried contagious diseases, I would have already caught them all—so many came one by one to welcome me and say how sorry they were about Henry.

I liked it. And I didn't like that I liked it.

As I sat and listened to the water gently colliding with the short cliffs, all of the thoughts that had been shut out by the chatter flooded back into my mind.

Will Henry ever wake up?

Where do we go if he does?

Am I a bad person?

I felt my sadness shift to anger, like a set of dark clouds suddenly drifting over the lake. All I could think about were the people who were to blame for this tragedy. It was Mrs. Grisham's fault. And Henry's fault. And it was most certainly the fault of those stupid teeks and their hideous stories.

But what about you, Ember?

I was in a battle to the death with my own mind when Mr. Amos appeared out of nowhere.

"Come inside. There's someone you need to see."

For a moment, the dark clouds disappeared.

Henry. He must be talking about Henry.

Before he could say anything else, I rushed around to the front porch and in the door.

"Where is he?" I asked.

Mrs. Freeman, looking pleasantly surprised, said, "I didn't expect you to take this so well. He's in the bedroom."

I ran to my bag and pulled out Henry's wooden sword. I had been dreaming about doing this ever since he became unconscious. Brandishing the sword, I burst through the door, gleefully shouting, "To war, my brother!" But not only was Henry still lying unconscious in the dim room; he was accompanied by the shadow of a man in a muddy overcoat at his bedside.

"Who are you?"

"He kept it," the man murmured, gesturing to the sword.

I had no idea what he was talking about.

"Who are you?" I asked again.

"Oh no." Mrs. Freeman rushed into the room. "Ember, this is Mr.—"

"Why are you with Henry?" I said. "He's sick. Who are you?"

The man rose from his knees and stepped into the light coming from the doorway.

"I know you. You're the man who jumped into the Interlink track. Get away from Henry!"

With Mrs. Hernandez right behind, Mr. Amos entered the room, saying, "Wait. Ember. You don't know who this—"

"I know him," I said. "I know all about him."

I gazed at the strange man, a fury building inside of me. His face was red, and his eyes were swollen. He looked like he was aging, moment by moment, right in front of me.

"I found your stupid hideout," I said. "I know everything. I know about your stories. I know what they did to my parents. What people like YOU did. And you won't do it to Henry. Not you. Not anyone."

"I know you found the hideout," the man said in a weak voice as he stepped toward me.

Sky appeared at the doorway, but I ignored him. "It wasn't even hard. Pretty bad hideout. The A.O. found me there. That's how this all started."

"The A.O.?" Sky asked, entering the room and making Mrs. Hernandez jump.

"Azaz Aylo," I told Sky. "Everyone knows her." I turned back to the man. "She wanted to take me in, but because I found your stupid hideout—"

Sky interrupted, "She wanted to *what*?"

"Let me live with her," I said.

His face twisted into a mess of offense, disgust, and disbelief.

"What? What's that look for?"

Sky opened his mouth to speak, but the stranger cut him off. "I opened the door," he told me, stepping even closer.

I turned to face him. "Why would you do that? You're lying."

I remembered something Mrs. Grisham had told me.

"If it opened, someone opened it for you."

"Ember, please, listen," Mr. Amos said. "It's not what you think—"

"Why would she take *you* in?" Sky yelled over him. "Who are you?"

"Sky, not now," Mrs. Freeman urged.

I ignored Sky and remained singularly focused on the man. "Why did you open it?"

He was a shadow of a man, growing dimmer with every word I said to him. He opened his palms and reached out his hands.

"I wanted you to see it. I thought ... I had no idea you were so ... I wanted you to see it."

"Why!"

"Do you not remember?" he asked. "The stories—"

"I hate the stories—"

"—the stories from your book."

Cold rushed over me.

"What ... did y-you say?"

The man dropped his head and spoke in a whisper. "Remember ... we wrote, 'May the past guide you into the future.'"

No. It can't be. No way.

"Who are you?"

At that moment there was a sound from Henry's bed. He was turning onto his side. Mrs. Hernandez clutched her heart and exclaimed, "*¡Gracias a Dios!* He's moving."

As I rushed to Henry's side, the man did the same thing.

"Henry," we said together.

I ignored him as I watched my brother.

"Henry, it's Ember. Please wake up. Please."

The man's hands were clasped in a prayer position as all of us waited to see if Henry would move again, but nothing happened.

"Did he ... oh no. Why did he stop moving?"

I waited for Mrs. Hernandez to give me an answer.

"I don't know." She rushed to check his pulse. "Oh, thank God. He's alive. I think that was a good sign."

As I let out a sigh, I heard the man do the same. For a moment I had forgotten he was there. My fury returned.

"Who are you?" I demanded through gritted teeth.

The man looked at me, his swollen eyes glistening.

"I'm Adam Aaronson. Your dad."

The whole room froze, and so did I.

I studied the ragged, tired face in front of me.

This man couldn't be my father; it was impossible. My father was strong and tall. He was the smartest, bravest man I had ever known. The man before me now was fragile—pathetic. But when I looked into his eyes—his swollen, desperate eyes—I realized I did in fact recognize them. I wished I didn't, but I did. He stood there, compulsively scratching himself while he waited for me to answer. But I had no idea what to say.

This was my father. But I didn't know him.

I overheard Mrs. Hernandez behind me whispering to Mr. Amos, "But . . . Adam Aaronson is dead."

"I thought so too," Mr. Amos replied. "But I got word a few days ago that he was with the Amadi girls at the Oarsmen Outpost."

I noticed Mrs. Hernandez backing away from the door, gesturing for Mr. Amos to join her.

"I wish those girls wouldn't stay at that Outpost. The whole Amadi family needs to accept that the Oarsmen ended years ago. They can't bring back the dead by living in that silly Outpost and pretending they're coming back. There are no Oarsmen anymore. Why hold on to nothing?"

Mr. Amos lingered for a moment, his eyes glancing back to me and the man. To me and my father. I noticed he was holding the torn page from the journal I had drawn on that morning—the page where I had written my father's name.

"It's not nothing . . . until they stop holding on," Mr. Amos said. "Then it's nothing."

Sky left to go into the main room. Mr. Amos followed along with Mrs. Hernandez, leaving me with the stranger who was my father. I looked away from him and focused on Henry.

"I wanted to find you sooner," he said. "I wanted to get you out of Oasis . . . to a place like this."

When I looked at him, he was scratching his arm and swallowing in pain. He blinked his eyes, and they remained closed for so long that I thought he might be passing out. But then they reopened, making me look back at Henry. I heard my father make a loud, gross swallowing noise and remembered what Azaz had told me about how the stories had ruined my parents. My father did seem ruined—irreparably.

"How long have you been looking for us?" I said.

"Since the moment I was taken away. They injected me and sentenced me to years of sleep, and even then I looked for you both in my dreams. And I know your mother—" He couldn't go on.

"She what?"

He swallowed air as if it were lead and rocked back and forth like a ship in a thunderstorm.

"She … what?" I asked again.

His unsteady hand pulled multiple pieces of paper from his shirt pocket as he cried softly.

"I wrote you this when I woke up. For when … in case I never …"

I took the papers from him and began to read while he continued rocking back and forth.

> *Ember and Henry,*
>
> *I've heard it said that we don't really die until the story of our life stops being told. This is our story. Tell it and we will keep living.*

I flipped through the pages, stopping at paragraphs and sentences that caught my eye.

> *… The world was very different when your mother and I first met … loved you with every fiber of our being … Your mother was born with a disorder in her brain. I dedicated my life to technology that I believed, and still believe, could help her …*

... There was a war. You've probably heard of it. It was a senseless war. Don't let anyone tell you otherwise ... I could join them and fight, or I could go to Oasis and work in their lab. Your mother was pregnant with you, Ember, at the time. I took the job in Oasis to be able to meet you.... Your mother's dream was to be your mom. She would want you to know that, both of you ...

I stopped reading. I couldn't stand it.

I had parents who loved me. And one of them was right next to me.

As I glanced back at my father, I noticed he had collapsed to the ground without me even noticing. He lay there motionless.

"Mrs. Hernandez! Mrs. Hernandez!"

She rushed into the room and checked his pulse. Mr. Amos came right behind her.

"Is he okay? My God. Is he?"

"He's breathing," Mrs. Hernandez said. "He's breathing. Get him into the bed."

I stood there and watched them lay my father on the bed, next to Henry. I couldn't move. After all this time, my dad had come back for me. But as I stared at the feeble frame of a man barely alive, I wondered if it was already too late.

CHAPTER TWELVE

THE OARSMEN

(Sky)

Nothing made sense.

That's why I was following Rosa up to the cliffs. Not just following—I was actually running after her. She had told me she was going to check on Ember, who had decided to get away from everybody to think. Rosa was worried about her. I just wanted some answers. But before we reached her, I wanted something else.

Oxygen.

As we neared the water, I couldn't keep up with Rosa. I felt light-headed. I slowed down, clutching at the massive stitch in my side. My legs didn't seem to be able to run as fast as my mind was racing.

"A special life prepares you for something special."

The words from Mr. Amos seemed to mock me. There was nothing special about my life. But *maybe* there could be?

No way.

I replayed the scene that had happened earlier with Ember. How she'd brought up Azaz Aylo, how she'd said the A.O. had wanted to take her in. But why? Why would Azaz care about Ember?

Then to see her with the stranger, the man calling himself her father. While Ember spoke to the man named Adam Aaronson, I stepped into the main room, where Mr. Amos was.

"Who is he?" I asked.

"An Oarsman," Mr. Amos mumbled, mostly to himself.

He looked at Mrs. Hernandez, who was nearby. "You'll want to look at him, Val. He was injected too."

This shocked both of us.

"What you say?" Mrs. Hernandez said, standing from her chair and rushing back to Mr. Amos.

"He was injected seven years ago," he replied.

"But—"

"But he woke up. He woke up a few months ago. I know. I couldn't believe it either. It was an act of sheer will or providence . . . but he woke up. And he walked here, probably hundreds of miles. I didn't ask him yet, but," he whispered privately to Mrs. Hernandez, "what if it's not just the Amadis? What if there are more Oarsmen, enough to—"

"Enough." Mrs. Hernandez turned away from him. "No more of this today."

She walked back to the chair, sat down, and dropped her head into her hands. Mr. Amos turned to me, and I knew he still had more to say.

"But he's fading into nothing. His mind is there, but it comes and goes. They told me he doesn't sleep, and when he does, he wakes up screaming. He was a good man, a brilliant man . . . I hardly recognize him."

"You knew him?" I asked.

"I did. And his wife. But I didn't connect them to Ember and Henry until this morning." He moved to the doorway to peer inside. "He's been looking for them. He came all this way . . . I hope she's not cruel to him."

When I finally reached the edge of the cliff, I found Rosa standing there, laughing between deep breaths.

"I was starting to think you weren't coming," she told me.

Behind her was a cotton candy sky. The last bits of pink clouds were starting to fade to a bluish gray. The sight was beautiful. Just then I saw

Ember walking toward us.

"What are you doing here?" she asked both of us.

I looked at Rosa, but I was still gasping for air.

"We were worried about you."

Not me, I wanted to say but couldn't.

"I'm fine."

Her eyes looked glassy, as if she had been crying. Ember might be a lot of things, but "fine" was not one of them.

"I heard about what happened," Rosa said. "About you meeting your father."

"Yeah, I'm … It's a lot to take in."

I guess I had wanted to talk to her, to tell her I understood what it was like to have people let you down. But before I could, Rosa said something that shocked both of us.

"I just wanted to come here to tell you that your dad—Adam Aaronson—is a hero. A real hero."

"How?" Ember moved closer to Rosa for an explanation.

"Adam Aaronson was the first man to publicly defy Topos. He's practically a legend to the kids around here."

"Why would he do that?" I said.

"He was working on a new technology about connecting computers and the human brain. At first Topos didn't really want to control people's minds, they said—they just wanted to read them. And the experiments started out with all volunteers. At least that's what they say. But my dad said that they told young men that they could either fight in the war or volunteer in the lab as subjects—the lab Adam Aaronson was in charge of—"

"You don't have to say his whole name every time, you know," I said.

"—so Adam Aaronson went along with it for a while—years, I think. I don't remember. My brother would know. He loved Adam Aaronson … um …"

Rosa cleared her throat.

It occurred to me that I had never seen Rosa's brother in Cherry Harbor. No one had ever mentioned him before.

"Anyway, they said, 'You can either fight or lie on this table and think of a number five times while we scan your brain.' So obviously people did that. But then Adam Aaronson noticed that they were bringing in subjects who were unconscious—hundreds of them. And when he looked into it, he found out Topos was injecting people with this teal thing and putting them to sleep. They wanted to study dreams, or watch dreams, or something, but Adam Aaronson thought it was unethical, which it was. So, he refused to work on anyone who came in unconscious, and they couldn't get rid of him because he was so smart, and they needed him to run their lab."

I looked at Ember and could tell she was fascinated. But none of this impressed me. "What's the big deal? He didn't do anything."

Rosa rolled her eyes. "I'm not finished yet. He was also a member of the Oarsmen."

That word again.

"Okay. Who are the Oarsmen, anyway? Amos was talking about them today too. What's the deal with them?"

Rosa looked out at the wide-open stretch of water. "They're heroes."

"Heroes? Like you think Adam Aaronson is a hero?"

"Can you just please let her talk?" Ember blurted out while giving me a look of anger.

Rosa continued to look at Ember. "Adam Aaronson is a hero. And so are the Oarsmen."

I looked back at Ember, waiting for her to put an end to this. She was from Oasis. She knew better. But she didn't seem annoyed at all, not with Rosa anyway.

Is she actually buying this?

I knew I should have kept my mouth shut, but that never stopped me before.

"Topos was in charge, not him. He should have just done what they asked."

"But what they asked for was wrong," Ember said, with a real bite to her voice. "You heard Rosa."

"What's 'wrong,' anyway?" I asked Ember. "Just because Rosa thinks it's wrong doesn't mean it's wrong."

"I don't just *think* it's wrong; that's not—" Rosa began to say, trying to back out of this discussion.

I wasn't about to back down.

"And anyway, who cares? Who cares what's 'wrong'? Who cares if they watch your dreams? Your dreams aren't important."

"But they're yours," Rosa said quietly.

"Yeah! They're mine," Ember repeated much more loudly.

I shook my head and stood directly in front of Ember.

"What's yours? Topos built the lab he worked in, the city the test-subjects lived in. Topos gave everyone food and a place to live and things to do, and basically gave them *everything*, so why is it so bad for them to get some dreams in return? He doesn't sound heroic to me at all. I bet the Oarsmen, or whatever they're called, aren't either."

Rosa sighed. "You're wrong. They're heroes."

If I heard that word one more time, I might throw up. "It doesn't matter anyway. Nobody cares."

"I care," Rosa said. "I care a lot, actually."

I laughed. "You care about everything."

"Well, you care about nothing," Ember barked out, now defending her new girlfriend.

I was outnumbered and needed to get out of there. But I just kept digging my hole.

"I'm just a realist. I know enough not to mess with people in charge. Rosa, I know all your made-up stories are about 'heroes,' and how they always 'do the right thing,' but no one in the real world cares about that. Ember knows that."

"You don't know what I know," Ember said.

Rosa frowned. "You know they aren't made-up."

I no longer felt like being argumentative. Now I was just angry.

"I know a lot more than you or any of the people around here know," I said to Rosa. "You live in this little bubble, believing all these little lies. Making up all these stupid little stories. And now you're going to lie to Ember about her dad just to make her feel better. But she doesn't need to feel better. She just has to accept that her dad is a nobody. That he left her. Because he's not a hero! He's just an ordinary jerk who picked the wrong side and suffered the consequences. She can handle that, but you—"

"Stop it! Just stop it!" Rosa said to me as she burst into tears and then stumbled away.

Ember and I watched her run back toward the trees. She was going to go back through the grove alone, even though it was almost dark out.

"You're really a jerk, you know that?" Ember told me.

"No, I'm not. I'm just being honest."

"You're being mean. And there's no reason why. Rosa didn't do a thing to you. She was just trying to make me feel better. Besides, what if she's telling the Truth? Is it so impossible that my dad isn't just a—what do you call him? —ordinary jerk? Just because yours obviously was."

"I don't care."

Ember gave me a disgusted look. "It's sad."

"What's sad?"

"For someone so worried about lies, doesn't it bother you that you're lying to yourself?"

Before I could reply, Ember took off into the trees to follow Rosa. Part of me wanted to follow her, to tell her she was wrong, but I remained there. Because I wasn't sure that she was wrong.

That's what I get for coming to check on her.

Spotting a tree branch above me, I tried to rip it out in anger. I thought destroying something would make me feel better. But it was stronger than me.

"AGH!"

I yanked at it wildly and even propped my foot against the trunk for leverage. When it finally came loose, I chucked it into the water and sat back down. Then I let out a long sigh.

"I am so stupid," I said to the stars.

"I'd have to agree, my boy."

The voice made me jump. I stood up as I saw Mr. Amos emerging from the trees and chuckling at me.

"What the heck?" I shouted. "Are you following me now?"

"Mrs. Hernandez just wanted me to check on the three of you. I tried to tell her it was fine, but well, you know her. Then I saw Rosa running toward the Sticking Place, crying. Probably to tell her mother, God help you. Then Ember right after her."

I couldn't make out his expression in the dark until he got closer to me.

"You need to be careful with your words," he said.

"You're not my dad."

Mr. Amos sat down next to me, and he laughed. "Oh boy. With that attitude, you're lucky I'm not."

It was a stunning night—a full moon. The air was only a bit cold. Snuggled next to another warm body, I could have sat there forever, perfectly comfortable. Of course, with Ember and Rosa gone, Mr. Amos was the only person I could snuggle up with, and I would rather be dead.

"A word of advice, my boy." Mr. Amos slapped my back. "About the ladies."

"I noticed you're single."

"A twist of fate. But I wasn't always. In fact, I had a reputation of being good with—"

"Please stop."

For a moment, neither of us said a word. Then I finally spoke.

"I blew it. I really blew it."

Mr. Amos clasped his hands together and leaned his elbows on his knees. "Seems you did."

"So, what even are the Oarsmen anyways? What makes them so special? What's up with you people?"

Mr. Amos chuckled. "Is this how you talked to the girls?"

"Yes," I said with a sigh.

For a moment we sat there, and I was so cold my body began to shake.

"Do you really want to know? About the Oarsmen?"

"What the heck," I said. "Yeah, I do. Ugh. I actually do."

"Look at me. In my eyes. Look at me. Now take my hand." Mr. Amos held out his hand. "You shake this hand, and you are promising to never tell anyone what I'm about to tell you. Can you promise that?"

I nodded.

"Then shake it," Mr. Amos said. "No. While still looking in my eyes. You have to do both."

It was surprisingly difficult to grab his hand without breaking eye contact, but I managed it.

He gripped my hand, holding it in place. "That was a promise. Man-to-man. You keep those."

After we dropped hands, I had to shake out my wrist to try to get the feeling back, checking my fingers for any damage made by my first man-to-man promise.

"There was a war. Actually, let's start before that. There was a country and a corporation, and then there was a war," Mr. Amos said. "It's not that Topos took control. They were given it. Bit by bit, until they had it all."

"I know this. I know all about Topos."

"I highly doubt it. Topos wants to create a new world, but they can't create a new world with the same old man. Man has to change too. But men don't change, not really. Despite our advancements, our break-throughs, our brilliant new ideas, we still want the same things our ances-tors did. We still make the same mistakes. But the leaders of Topos are arrogant. They think human beings are containers that can be filled with whatever they want, and if they just empty us out, bit by bit, then we can be made new.

"I used to think that was true. But then I found myself emptied out—of everything, I thought. And there was still something there. Something ancient—something that's been there since the beginning of man. It's in all of us, and we can't escape it. Topos doesn't understand that. But the founders of the Oarsmen did.

"There were four founders. We called them the Gang of Four. They formed right after Topos sent out a memo with the headline 'Focus on the Future.'"

Mr. Amos quoted the memo in a whisper.

"'Don't look back. It's time to leave the past in the past...' It was a relief. The recent past was war, famine, death—no one wanted to look back. It started as a purging of bad memories, but it became a purging of all memories. It was cathartic, it was freeing... and then it wasn't. Then your favorite song would disappear . . . your favorite book. The stories you'd learned in school. Gone."

As Mr. Amos looked out over the water, I felt my body shiver again. But this wasn't from the cold.

"No one cared, really," Mr. Amos continued. "No one except the Gang of Four. If something started disappearing—a book, a story, art from a certain era, or even weapons—they would collect as many as possible. But they kept getting caught."

"Bet they did," I said under my breath.

"*But* they didn't quit. They were slowly forming a rebellion, and Topos knew it, but they still couldn't snuff it out. Every time they tried, they missed something. The Gang of Four were said to have a secret location where they were building an armory to house some kind of new weapon to resist Topos head-on. But they never told any of the other Oarsmen where it was or what was in it because there were rumors of a spy in the mix... and there was one.

"Turned everyone in. Then everything changed. Before, Topos was more of a nuisance. They changed the calendars and restricted travel, but it was livable. For most people, it was fine. Then two of the Gang of Four disappeared. The Oarsmen went underground. But they kept growing, with more and more members, until ... Day Five, August 3 ... In one night, thousands of people disappeared. They let the kids and babies stay, but anyone older than that was gone. Overnight. Anyone suspected of being an Oarsman. They were all gone."

"So, they're gone. It's over—the Oarsmen?" I asked.

"That's probably enough for now." Mr. Amos stood up. "Let's go back home."

"But why are they called the Oarsmen?"

Mr. Amos was walking away. "You ever seen anyone row a boat?"

"Do what?"

"Another time, my boy. Another time."

As I followed him back through the trees, I felt my mind spinning.

Could all that be True?

I had run up to these cliffs with a head full of questions. Now I only had more.

I also had a couple of girls I probably needed to apologize to.

CHAPTER THIRTEEN

ATTACK

(Ember)

I'm not sure how I navigated through the trees alone, but there was no way I was going back and asking Sky to guide me. I would have rather been lost, which I was once or twice. But I kept up my pace because I wanted to get back as quickly as possible to check on Henry, and to talk to my dad.

My dad.

Those two words still felt strange echoing in my head.

As I wandered down the path in the woods, I replayed what Sky had said about him.

"He's just an ordinary jerk who picked the wrong side."

But what if he was wrong? What if Rosa was telling the Truth? What if my dad was a hero, even if he did pick the wrong side? That didn't seem right to me. But then I remembered him as he was when I was a kid, towering above me, picking me up in his strong arms, he and mom dancing in the kitchen. I remembered the night he was taken away, I never heard him cry or beg for his life. An ordinary jerk would have begged, would have screamed. But he didn't. What did Sky know about anything anyway?

As I neared the Sticking Place, the sound of gagging cut through the darkness. I stopped and looked around, but I couldn't make out anybody in the soft glow of the moonlight. I waited and heard more gasping sounds. I realized someone was throwing up nearby.

I followed the sound and found my father, keeled over, vomiting into the grass as quietly as he could. The hem of his pants was splattered with puke, and his shirt was soaked in sweat.

"Holy Administrator. Help! We need help."

"Shh, please don't call anyone," he whispered. "I'm fine." Then he threw up again. I walked to his side, avoiding the circle of vomit that surrounded him. He was convulsing and gasping for air. Then he would scratch his arm so intensely it broke his skin, making him bleed. There was blood all over his hand.

"You're sick," I said. "Let me get someone."

"No, please. This is normal for me. There's nothing anybody can do."

"You weren't this bad earlier."

"I wasn't." He threw up again, this time on my shoes. "Most nights are like this. I'm sorry you have to see this, Ember."

He put his hands on his knees and then on his hips until he was standing up straight. "I'm okay now."

"You don't look okay to me," a voice from behind us called out.

Mr. Amos was walking over to us from the woods.

"You need to be resting," he said to my father.

"I didn't want to get sick inside your home."

"My home is your home. The ladies will get you fixed up in a couple of days," Mr. Amos told him. "You'll see. They're incredible."

My father's eyes became misty. "It won't work. I should have told you. But it won't work."

He slumped over, stumbling toward the ground. Mr. Amos grabbed him before he hit the dirt.

"Let me help you over to the porch." Mr. Amos took him by the arm to give him some support. I followed them to the porch, but then, watching my father run his bloody hand through his hair, I felt an overwhelming desire to leave.

"I can let you two talk," I told them.

"No," Mr. Amos said. "Stay. Please."

As I leaned up against the porch railing, I looked at the two men as the light of the full moon washed over them—Mr. Amos, a picture of health; my father with vomit on his cheek. They both rocked back and forth, though only Mr. Amos was in a rocking chair.

"It still runs in my veins," my father said in a weak voice. "I don't think it ever comes out. Nasty stuff. They don't plan for anyone waking up."

The more I looked at him, the less I recognized him under the thick layer of sick that covered him like a blanket. He was pale and paper-thin, his eyes watery and dazed. Even breathing appeared to be a struggle for him.

"I'm glad you found me," my father said to Mr. Amos. "I needed someone I could trust." Mr. Amos responded with seemingly outsized gratitude. "I can't tell you how much it means to me—after everything. That you still—"

"There isn't much time," my father interrupted, his voice barely a whisper. "It's time for the Oarsmen..."

He stopped and grimaced, one hand clutching at his stomach.

"Adam, let's—"

My father waved off Mr. Amos. "No. The Oarsmen. There are new Oarsmen all around the country. I met some of them on my way here. It's time to finish what we started. Bring down Topos once and for all. We're ready."

I remembered Rosa saying that my father was a member of the Oarsmen; what that meant, I had no idea. Mr. Amos looked as if a small electric shock had just jolted his rocking chair.

"So, the Gang of Four are alive? I thought they would get out somehow. You did. Praise God. Are they at the Armory? Have you seen it? Is it intact?" He was growing more and more excited. "The Amadis! My God. The Amadis won't believe it. They've dreamed of this, Adam. I mean, dreamed for so long. How many are there?"

My father looked at Mr. Amos vacantly.

"What?"

"The Gang of Four are gone," my father whispered.

"But—"

"We're still regathering."

"But ... without the Armory?"

"There is still a way to get to the Armory."

"How?" Mr. Amos asked.

"I'll need your help. You know Oasis like I do. There's something we need there."

"What is it?"

"A map—to the Armory."

My father had spoken these words as if they were his last gasp. His body wilted in the chair as he closed his eyes and nodded his head. He was asleep.

I rushed over to wake him up.

"Let him rest," Mr. Amos said.

I backed away from my father slowly, making sure his chest was still rising and falling. "How long is he going to be like this?"

Mr. Amos seemed distracted and didn't respond.

"Hello," I said, waving my hand in his face.

"I'm sorry. I'm just taking it all in. I thought it would be years before we would have the means to challenge Topos, but if we can find the Armory ... If the Oarsmen really are—"

In that moment, I couldn't have cared less about some Armory or the Oarsmen.

"Yeah, they're returning or whatever. That's great. Bet my dad would like to be alive to see it."

"Of course." Mr. Amos put his hand over his heart and looked at my father. "Of course. What will help him is the same antidote that will help your brother."

"Where is it? Where do I get it?"

"Mrs. Hernandez is working on it. She's probably in the lab, working on it, right now."

"The other woman helping Henry? The one who sings?"

I knew the answer to that question, but I asked it to emphasize how insane it was that the life of my father and my brother was in the hands of some lady who, up to that point, I had only seen singing and running around with weird dried leaves.

Mr. Amos gave me a look that said, *Excuse you, young lady*, without him having to say anything.

I don't have time for this.

"Where's the lab?"

At that moment, Sky appeared, coming through the trees. He stopped abruptly on the porch steps, noticing my father. "Is he alright?"

"Does he look alright?" I turned back to Mr. Amos. "Where's the lab?"

Sky stepped closer. "Mrs. Hernandez's lab? I know where it is."

I looked back at Mr. Amos to verify that was true.

"He does."

I took a long, angry inhale through my nose. "Fine. I want to go there now. Let's go."

"Um, okay," Sky said.

"Watch him," I told Mr. Amos, pointing at my father. I started to walk away, then turned my head back. "Please."

On principle, I was not going to be the first one to speak, so Sky and I walked silently through the trees. When the town was in eyeshot, he said, "Look, I don't think I said what I wanted to say earlier."

I started walking faster. "You mean you didn't mean to call my dad a jerk?"

"Well, um, yeah. I didn't. I mean, I did, but I shouldn't have. It's just—"

"It's just that you have major issues, and you took them out on me. Well, I'm sorry that my dad's a hero, and yours isn't."

Sky stopped walking. Maybe on any other night I would have felt bad, but not this one.

"I think I should go back now," he said, without one hint of anger. He pointed at a shack down the road. "That's the lab there, the one with the blue door. I can come back and get you if—"

"I'm fine."

"Okay."

We parted ways. I could feel all the horrible things I had hoped to say to him boiling under my skin, turning into a hot goo that gushed through my whole body. I reached the blue door at the point of the explosion. Mr. Hernandez opened the door, laughing until he saw who it was.

"Oh. *Hola.*"

Mrs. Hernandez was standing in the room behind him, crouched over a small wooden table overlaid with a plastic tablecloth, wearing a floor-length cotton gown over her clothes, oversized safety goggles, and disposable gloves. The cool night air was gently flowing in through the open window, which carried the faint gasoline-like smell from the small room.

"I need to talk to you about the antidote."

Mrs. Hernandez didn't turn to face me. "Ah." I saw her place a small glass bottle on a scale; then she spoke to her husband. "I need a moment, *mi amor.*"

Mr. Hernandez invited me inside, then stepped out and closed the door.

I noticed a small vial of glowing teal liquid on the table.

"Touch nothing," Mrs. Hernandez extracted some of the teal liquid and held it up to the light. "How can I help you?"

She still hadn't turned to face me, which I found made the angry-goo-in-my-veins sensation much worse.

"Is that the antidote?" I asked.

"It will be," she said coldly, dropping tiny bits of the teal liquid into the container on the scale.

"Is it done?"

"No."

I took a step toward her.

"Stay where you are," she warned.

"Is it close? Are you even close?"

Just looking at the way her whole back tensed, I suspected the angry goo was in her veins too. She removed her gloves, walked to a small table a few steps away, and made a note in a tiny notebook. She could have looked at me then, but she didn't.

"It's a slow process," she said, putting her gloves back on.

Slow process?

That's all she wanted to say to me? Me? With a dying father and an unconscious brother?

"Are you really the only one who can make this antidote? There's no one else in this whole stupid town?" I said.

Her hand shook with anger as she dropped a few more bits of glowing teal liquid into a different glass tube. She picked it up, swirled it, and put it back down. Then she just watched it, motionless. I couldn't stand there watching her do nothing for one more second knowing my dad was back in the woods, dying.

What in the world is she doing?

"Look! I get it. You don't like us; you don't care. But this is my—"

She cut me off, ripping off her gloves and finally looking at me.

"Don't care? *¡Ay, Dios mío!* Don't care? Is that why I am here, making an antidote for your *papá?* Is that why I visit your brother every day? Do you have any idea how hard this is for us? Helping you! Helping you when it's people like you who—"

She stopped herself.

"People like me? Like *me?* It's people like *you* who cause all the problems. People like you who don't care enough about anyone to get in line. All you do is make life harder for everyone. You're the cruel ones. You're the killers."

"Then where is my son?" she said quietly, tears forming in her eyes.

"Your son?"

"My son. Where is he?"

"I-I don't know. Why would I know that?"

She wiped away the tear falling down her cheek. "Because it's people like you who took him from me."

I should have fought back; everything I had ever been taught told me she was lying. But something about the way she held back tears looked eerily familiar to me. I had never known this woman before, but I knew those eyes. They were the same tear-filled eyes my mother had the night she was taken, filled with sorrow, filled with fear. Nothing about Mrs. Hernandez's round face and dark features resembled my mother at all, at least not how I remembered her. But still, in the eyes of this strange woman, I saw my mom, looking at me.

"His name was Manny," she said. "He worked with the Amadi girls at the Oarsmen Outpost. Until one day he was captured on the road to Oasis. All the girls found was a teal hat."

"Topos," I said under my breath.

"They took him, like they took your *papá*."

I saw my mom again, hiding me in the wardrobe, handing me Henry and telling me to keep him quiet. Mrs. Hernandez's voice spoke over the memory.

"Are you sure we're the cruel ones?"

Just then the wail of a siren cut through the air.

WEE-OOO

WEE-OOO

WEE-OOO

"What is—"

Mr. Hernandez burst through the door and yelled to his wife.

"I have to go. Go to the house and hide. There's a knife in my drawer, in case—"

"Go," Mrs. Hernandez said. He kissed her and ran, and I followed him into the street. Mrs. Hernandez was yelling for me to come inside, but I ignored her and headed for the siren. There were men pouring out onto the dirt roads, carrying torches, bats, knives, and shovels. I lost sight of the back of Mr. Hernandez in the crowd. I couldn't see above the heads of the men and flaming torches, but I recognized Mr. Freeman in front of me.

"Who're they?" he yelled.

They?

I ran to nearest front porch, where an old man with a cane was coming out of the door with a baseball bat. I sprinted up the steps, and that's when I saw it.

Everyone saw it at the same time.

Topos.

I could only just make out the sea of teal set against the darkness, the glow from the Teal Lady was far too big for a syringe, even for hundreds of syringes. The glow lit up their faces as they marched toward us.

A man stepped in front of the crowd.

"What do we need to do, Mayor?" Mr. Hernandez yelled.

"I will meet them and speak to them," the man they called the mayor replied. "I'll find a diplomatic solution if I can … If I can't …"

"We'll be ready," Mr. Hernandez said.

The men broke off, assembling into groups under the direction of Mr. Hernandez. I saw Mr. Freeman running toward the old man with the cane who was just a few steps in front of me.

"How's that gun comin' along, Borey?"

"I'm afraid not well," the old man replied.

"Well, we can make do with—" He noticed me on the porch. "Ember. Ya shouldn't be here." I waved him off and watched the silhouette of the mayor against the teal sea getting smaller and smaller. He must have just reached them. The whole town went silent.

I heard Mrs. Hernandez's words echo in my mind.

Are you sure we're the cruel ones?

A woman screamed as the mayor's body fell to the ground. The man leading the T-Force slung the mayor's limp body over his shoulder. I could just make out his face. It was Commander Daley, the Commander of the T-Force. You never saw him in Oasis, which was part of what made him so threatening. But I had seen him once, coming out of Azaz's office, looking ready to kill. He had that same look now. For some reason, no one moved as he approached and laid the body on the ground. I could hear the muffled sobs of the woman who had screamed; she must have been his wife.

Mr. Freeman stepped in front me and blocked my view of the scene, but I heard Commander Daley yelling.

"We're here for Ember and Henry Grisham. Hand them over and no one gets hurt."

Mr. Freeman stood taller in front of me as my stomach turned to ice.

Me? They're here for me?

Even worse, they were there for Henry. I knew I had to get back to him, to hide him. I heard another familiar voice that I couldn't quite place.

"I see her, sir."

Cade Carter.

Cade Carter was in the front row of the T-Force. My mind scrambled.

Is Cade Carter in the T-Force?

He was holding a weapon I had never seen before, a gun with a glowing teal canister with a needle sticking out of the barrel. I imagined it spewing Teal Lady–laced needles into the crowd, putting them into perpetual sleep.

Then I realized what Cade had said.

"I see her."

Me. He's talking about me.

All these thoughts came in a matter of seconds, and I peered out from behind Mr. Freeman to see Cade's finger pointing right at me. That's when the fight really started.

Cade came running straight for me, and the men of Cherry Harbor rushed the T-Force, slicing them with shovels and lighting their uniforms on fire. Worse than I could have imagined, a spray of needles traveled at bullet pace to their targets, sending the men of Cherry Harbor into full-body spasms and shrieks of terror until they finally collapsed to the ground. It was the fastest I had ever run in my life, and still, even with the men of Cherry Harbor trying to stop him, Cade was right behind me. Thorny vines ripped open my skin as I plunged into the trees. I looked behind me and saw Cade's face as he pursued me. It was like I was an animal instead of a girl he knew, who he had worked with. My foot got caught on something and I tumbled forward.

"Help! Someone help me!"

CHAPTER FOURTEEN
PICK A SIDE
(Sky)

I was lighting the candles in the Sticking Place when I heard her screaming.

Mr. Amos had run off so quickly after the siren sounded that I hadn't had time to truly grasp what was happening. I had come up behind him as he opened his knife box and rushed to the door. I barely had time to ask what was happening. When I did, he answered so plainly.

"We're being attacked."

I heard another terrified shriek.

"That's Ember," I said, crushing the matchbox in my fist.

Without another thought, I ran out the door and straight toward the grove, feeling the damp brush squashing under my feet as I called out her name.

"Ember!"

My eyes had to adjust to the darkness outside. Once they did, I saw her sprinting toward me, her overalls covered in mud, her hair flying wildly.

"Help me!" she screamed out again.

Another figure emerged into view right behind her, close to over-taking her.

"Stop right there," the figure called out.

I recognize that voice.

"Cade?" I yelled to him, gasping for air as I ran. "What are you doing?"

He was holding some kind of new weapon. The glow of teal lit up his face. I saw the barrel pointing at Ember's back. I was just steps from her; the weapon was pointed right at us. I had no other choice.

Ember cried out as I tackled her to the ground and the needle flew over our heads and hit the tree behind us.

"Are you okay?" I said to her. She was clutching at her chest in shock, but there was no time to help her. Cade was aiming his weapon again, this time at me.

"What are you doing here?" he snarled in a tone I had never heard from him before.

"You've got to tell someone to call this off, man." I crawled in front of Ember as the barrel of Cade's weapon shifted in her direction. "Seriously, there's been some kind of mistake."

"Move!" he yelled. "Move, or I shoot you both."

I didn't move.

Moments before Cade would have pulled the trigger, I heard the voice of a woman yelling through the trees.

"Drop it or I shoot."

Only I could see Mrs. Hernandez was bluffing. She had nothing to shoot with, only a baseball bat, which was almost half her height in length. But Cade wasn't facing her, and she sounded so convincing. I capitalized on Cade's moment of indecision and lunged for his legs, tackling him to the dirt. He tried to crawl to his weapon, which had fallen to the ground, but I was holding him back.

"Grab his weapon!" I yelled to Ember. "Shoot him with it!"

Ember's hands were shaking uncontrollably as she picked up the weapon. She tried to aim it. "I can't do it."

"He'll be okay. Just do it."

"No ... I can't," she cried as Cade writhed and fought as hard as he could.

"Stop it!" I screamed out, holding him down. "He'll live. Ember, trust me."

The shot finally came, but not from Ember. It was Mrs. Hernandez who had taken the weapon and pulled the trigger. She'd hit Cade right in his poster-boy face.

Ember looked at me in horror, trying to tell me something but unable to say a word.

"They have an antidote," I said. "He'll recover."

"You're sure about that?" a deep voice growled in the darkness.

When I saw the burly figure and jet-black hair that blended into the night, I knew who it was.

"Daley?"

Oasis T-Force Commander Byron Daley emerged from the shadows into blue moonlight. His uniform was ripped across his right shoulder, revealing freshly burned, bubbling skin.

"Trotsky," Commander Daley sneered.

I hadn't heard that name in a while. It hardly felt like my own.

I had known the Commander since childhood. I had been told he used to be a likable guy, but since I had met him, I had only known him to be the way he was now—angry.

"Shooting my men in the face, that's what you do now?" he asked me.

"Call this off, Daley. These people did nothing."

I could hear the distant sound of screams getting louder and louder.

"They have two fugitives," the Commander said. "Maybe three."

I stood my ground, not afraid of him. "Someone will find out you went rogue. You'll be removed."

"Rogue?" The Commander cackled. "*I'm* not rogue."

"H233 isn't supposed to be used on innocent people, and never like this. I know the rules."

"*You* know the rules, huh? So, you ignore them on purpose?"

"Why did you even come?"

"The girl." He pointed to Ember. "She was working for us, and she turned. Attacked two of my men. Azaz wanted to wait." He looked at

Ember. "Guess you got into her head. Azaz thinks you'll change your mind and come back. Me? I don't believe in second chances."

I knew that last line of his was meant for me.

I smiled. "The last time I checked, Commander, Azaz is still your superior."

His eyes thinned as he gave me a smirk. "I received direct orders from the Administrator himself this morning to come here. This is his call, not mine, and not hers."

"The—the Administrator sent you? For m-me?" Ember said.

Commander Daley took a step in her direction, but I stood in his way.

"You need to leave," I told him.

He smiled his signature twisted grin. "Have you ever heard of a group called the Oarsmen?"

Oh no.

"The what?" I said, lying.

He laughed at me. I was never a good liar.

"You picked your side, Trotsky." Daley moved closer to me while he reached for his syringe. He could have fired his new weapon from where he stood, but I knew he wanted the satisfaction of a close-contact attack.

"Sky, watch out!" Ember cried out behind me.

I saw the glow of a flaming torch coming through the trees behind the Commander. Bradford peeked out from behind one of the trunks, making a sign that I thought meant he wanted me to stall.

"Wait!" I held out my hands. "I do know something—about the Oarsmen."

This stopped Daley in his tracks; his voice gave away his desperation.

"Tell me what you know. Tell me now!"

I saw Bradford gesturing to a group of Last-Year boys who snuck over to meet him where he stood. I just had to hold him there a little longer.

"Wow. These Oarsmen really did a number on you, huh? What did they do? Eat your lunch?"

Before the Commander could answer, Bradford came up from behind and lunged at him with his torch.

"Run!" Bradford told us just as the Barlow boy took a swipe at the back of the Commander's knees with a shovel. While he was down, Mrs. Hernandez raised her bat and hit him squarely on the top of the head.

Daley was knocked out cold.

I stood there for a moment in shock. Mrs. Hernandez dropped the bat and rushed over to Ember to make sure she was okay. I stared at Daley, wanting to make sure he was out. Part of me was angry I hadn't been able to do it myself. The other part of me couldn't believe what I had just been a part of.

"Go!" Bradford yelled. "Go before he wakes up. It won't be long. We'll hold him off."

I turned and followed Mrs. Hernandez and Ember, who were already rushing away through the trees. When I looked back, the young men were circling Commander Daley with their shovels and torches.

Despite the adrenaline flowing through me, I felt like I was trudging through mud as I replayed in my mind what the Commander had said.

Is he right? Did I pick a side?

As the doors to the Sticking Place opened, I wondered what side I had been on before.

And who's on my side now?

Without meaning to, had I just joined some kind of rebellion?

Then I remembered Mr. Amos's words.

"A special life prepares you for something special. That's your life, Sky."

But was it? Was it really?

Who am I?

Mrs. Hernandez thrust a medicine bag into my arms. "Hold this."

Stepping into the room, I watched the woman bustling around, giving directions while throwing tinctures and pill bottles into the bag. Mr. Aaronson sat in a chair, his face as white as snow. "Henry needs this one in the morning, and this one at night," said Mrs. Hernandez. "This one is twice a day, but these two can't be mixed and—"

"Are you leaving?" I asked her, unable to keep up.

"*Sí, sí.* Those men . . . they are after Ember and Henry."

Ember emerged from the room where Henry was lying and avoided meeting my eyes when I looked at her. I could read the guilt all over her face; it was a feeling I knew well.

"How did they know you were here?"

She held up an object I was very familiar with—a Tracking Token.

"This was in Henry's pocket. I forget it was there." She threw the token against the wall. "Oh, I'm so stupid!"

"What do they want with you guys?" I asked her.

"They just . . ." Ember paused. "It's a long story."

"We don't have time for long stories." Mrs. Hernandez took the bag from me, placing it on the table. "There are more of them. And they are going to be here soon. We need to go to the Outpost. It's well-hidden. We can hide them from Topos there, at least for a little while. Help me pack. I don't see how he can travel."

"He's fine," Ember said, gesturing to her father.

"Not him. Your brother," Mrs. Hernandez said, still stomping around the room and tossing medicines to whoever would catch them and put them in the bag. "He really shouldn't travel, but what choice do we have? *¡Ay, Dios mío!* Ember, are you writing this down?"

When I looked over at Ember, she appeared to be frozen in place.

"These are the ones for your father." Mrs. Hernandez showed the tinctures to her and Mr. Aaronson. "If he passes out again—"

"You can't expect her to take care of us both," said Mr. Aaronson, looking protective yet helpless. "I'm feeling strong."

"*¡Ay!* Strong now. Maybe. But you could relapse any second."

"I'll go with them," I told them before I could think about the words coming out of my mouth.

Ember gave me a desperate look. "You will?"

She wants me to come.

I walked over to her and offered her my hand to help her up. "I will."

She actually took my hand.

"Sky," she whispered, "you said they have an antidote in Oasis?"

Mrs. Hernandez spun around to face us. But before I could answer, Mr. Amos burst into the room, looking frantic. When the doors opened, the distinct smell of smoke filled the room.

"They're taking everyone." He heaved, catching his breath.

"Is that ... blood?" Ember pointed to the knife in Mr. Amos's hand.

Mr. Amos looked as if someone had died as he faced Mrs. Hernandez.

"Fire ... They set your lab on fire."

Her eyes grew wide as she gasped. I knew exactly what she was thinking, and so did Mr. Amos.

"It's too late." Mr. Amos closed the door. "I tried to get the vial. It's gone."

"Gone ...," Mrs. Hernandez repeated, pressing her palms together in front of her lips.

Her shadow from a nearby candle seemed to float across the wall behind her.

"Jay is leading whoever he can to the Outpost," Mr. Amos continued. "These people won't stop until they get the kids."

Mr. Aaronson stood, clenching his fists. "Well, they can't have them."

"They won't come here," Mrs. Hernandez said.

Mr. Amos laid down his knife on a metal box. "I told them to come here."

"You WHAT?"

"I told them to come here," Mr. Amos repeated. "That the kids are here."

Mr. Aaronson began to shake with anger, then started to wobble and sat back down again. Ember looked angry as she stood by his side. Mr. Amos raised his hands for everybody to calm down.

"It's not what you think. Listen. I would never ... I have a plan."

"What is it?" Mr. Aaronson said between gritted teeth.

"There's a hiding place. You all hide in there. I'll make it look like you escaped."

Ember crossed her arms. "This better be a good hiding place."

Mr. Amos began to frantically clear the far corner of the room of all metal boxes and briefcases and wooden crates.

"Give me a hand, will you?" he asked me as he pushed on a very large glass showcase filled with trinkets. After helping him shove it out of the way, I tried picking up the few remaining objects on the floor.

"Gah. What the heck is that? It's so heavy."

Mr. Aaronson and Mr. Amos answered me at the same time. "Old cannonball."

Ember helped me roll it out of the way.

"Why would you even have this?"

But Mr. Amos didn't have the time to explain.

"Get me a hammer."

I looked at Mr. Amos for a second, then looked at Ember to see if the word "hammer" meant anything. She had the same blank, puzzled look that I probably had on my face.

"My gosh . . . ," Mr. Aaronson said, rummaging through Mr. Amos's boxes.

"The one in the corner," Mr. Amos said. "Yes. That's it. Thank you."

Mrs. Hernandez held a candle over Mr. Amos for extra light while he used the back side of this instrument he called a "hammer" to rip out the nails in the floorboard. I picked them up and hid them in a box.

"First thing I put in." Mr. Amos ripped up multiple floorboards. "Extra storage."

Ember examined the space on her hands and knees. "But it's filled with junk."

Mr. Amos ignored her as he and Mr. Aaronson pulled out large maps, dusty journals, and multiple unmarked thin metal boxes and hid them around the room. The small, thin gap in the floor looked no more than sixteen inches tall. I was almost afraid to ask my next question.

"So, we ... get in there?"

"They're coming," Mr. Aaronson said, peeking through the front curtains.

I went to look for myself. There were Agents marching blindly through the smoky grove. Some of the oak trees were damp from the rain yesterday, so they hadn't ignited, but fire was still traveling irregularly through bits of brush.

Mr. Aaronson emerged from the bedroom, carrying Henry in his arms. "Go ahead," Mr. Amos said to us.

Ember got in first, then I followed. We had to lie flat and shimmy sideways on our stomachs since there was no other way to get in. The air was dry and dusty, making me want to cough. Mr. Aaronson handed Henry off to Mr. Amos, then slid down into the space that was almost full. Ember mumbled something as she tried to roll onto her side to make room, but she couldn't. We all had to lie flat.

How are we going to get everyone down here?

"Mrs. Hernandez, you go next," Mr. Amos instructed. "We'll lower Henry in last ... Wait." I heard his footsteps across the floor above us. "They're close. Very close."

"Give me Henry," Mrs. Hernandez said to him. "Do it."

"We don't have much time!" Mr. Aaronson said.

"Lower Henry down here," Ember called out.

More footsteps sounded above us.

"What are they doing?" I asked Ember in the darkness.

"I don't know."

"Start covering them up," Mrs. Hernandez said.

Ember squirmed, trying to get back up, but she couldn't move. "Wait! What are you doing with Henry?"

I could only barely hear Mrs. Hernandez speak. "I will take care of him. Trust me."

I wondered who was holding Henry now.

"Hold them off as long as you can," Mrs. Hernandez said from above. I assumed she was talking to Mr. Amos. "We'll go out the back. We have no choice. God help us all."

"Stop her!" Ember shrieked.

We heard the quick shuffling across the floor, then heard Mr. Amos above us.

"Get as low as you can." He threw the floorboards back in place, then slid something back over the top.

"I have to get out of here," Ember said.

"Quiet, Ember," her father told her.

I couldn't breathe. I felt like I was trapped in a cage.

"Henry!"

"Ember, you have to —"

"They're here," Mr. Amos's muffled voice said. "Nobody speak. *No one.*"

We heard Mr. Amos greet them on the front porch, stalling for as long as he could. When the doors opened, I heard Commander Daley's booming voice.

"Where are they?"

He obviously had gotten away from Bradford and the other guys. I tried not to think about what might have happened to them.

"I am charged with removing Ember and Henry, and I will complete my mission."

I wondered if he was going to say my name as well.

"They're right over… Oh my. They were here just a moment ago." Mr. Amos sounded like he was giving his finest performance above us. "They must have… Oh no. I can't even believe it."

I could just make out the sound of the back door creaking open, and desperately hoped Mrs. Hernandez and Henry were far enough away by now.

"You—search out the back door," the Commander barked. "You. Search the room."

A pause, then the Commander asked a question.

"Do I know you?"

"I don't think so," Mr. Amos said in a muted voice.

"You. Take him for questioning."

There was movement above us as they took Mr. Amos. I heard another door open; another set of steps began to thud.

"They're looking for Sky! And Henry and Ember! Where are they? We need to warn them. I have to—"

I almost choked.

Lincoln! What is he doing up there?

But I knew why he was there. It was just like Mr. Amos had said: he cared about me. I could just imagine that little guy running through all the fighting because he wanted to warn me. He had no idea what he was getting into, or maybe he did, and that didn't stop him. Maybe whatever it was that made him such a dork also made him brave. Still, I wished he hadn't come.

Seeing the Agents must have left him speechless.

"Uh. I . . . um. I . . . oh no."

"Unbelievable," Ember whispered with disgust.

Mr. Aaronson shushed her.

"So, you know . . . *Sky*?" Commander Daley asked.

No, no, no. Say no. Please say no.

"Yes. He's my friend."

Of course.

"Take him too," Commander Daley ordered.

I could almost see his smirk in my head.

"See if 'Sky' comes looking for his *friend*, since he's a *hero* now." All the Agents snickered. "Don't inject anyone. I want them conscious, so we can *talk*."

CHAPTER FIFTEEN
TO BE A HERO
(Ember)

"**H**oly Administrator," I said, marveling at Sky, who had just, without warning, stood up and burst through the loose floorboards, tipping the glass shelf and shattering it.

"It just, uh. Seemed like the best way."

"No, that was good. Just ... whoa."

I crawled out of the tiny space under the floor. We had been under there for what felt like an hour. There was an eerie silence that surrounded the tiny shack. I walked to the window and peeled back the curtain. No one.

I heard my father groan as Sky helped him up; his feet seemed unsteady beneath him.

"Make sure he doesn't—"

Fall. I was going to say fall, but before I could, Sky had his arms wrapped around my father, holding him away from the ground.

"I got him. It's okay. I got him."

"I'm alright," my father said as Sky sat him down on a metal box.

Sky must have seen me reach for the doorknob.

"Whoa, whoa. What are you doing? We don't know they're gone."

I peeled back the curtain again and gestured for Sky to come look with me. "They're gone."

"Blast it." He ran his hands through his hair. "They took them. They took them to Oasis."

209

I opened the door and was greeted by a smell of burning brush so overpowering I could taste it. I held my breath and stepped onto the hazy porch. The fire had arranged itself in haphazard patterns on the ground as if it were a message Topos had left behind.

"You're next."

I had the thought to call out for Henry, but Mrs. Hernandez had taken him over an hour ago. If they'd made it out, he was far away by now. If they hadn't, he wouldn't be able to respond to my call because he ... I shuddered.

Only a few of the large trees had surrendered to the power of the fire, but no doubt more would fall. They would all fall eventually. Sky joined me on the porch, my father walking behind him.

"What now?" I asked, staring at the flames.

"Let's take a walk," my father said.

The grove floor was littered with needles, but all their victims had vanished. No one had to ask where they had gone; we all knew— Sleep Camp. That unknown, dreaded place where you went and never returned from.

Except for my dad.

He had gotten out. I guess I had taken that fact for granted in the confusion of his coming. As far as I knew, no one ever left Sleep Camp, and no one ever defied the perpetual sleep of the Teal Lady. Except for my dad, who was standing next to me, ripping his skin with furious scratching, gulping for air like he was underwater. I very gently took his arm.

What did they do to you there?

The smoke grew thicker as we reached the end of the grove, and when we emerged on the other side, I saw a building engulfed in flames in the distance. The fire was working desperately to spread to the closest structure but hadn't yet been able to make the jump.

The lab with the blue door had been reduced to a pile of rubble. Whatever hope of an antidote that had been contained within those walls was gone now, turned to pure ash. I found the brutality of it all overwhelming, the chunks of hair on the dirt, blood smeared on the collapsing wooden porches. But it was clear it bothered Sky even more. He approached every new piece of destruction with growing disgust. I knew what Topos was capable of; I had seen it seven years ago when they took my parents, but I had forgotten. I wondered if Sky hadn't known until now.

He ran to the door of a burning building, calling Lincoln's name. He looked like he wanted to go inside.

"He isn't there," I said, assuming this was where Lincoln had lived. "They took him."

But he just kept yelling his name.

"Lincoln? Lincoln!"

He rushed into the burning building. My father didn't hesitate, starting to run after him.

"Sky, don't go in there. It's—" He was taken over by a coughing fit in the face of the smoke and couldn't go on.

"Sky. Come out. He's not there."

I couldn't see him behind the wall of smoke. Was he in there, burning? Just hours before I had hated him, but now everyone was gone, and we needed him. I couldn't handle any more loss.

"Sky, please!" I begged.

He came running out of the building with his shirt on fire, screaming. My father threw him to the dirt. "Roll!"

Sky writhed in the dirt until the flames subsided.

"Are you hurt?" I asked.

But he had nothing to say about the small patch of bubbling flesh on his arm.

"You know what I'm going to do?" he seemingly announced to the whole world. "I'm going to be a hero. I'm going to get my friends. I'm going to Oasis. And Daley will wish he had never been BORN."

I was ready to talk him down, to help him come to his senses. We couldn't go to Oasis, not now. But before I could say anything, my father spoke.

"I'm coming with you."

"You're—you're what?" I said. "You can't go anywhere. We need to get you back to Mrs. Hernandez, to someone who can help you. To Henry."

"There isn't any time."

"Time? Time for what? If we can get you help, you'll have plenty of time. As much time as you want."

I felt desperate for this not to be happening. A trip to Oasis could kill my father, and I could think of no reason worth the risk.

"We can't go." I turned to Sky. "You'll have to be a hero by yourself."

That didn't seem to faze Sky one bit.

"Good," I said. "So that's that, then. Now we just have to find Mrs. Hernandez."

"She's at the Outpost. It's about half a day's walk from here, but it's hard to find if you don't know the way," my father replied, which made me think he had come to his senses. "But I have to go to Oasis."

"Why? Sky doesn't need you to, right? See? He's fine. You don't have to help him. You can rest."

"I'm not going to help him."

"What?" Sky said.

Then I remembered the conversation on the porch with Mr. Amos earlier that evening.

"The Oarsmen. This is about the Oarsmen?"

"Again?" Sky said. "How are these boat-people suddenly all anybody can talk about anymore?"

Although I could have imagined that exact sentence coming out of my mouth, I didn't appreciate the way he said "boat-people." My dad was one of these "boat-people," after all.

"Is this about that map? To . . . what, again?" I asked him.

"The Oarsmen Armory," my father said.

Sky inserted himself between me and my father. "So that's real?"

My father looked at him and chuckled. "Very real."

"No, I mean *real* real? As in it actually exists? It's not just a metaphor or something? A story?"

"He said it's real." I moved Sky out of my way. "And the map is in Oasis?"

"Did you say Oasis?"

"Yes, Sky. Keep up." I turned back to look at my dad. "Can I talk you out of this?"

That was the first moment I saw my father as he used to be, when he grinned at me with a look of the sweetest defiance.

"No."

With that one grin, it was settled. There was no way my dad wasn't going to Oasis, and there was no way I would let him go alone. So, me, my sick father, and a guy I just met were off to face off against the most powerful corporation in the world in their own capital city, all to get a map to a place that was important for a reason I didn't understand, and yet, at the time, it was the only reasonable thing to do.

It took another hour or so to get supplies from the Sticking Place, a bandage and a new shirt for Sky, and we crossed the threshold from the burning little town back into the seemingly endless sea of dirt without fanfare. You would think a life-changing moment like that would be accompanied by a brand-new feeling, but no. I walked on with the exact same sense of dread that had been growing in me since we'd made our plan to leave. That was the only part of the plan we'd made—the leaving part. Everything beyond that point was unnervingly unclear.

I seemed to only make the walk to Oasis in the dead of night and under terrible circumstances. I wondered what was worse: the last trip, when I had been dragging my unconscious brother through the dirt, or this one, slowing down every few minutes to give my father time to vomit. The itch on his arm spread over his whole torso, sending him into sudden scratching fits that made him stumble, but he didn't fall because of Sky, who walked at his side the entire time. It shocked me how carefully Sky watched my dad, as if he had known him for a long time. I looked for signs of insincerity, waiting for Sky to ditch us and run off on his own. But he hadn't done that. He was with us—truly with us—and that surprised me.

I like this guy.

During one of our many stops, I motioned for Sky to join me. We faced away from my father to give him privacy.

"I just want to say thank you," I said, looking up at the full moon.

Out of the corner of my eye, I saw Sky raise his eyebrows.

"Don't look so surprised."

"What? You're not even looking at me."

I made the universal *I'm watching you* gesture. "But I still see you."

Sky laughed. "So, you're thanking me for…"

He's going to make me say it.

"Oh, you think you're funny."

"No, no." He smirked. "I'm just curious. I think you're thanking me for…"

He was waiting for me to fill in the blank.

"For…saving…"

"For *helping* me," I said.

"For saving your life; got it. You're welcome."

"Very smooth." I rolled my eyes and walked away.

Actually, it *was* smooth in Sky's own way. But what was he doing? I thought I must have misread him. Surely now—in the middle of nowhere, on a mission that would probably end with us all in Sleep Camp—he hadn't chosen that moment to flirt with me. But flirting or not, I wasn't going to let him take any of my attention.

Surely he wasn't flirting. Right?

It turned out that my attention was needed elsewhere.

"Ember!" my father yelled. "Get back."

I didn't see it at first; I only heard it, a rattling sound right where my next step would have been. I shrieked in terror. The snake's body was spiraled upward, with its head and tail elevated highest, ready to strike. I had only seen a snake one other time in my life, on the Fibonacci. Real life was much worse.

"Get back," Sky said, trying to shoo the snake away.

"Stop," my father called out. "Do. Not. Move. Ember, back away slowly."

After I'd taken two steps, the snake snapped at the air where I had stood. I screamed again.

"Slowly," my dad said.

Slowly felt so unbelievably wrong when every fiber of my being was demanding I run. But I listened to my dad and stepped away holding my breath. The snake held its ground, waiting in the strike position for what felt like an un-survivable amount of time, before slowly spiraling back to the earth, lengthening his body through the dirt, and slithering away. My skin crawled as I watched it, waiting for it to change its mind.

My father let out a long exhale. Without thinking about it, I ran into his arms and cried. It seemed like the wrong time for me to lose my nerve. But it wasn't the snake that shook me; it was the idea that the snake was the least of our worries.

Because even if I slowly walked away from Topos, they would still strike.

We walked on together until the glow of Oasis could guide us the rest of the way. The great arced wall of the city came into view. I used to think those walls were to keep me in; now they were there to keep me out.

"This way." My father led us in a wide circle around the city. The closer we got to Oasis, the stronger he looked, as if the idea of what he was there for had overcome the Teal Lady corrupting his veins. We came to the same bit of wall I had used to get out. I wouldn't have recognized it if it weren't for the tiny drawings of oars on the bottom of the wall. I hadn't noticed that before.

My dad removed his wedding band, just as Mrs. Grisham had. He ran it across the wall until it clicked into place, and he drew a circle with it. I heard the familiar clicking sound and the round door slid open.

"What? How?" Sky said.

My dad looked back at him and gave him a satisfied wink. "There were Oarsmen in city construction."

"Right...of course there were," Sky said, rubbing his wrinkled forehead.

I could hear the high-pitched whine on the other side of the door.

"Cover your ears," my dad said to me at the same time I said it to Sky.

I got on my hands and knees and followed my dad, crawling through the door and then traveling down the dark, descending tunnel. The whining sound was just as painful as I remembered, maybe more so now, watching my father trying to survive it. Over the wail, I swore I heard something else—a voice, a deep, booming voice, coming from underneath the high-pitched sounds the walls made. I grabbed the back of my father's shirt, hiding my body up against the wall and gesturing for Sky and my dad to do the same. I had to pull Sky into position seconds before the body of the deep voice walked past the opening of the tunnel just steps in front of us. I could only make out a few of his words: "code," "girl," and finally, "Oarsmen Armory."

"Daley," Sky whispered in my ear, but I already knew it was the Commander. I knew that voice. It had been haunting me since I'd heard it above our hiding place under the floor. It occurred to me that I had seen him but never heard him speak. But I knew that voice from somewhere— somewhere deep in my memory; I just couldn't place where. Luckily, Commander Daley had no intention of turning onto our corridor and no inclination that anyone would be there, especially not us. At least that's what I imagined. He moved away quickly, and his voice was overpowered by the wail again.

Sky took it upon himself to be the first to make sure the coast was clear, and it was, so we moved on, following the thin trail of lights at our feet. I spoke to my father in front of me.

"He was talking about the Armory."

My father stopped. "He was?'

"Yeah. And he said 'code' and 'girl.'"

My father walked again, much faster now. "We don't have much time."

"Time for what?" Sky said.

But before he answered, we came back to the same words written on the wall that I had seen before. Sky read them out loud, as if he had read them many times before, but now he finally understood and so did I.

Outside of Oasis
Are people the same as us?
Regardless, we are the same as them.
Silly question
Men are all the same, I think.
Equal, yes.
Naturally.

"Oarsmen," we whispered together.

My father looked at the wall like it was an old friend. "An old code. Probably shouldn't be using it anymore, but we've hardly been able to vote on a new one … I can't imagine why they didn't cover that up the day they found this place."

As we approached the narrow entrance to the hideout, my father removed his wedding band. But instead of a circle, he drew an X that spanned the length of the door. It slid open, and I crouched down to step inside.

So much had changed since I had been in the hideout, it was hard to believe it had just been a few days. I had thought that the scribbling on the walls was a kind of portal to my parents, just like my book had been. I had no idea that it was my father who had brought me here.

"Why?" I asked him. "Why did you want me to see this place?"

My father guided me over to the place on the wall where he and my mom had written their names. He placed his hand on her name as if by doing so, he was touching her.

Julia Aaronson.

He looked back at me warmly. "So you would remember."

"Remember? I've never been here before. Not before a couple of days ago."

"Remembering is much bigger than what's happened to you in your own life. You needed to remember what happened *before* you. That's what this place is."

"And this place was for the Oarsmen?"

My father still hadn't taken his hand off my mother's name. "She loved it here. She's the reason I joined the Oarsmen in the first place." He paused for a moment before he spoke again. "It doesn't seem right that I'm here without her."

For the first time I thought of my mom in her current state, asleep for seven years while life moved on without her. All because she was an Oarsman.

"She would love to see you here," my father said to me. "It would make it all worth it to see you carrying on with what we started. That's all she wanted. That's why she gave you that book."

"She gave me the book because she wanted me to be an Oarsman?"

"Because she wanted you to remember."

"But would she have wanted me to remember so I could become an Oarsman? Would she have liked that?"

My dad smiled. "She would have loved it."

"Then that's who I am." I put my hand on the wall over my father's. "I'm an Oarsman, like you, like Mom. I'm an Oarsman."

The wall seemed to let out a spark of electricity that ran through us both. I saw my mother, smiling in her perpetual sleep. Somehow, she had heard me. I could feel it. I could feel our whole family finally together again, a family of Oarsmen. Any doubts I might have had were washed away by the love I felt in that moment. Fear lost its grip. Even the image of my whole family locked away forever in Sleep Camp and the fact that I had no real idea what it meant to be an Oarsman didn't bother me.

I remembered what family felt like.

I remembered.

And that was enough.

CHAPTER SIXTEEN
BURNING ALIVE
(Sky)

T his place...
I could remember it well, even if I tried not to. I didn't want to. But watching the scene in front of me with Ember and her father brought everything back.

It brought me back to this hideout. To the feeling of wonder I felt when I'd found it for the first time as kid while exploring with my best friend. To the secret trips we took there together, and the even more secret trips I took alone. To my mom finding me, yelling at me.

"I told you not to come back here. It's lies. It's all lies!"

My eyes drifted toward scribbling on the other side of the room. I walked over to it and couldn't help but study it again.

"Tyndale," Mr. Aaronson said, moving toward me. "Amos wrote that."

I backed away from the wall.

Of course Mr. Amos wrote it.

"You know the story, then?" Mr. Aaronson asked. "It's the man who was killed for translating the Bible. He was betrayed by a friend—"

"I know it," I interrupted, walking away and pretending not to give it a second thought.

But that's all I could do—give it one more thought. That's all I had been doing since reading about this man named Tyndale years ago on that very wall. Then *hearing* about him. I could still picture Mr. Amos dressed up and talking in a strange voice. "*No man should have to go through another to get access to the Truth. I will get this book to the people, and when I'm finished, the poorest, lowliest man will be more righteous than you."*

All for a book.

It still blew my mind. Having to run away from home, working without any hope he could finish, being betrayed by a supposed friend—I heard Mr. Amos in my head again. *And once he gained his trust, he betrayed him—* then strangled and burned at the stake. All for a book?

Lies. All lies!

But was this story really and truly a lie?

I glanced over to Ember and her father, who were standing close together and reviewing the small sketches on the bottom corner of the far wall. Mr. Aaronson was excitedly telling her a synopsis of every story. She was finishing his sentences, and every time she did, Mr. Aaronson's face would light up. It looked as if he were being lit from the inside out.

All because of these stories.

I pictured Tyndale. This man being put to death. A loser on all counts, at least in the way I would've thought about it. A man on fire in front of his enemies. I could almost hear him. *"I pray their eyes will be opened."*

Those were his last words. At least, according to Mr. Amos.

Lies …

It had seemed like a lie before my world turned upside down, before I'd accidentally joined a rebellion, before the teeks turned out to be the best people I've ever known.

There was a question I couldn't shake, one that kept rolling around in my head: Who decides what's True, anyway? Do I get a say in it at all?

I could feel myself being sucked backward into a memory. The image of Tyndale slowly vanished and was replaced with the image of my mother in a noisy boardroom. Everybody dressed up. Adults chattering and clinking their champagne flutes. A man asking my mother a question.

"Will your husband not be joining us?"

Without hesitating for even a second, my mother had responded with, "Oh no, not today. He's very busy today."

I couldn't believe it when it happened right in front of me. I felt something rushing through me—racing inside of me—wanting to claw its way out of this boardroom. I wanted to tell this man the Truth.

My father isn't "busy." I don't have a father. I've never had one!

The only lies had come from my mother. About my "father." About the Holdouts. About my whole *life*—the lies had come from *her*. The very word whirled around me. It felt like all the scribblings around me had one glowing word on them: *Lie. Lie. Lie. Lie. Lie. Lie.*

The word had somehow lost its meaning. I felt the anger build up inside of me again, the same anger that had sent me out of Oasis to find out the Truth.

"We're wasting time," I said, forcing all these thoughts out of my head.

I stared at Ember and her father. Watching them together made my skin feel hot. Not warm, but hot, like fire. Ember shot me an irritated look, and I tried to relax.

"I'm sorry," I said. "We can't get distracted. We have a job to do."

I walked to the center of the room, shaking my wrists, trying to fling off memories.

"He's right," Ember said, leaving the moment with her father. "Azaz knows this place. They all do. It's not safe. So, what's our plan?"

It took me a moment to realize the question had been directed at me. Both Ember and her father were looking at me, waiting for an answer.

"Um . . . yes. I do have a plan."

But I didn't have a plan. I hadn't had a plan since I left Oasis.

"They're probably holding Lincoln and Mr. Amos in Building One, on the sixth floor," I said, surprising myself with how confident I sounded.

I could see Ember shudder as if she knew I was right.

"I'm sure the map is in that building too. That's where they keep the most important contraband," Mr. Aaronson said.

There was only path to Building One from where we were, and we all knew it—the Interlink track.

"Won't it be running?" I asked. "It's almost morning."

Ember grabbed my arm, thinking out loud. "Wait. What day is it?"

"Saturday," her father replied.

"No." She looked at me. "What *day* is it?"

"It was Day Four when they attacked us," I said. "So, it's Day Five now."

I was still going by the Oasis calendar. This whole "weeks" thing that these other people had still hadn't sunk in yet.

"That's what I thought. I've been counting days to see how long Henry takes to recover. So, the Interlink only runs every hour . . . or two on Day Five?" She looked at me for confirmation.

"It runs every two hours, unless there are Envoys visiting; then it's every hour, but we have no way to know if they're visiting today," I told her.

"We can make it in an hour," Mr. Aaronson said. "We'll have to move fast. We'll go to the door and watch for the Interlink. Once it passes, we have an hour. We need to be ready."

As we left the hideout and walked up the dark path, Ember took the lead and repeatedly reminded us to stay close to the wall. As she moved quickly, I felt my arm being tugged by Mr. Aaronson.

"I need you to do something for me," he whispered, making sure Ember couldn't hear. "If anything happens to me, you take Ember and get her out of here. No matter where I am, no matter what I do, she goes with you. That's your job. Do you understand?"

I had a dozen questions I immediately wanted to ask him, but I could tell this was one of those man-to-man exchanges where most details were left unspoken.

"Okay," I nodded. "I got it."

We moved again and caught up with Ember, who had been waiting for us with her arms crossed. When we reached the door and opened it, we were met with a rush of air from an incoming Interlink.

I swallowed. "I guess it's now, then."

"I'll take the lead," Mr. Aaronson said. "I know this route the best."

"We're at the Charrington stop," Ember added as she looked around. "That means we're almost nine stops away from Building One. I'm not sure how long that will take for us to walk there."

Watching Mr. Aaronson trying to move as fast as he could but still slowly trudging along, I knew it was going to take us longer than we thought. We were quiet as we walked. I could feel the adrenaline inside of me waning. I was getting tired, which made me worry about how Mr. Aaronson felt. But he seemed to be showing fewer and fewer signs of illness. I remembered how Mr. Amos had described his waking up from the Teal Lady as an act of "sheer will or providence." I didn't know what providence was, but I could see "sheer will" written in bold across Mr. Aaronson's entire demeanor. Eventually, he told us we needed to switch to the other side of the track in preparation for our exit.

"We'll want to be on this side when it comes," he told us.

Moments later he stopped and pointed. "This is it."

Ember and I looked up at the seven-foot wall.

"How do we—" Ember murmured.

"Stay as close to the wall as possible," her father said. "We have to wait for the next Interlink."

I laughed. "Are you crazy? It'll flatten us. Besides, if there are no Envoys visiting, it may not come for another hour. We need to get out now."

Mr. Aaronson forcefully gripped my forearm. "You go up now and you're in full view of every T-Force Agent working this station."

I knew what he was talking about. Everybody knew that the T-Force Agents assigned positions as Interlink guards were the slowest and dullest in the force. But they weren't so thick that they wouldn't notice three people crawling out of the Interlink track.

"When it comes, flatten yourself against the wall and don't move, not an inch," Mr. Aaronson explained. "You'll be okay. I've done it . . . many times."

I stared down the track at the faint light reflecting off the curved wall at the farthest end of the track that was visible. My body shuddered. "I guess the Envoys are here."

"It's coming." Mr. Aaronson pushed us into position. "Up against the wall. Don't move until I say so. No matter what, *do not move*."

The faint whiz of the Interlink grew louder and louder until the bright headlights turned the corner and shone straight on us. Mr. Aaronson pinned Ember to the wall with his arm tightly pressing on her upper back. We all faced the wall. With the Interlink barreling closer, I noticed Mr. Aaronson's knees begin to buckle. He was losing his balance, starting to fall backward, ready to be sliced in half—

I flung my arm around him and pinned him against the wall. The Interlink slowed to a full stop. I heard him let out a gasp of air.

"Wait . . . ," Mr. Aaronson whispered, as if forgetting he'd almost just died. "Wait . . . wait . . . Now."

He led us around to the back of the Interlink as the passenger doors opened and people flooded out. "I'll go first. Wait for my signal."

We watched him climb up a ladder on the bottom level of the Interlink and make the small leap to the concrete platform.

"Ember," Mr. Aaronson whispered instructively, and she climbed up the ladder and jumped.

She did not stick the landing, but thankfully, the bustle of Envoys covered her as they darted back and forth, asking the Agents for directions in the most distracted and pretentious way. I knew that even if someone had noticed a random girl spring up from the pit of the track, it was of significantly less importance to them than finding the proper Agent to carry their luggage.

Ember did a double take as she examined the crowd.

She recognizes someone.

I reached for the ladder, but the moment I made contact, the Interlink sped away, almost taking me with it. I looked up to the platform. I was going to have pull myself up. I reached my hand up and Ember stomped it.

"Blast it," I said, pulling back my hand. She looked down at me in the track and discreetly shook her head.

I could hear her talking to someone. Her father, standing at her side, but facing in the opposite direction.

"I need to get to Building One. Scan us in. Please."

"No, no, no. You shouldn't have come. I can't help. I can't. I can't."

Who is she talking to?

I saw Mr. Aaronson turn to face whoever it was, and she gasped so loudly, I thought someone had hurt her.

"Please," Mr. Aaronson said.

I heard no response, but moments later Ember gestured for me to come up. I pulled myself up onto the pavement. The group of envoys was clearing, and Ember dragged me along behind a woman with brown hair done up in a tight but still messy bun.

"Why are you out today?" Ember whispered to her.

"You. They made me come here to talk about you. You shouldn't be here. Oh, I shouldn't be here. Oh. Oh!"

"Just keep walking. We're almost there."

The woman's entire body shook as she scanned her card and the bars to the Building One checkpoint opened.

"Go," the woman said. I saw her face for the first time, covered in layers of makeup, black streaks coming down her cheeks in the shape of tearstains. "I hope I never see you again."

"Thank you," Ember said as we stepped onto the grounds of Building One without drawing any attention to ourselves.

"Who was that?" I asked Ember as we paced across the grounds, trying to avoid being seen among the group of Envoys gathered on the lawn.

"My caretaker."

Mr. Amos stopped. "Grisham? They gave you to Grisham?"

"We can't stop." I pushed them forward. I didn't know why we couldn't; it just seemed like moving was safer for some reason.

"I can't believe it," he said under his breath.

"You knew her. How?" Ember asked him.

The Administrator's voice rang out over the grounds, and everyone instinctively looked to the eighth floor.

"My special guests, welcome to Oasis. First, I must apologize. I am not able to accompany you today on your journey through our City of the Future."

The Envoys let out a collective groan of disappointment.

"*But* I have left you in the care of my knowledgeable and wise A.O. of Topos, Inc. She will be joining you at the main entrance of Building One, along with the Oasis T-Force Commander, in five minutes. They will both make sure your time in Oasis is safe, eye-opening, and, most important, inspirational. I have given my heart and mind to this city, and I believe you will find, even in my absence, that I am accompanying you everywhere you go. Thank you very much for being here, and remember, the future is a door, and your dreams are the key."

"Holy Administrator," Ember and I both said.

"The A.O.—"

" —the Commander—"

"—is going to be here."

"We have five minutes," Mr. Aaronson said. "I have an idea."

CHAPTER SEVENTEEN
THE NIGHTMARE ROOM
(Ember)

"Welcome to the Oasis laboratory. We're so glad you're here," a warm male voice proclaimed all around us as the chandelier dimmed and a video projected onto the glass wall. "In case we're not friends yet, you can call me the Administrator. What's your name?"

The video paused on a shot of the Administrator grinning from ear to ear with sparkling white teeth. He looked so friendly and wise with his frosted gray hair and his muted teal dress shirt tucked underneath a comfy patchwork sweater. Both of his arms were reaching out toward us, waiting for a response.

It seemed insane when my father suggested the best way to sneak into Building One was through the front door of the laboratory on the first floor. Sky said he knew the way to the T-Force interrogation room and went to the main entrance of the building on his own. Dad was determined to get to the seventh floor of the building—the Administrator's office. I had no choice but to follow him.

The video replayed.

"What's your name?"

I wished I had asked Sky what his plan was or how he knew about the T-Force interrogation room, but we were surrounded by T-Force, and Azaz and the Commander were minutes away, so we had no time for details like where we were going, how we would find each other again, or what would happen if someone died.

That's how I found myself face-to-projected-face with the Administrator at the front desk of the Oasis Laboratory, ready to volunteer myself as a "patient."

A sharp, robotic voice suddenly cut in on the speaker system, saying, "State your name."

"Martha," I blurted out.

"Last name," the robotic voice demanded.

"Washington ... Uh, yeah, Martha Washington."

My father smiled at me as the video started again, the robot voice cutting in over the welcoming tone of the Administrator to state the name. "Well, hello, *Martha Washington*. Welcome to our lab." The chandelier twinkled. "I hope you're here to volunteer your services. Is that right?"

The video paused.

"... Yes."

The back wall lit up bright teal as the Administrator spoke again.

"How wonderful. We'll just need a signature from you first. Would you mind?"

The glowing words "Sign Here" appeared on the top of the welcome desk. There were tiny documents almost filling the entire desk, but they kept shuffling around and changing positions. My father signed our fake name under the massive "Sign Here" with his finger. The chandelier twinkled again, and all the digital papers vanished. As we looked up, the words "Thank you" were written on the back wall, as if by an invisible hand.

The Administrator continued. "Welcome to the Team. I can't wait to meet you. Right this way."

My father whispered in my ear, "The door will open, and everyone will be clapping. Keep your head down, and don't say anything."

Just as he'd said, the right side of the glass vanished into the wall, and we were greeted by a group of almost-too-beautiful young people in teal-and-black lab coats. I didn't recognize anyone, but I didn't expect to. I had never been here before. My father had his head so low I was afraid he might fall. He hacked into his shirt multiple times, and that kept the group of stylish lab coats away from him, which I think was his intention. He had told me that when he worked here, there was a secret passage from the lab to the seventh floor. I hoped they hadn't remodeled in the last decade.

The ceilings of the lab were two stories tall and seemingly propped up by exposed white beams that ran all the way to the floor. Individual cubicles were separated by glass panels spaced wide enough apart to leave room for the large, glowing Fibonacci screens, which arced in a kind of elongated C-shape. Every ten feet or so, there was a white seat with a hard, thick helmet suspended above it.

As they led my father and me down a hallway lined with perfectly spaced photos of the human brain in gold frames, the creepy-pretty people asked us a flurry of questions about where we were from and what we did. Neither of us answered, and they didn't care. They kept up their routine responses just like the video of the Administrator and kept congratulating us on our commitment to the advancement of the species.

Eventually, we arrived at a small and dimly lit room at the end of a hall. Where the rest of the lab was sleek and eerie, this room was just eerie. One by one the flock disassembled, talking about their plans for the rest of the day.

"I'm with writing today."

"Ooh. You're so lucky. I'm conducting again."

"At least I'm not stuck in recording," one whispered snidely. "I don't even know why they still have anyone doing that. It's so old-school. But you have to put the stupid people somewhere."

It was evident by the sour look on her face that the one lady staying with us was stuck doing recording, whatever that was. She dusted some sugar over the wound and turned to face us with an insincere yet beautiful smile.

"I'll start with you, girlie," she told me, and pointed to a long, padded table in the middle of the room. She pulled a piece of candy from her pocket and popped it into her mouth.

"Today we're just going to have you lie down and place this cute little cap on your head. I'll ask you a few questions, and I'll just kind of eavesdrop on your electrical activity. No big deal. Have you ever worn one of these before?"

She held up a shiny, teal, helmetlike thing, with a chin strap and silver wires spilling out. She called me over to the table like I was baby.

"C'mon, girlie. On the table."

I was walking over as slowly as I possibly could, my head racing. What was my father doing? Was this the plan?

What do I do now?

"Oh my," I heard my father say as he walked toward the helmet in the girl's hands.

"What?" she said.

"This is broken."

He took it out of her hands. It was quite a sight to watch my father in his vomit and mud-soaked jeans evaluating the wiring.

The girl looked at me with a puzzled face. I shrugged, and in that second my father ripped one of the wires. He held the helmet thing up to her, pointing at the wire.

"See?"

She examined it. "Ugh. Of course I broke it. I hate my life. Just—ugh. Just stay here. Just wait a second. I'll get a new one." She left the room, whispering under her breath about how she hoped no one would find out about this.

"She believed you," I whispered to my father.

"Well, it is broken," he said, then became very serious. "You don't want one of those on your head. Ever."

"So those were here when you worked here?"

He walked over to the doorway and looked out. "Unfortunately. Come on. Let's get out of here."

"What if they see us?"

My father held my hand and walked me down the hall. "They'll find out we're here. If they don't already know. Now, it's just about speed. Speed and providence."

We sped down another hallway. The Administrator's motto was written on the walls in a curvy, beautiful font.

"The future is a door, and your dreams are the key."

Soon the walls on both sides of us were glass windows. I glanced in them to see people lying peacefully on tables, with their foreheads furrowed in deep concentration, wearing the teal helmets. In the next room someone was sitting up on the table, head slumped to the side and eyes vacant. The farther down the hall we went, the worse the scenes behind the glass became. At least at first the people had looked peaceful, then blank-faced, but now the helmet-wearers seemed more and more agitated. They were lying on the cold metal tables, reaching to the ceiling and screaming, or else they were sitting upright, begging someone who wasn't there for mercy.

The sounds. I will never forget the sounds. They were like the soundtrack to hundreds of nightmares playing on loop at the same time.

"What is this place?" I asked my father. He was staring at a room covered in thick black curtains.

"Studying the mind, that's what they told me I would do. Finding ways to heal what's broken, restoring the natural function, the original design. It was such a noble cause…" His voice drifted away for a moment. "There is only one thing that covers a multitude of sins, and it's not a noble cause."

He was still facing the room with the black curtains covering the glass.

"Do we have to go in there?" I said.

His voice trembled. "We do."

There was a keypad on the side of the door. I saw my father looking at it uncertainly. Even if he could remember the code, what were the chances they hadn't changed the password?

Hold on—I still have my Travel Card.

I remembered Azaz telling me it would open almost any door in Oasis. I hadn't thought to use it earlier, in all the commotion, but in my mind, this piece of plastic was the only chance we had to get in.

"Wait." I pulled my sparkling gold Travel Card from my pocket.

My father looked at it, obviously understanding its significance.

"Worth a shot, right?"

He nodded and stepped away from the keypad.

I couldn't believe I was doing this. I was one mis-scan away from joining these people in their perpetual nightmares. If an alarm sounded, it would be me on that cold metal table. It would be me begging for mercy.

Thankfully, that wasn't the case.

The doors opened like I was supposed to be there, and we stepped in. Any relief I had felt by opening the door turned instantly to desperation the moment it closed behind me. My stomach twisted at the sight.

There was a man, eyes closed, banging on the glass in terror.

An old woman moaning in agony on the floor, waiting to die.

Behind her, a boy—maybe five years old?—was cowering in fear under his table, crying for his mom.

Others ran around the room, being chased by people I couldn't see or mumbling to themselves while drool rolled down their chins, or trying to rip the teal helmets off in a fit of rage. One moment, they would sing out joyfully, but then, without any warning, those songs turned to shrieks of anger and violent threats. The things these people said to the air were unrepeatable.

An elderly man came stumbling toward me with his eyes closed. I noticed tears streaming down his cheeks and had the urge to lean in, to ask him what was wrong. But before I could, he started to scratch the blisters on his face. Clawing at them. Gashing them. Cutting them and making them bleed.

"Get them off me," he begged. But there was nothing there.

"You evil coward!" he screamed in my face. "There is no love in you!"

"Ember!" my father yelled to me.

I ran to him as the man swatted his face and cried.

"This way," my father told me, shoving away a row of metal beds. "Give me your card."

As I handed it to him, it occurred to me that if my card didn't open this door too, we would be stuck.

A siren went off in the room.

Holy Administrator.

"No, no," my father said, swiping the card again and again. He threw himself against the door. "Please, God. Not this."

The man swatting his own face was coming toward me with his eyes closed. Had he heard the siren?

Does he know we're here?

My father was frantically throwing his body against the door. "Please, God. Please."

The old man pushed toward me like he was fighting an army of invisible people, then would suddenly stop and go back to his swatting, then start again, more and more determined.

"You evil coward!" he yelled. But I knew he wasn't talking to me. He was talking to whoever he was fighting in his own mind.

My father collapsed at the door, gasping for air. The siren wailed as I watched the old man fight the invisible coward. He seemed to have a sword now, and he looked like Henry, fencing the air.

I have no idea why, but for some reason I decided to encourage him. It was the only thing I could think of to do.

"You're winning!" I yelled to him. "You're winning!"

"You evil coward!" he screamed, slicing the air.

"You're winning!"

He was just steps from the door and crying out like a wounded animal.

"There is no love in you!"

That's the moment I think he must have won the fight, because at that moment in the chaos, everything seemed to stop. He had a moment, maybe ten seconds, where his eyes were open. Maybe fifteen seconds, and he used every one of them to type a code into the keypad.

The doors slid open.

I pushed my father through.

From the other side I tried to yell back, to thank the old man, but he had already returned to ripping open his scars. The doors closed, leaving him on the side with the siren, and us in an empty staircase.

It was in that moment that I finally understood the word "providence." The moment when the siren stopped and I heard the T-Force on the other side of the door come and leave. I imagined these people set off the sirens often, but still, there was no better word than "providence" to explain my father and me sitting alone, safe, on that dark staircase.

My father was leaning up against the concrete wall, with tears in his eyes.

"Who was that man talking about?" I said. "Who was he calling a coward?"

It was a quiet answer. "Me."

"You? You're a hero."

"Everything you saw in that room, I helped build. I was too excited about the potential of the work to consider the cost."

I came to sit next to him. "What was happening in there?"

"They're making dreams."

"*Making* them?

"When I first started, we were studying them. But Topos always wanted to create them, to implant them. It seems they've figured out how to do that."

"Why would they want to implant dreams?"

My father sighed. "Life is made up of stories. Control the story, control the life. If Topos has the power to tell you stories every time you sleep, that means they control almost half of your life. They want to manipulate who you are, until you become who they want you to be—someone who never resists them as they build their perfect world."

He stood up and gestured for me to follow him. We walked up the stairs and came to a landing. Standing out on one of the walls was a large, framed photograph with a bunch of people—maybe a dozen—posing together. My father stopped and pointed at it.

"Recognize anybody here?"

I moved closer to the photograph and scanned the men and women in it. All of them wore white lab coats. I spotted him right away.

"That's you," I said.

"Yes. This was the original team here. People from all over the world trying to make a difference."

I wanted to ask him more about this, but he kept walking. For a moment I stayed there, looking at the image of him. He not only looked younger, but he looked more full of life. He flashed a grin that he seemed utterly uncapable of doing now. His expression showed hope and promise. Images long gone right now.

"Come on." He walked up the stairs. "We used to use this staircase for emergencies, for when people got out of control or . . . we didn't want people to become frightened by the work we were doing, so Agents came and took them away."

"Where did they take them?"

He continued up the stairs without answering my question. Maybe I didn't want to even know.

"But you're not a coward," I told him. "You're an Oarsman."

This made him stop for a moment and face me.

"And now you know why I have to be. Why I have to find this map. I'll never be able to balance the bad I've done with the good I've tried to do. But if I didn't try, I think it would kill me."

The winding staircase was filled with old photographs and posters from the early days of Oasis. I followed my father upward as the pictures sent us back in time. I passed a poster with the face of a very young Administrator, smiling at me. Underneath were his words in bold-faced letters.

"I'm with you wherever you go."

CHAPTER EIGHTEEN
POWER AND LIES
(Sky)

I pulled my Travel Card from my pocket. It was sparkling gold—at least it used to be sparkling. Now it was starting to fade from years of use.

After I scanned in at the front door, I found no one in the foyer. All the Agents were busy touring around the city with the Envoys or patrolling the streets to make sure no *lowly* Tenants left their units. That's always how they did it. The Envoys hated the Tenants.

I hustled into the elevator, scanned again, and selected floor 6. The doors closed and the cabin shot upward, making my stomach drop. I knew whatever Agents were left in the building were truly bottom of the barrel, but still—they had the Teal Lady, and that didn't require much skill to use.

When the elevator doors opened again, I waited for a moment to see if anybody was standing in front of me. Then I stepped into the T-Force Executive Offices, looking around the room. Right off the elevator was an angular wooden desk with a metal face on which the T-force logo was embossed. I hated that logo. I used to have nightmares about being eaten by its creepy half-man, half-panther face.

What are *you* doing here?" a voice called out.

I spotted a guy a little older than me sitting behind the desk. A smug look. Impeccable hair perfectly in place.

I flashed my Travel Card at him as I approached.

"There are hostages in this building. I need to see them."

I didn't recognize this receptionist, and I hoped it was mutual. As he rose to his feet, I could clearly see his finger hovering over a call button, probably a direct line to the Commander. My heart started racing.

"State your purpose," the receptionist said.

"I just said, I'm here to see the hostages."

"I heard you. Why."

Great. A tough-guy receptionist.

The man's attitude made me want to crawl over the desk, grab him by his perfect hair, and slam his head into the wall. But I knew I needed to stay calm and act like he was the one who was out of line.

"You're new," I said in a dismissive tone. "You don't know who I am."

"Oh yes, I do."

I glared at him. "Then you know that I have access to wherever I want in Oasis."

"I know you *did*," he replied with a menacing emphasis on the final word. "But it is also my understanding that you turned."

I could feel my heart thumping in my throat, and everything inside of me wanted to show him exactly what being turned looked like. I leaned over the desk.

"You ever heard of spying?"

Spying? That's not going to work.

The receptionist huffed, but I noticed a slight quiver in his upper lip.

I decided to press further. "I understand, Agent—" I glanced down at his badge. "Rat Cell."

"It's Ratz-*zel*," the Agent sneered, his ears growing red.

"Like I said, Rat Cell, you're new here. And since you're just a receptionist, is it possible you don't know about top-secret missions? Or better yet, don't know anything at all?"

The receptionist's twitching lip opened into a snarl. He dramatically raised his finger to make sure I saw it and placed it back over the button.

"Why don't I call the Commander and find out? Then we'll see who knows nothing."

"I wouldn't do that." I reached over the desk and grabbed the Agent's wrist. "You'll feel like a real idiot."

He struggled to wrest his hand free from my grip. I could tell this guy didn't care about feeling like an idiot. All he wanted was to press the button and alert the Commander. I held his arm in place as he struggled to reach the button.

"He's with me," a voice wheezed from the hallway to the right. A lanky Agent came squiggling toward us. "Hate to break up this cute little game you two are playing, though."

As I dropped the receptionist's arm, I knew I recognized the voice.

"I.P.!" I called out. "What are you—whoa. You look awful."

I.P. Daley arrived at the back corner of the desk in a fresh uniform and teal hat. There were dark blue bags around his eyes and a kind of swollen look to his whole face. He gave me an animated grin.

"I look better than you, baby face." He turned to the receptionist. "He's with me, dude."

The receptionist's expression tightened into a series of angry horizontal lines. It was a satisfying sight watching him look up at I.P. I wasn't surprised—I.P. Daley had a special way of annoying people, especially since he was always looking down on them. Not because he was arrogant, but because he was just so stupidly tall. I guess he was a *little* arrogant, but he was the son of the T-Force Commander, so he had a good reason. Still, he was a friend of mine. A friend since I was a little kid.

"I'll scan him in," I.P. said. "Relax your face, man. It'll get stuck like that. I said, he's with me. Can't a sick guy have visitors?"

I.P. reached over the receptionist and scanned his card on the desk.

"You seriously need to learn to relax, man. Like, you're the receptionist. You take this way too seriously."

As I walked past the receptionist, I gave him one last smirk before following I.P. down the hall. When we were out of earshot, I.P. turned toward me. "Holy Administrator. Where have you been?"

"Where have *you* been?" I asked, watching I.P. scratch his arms and blink his sunken eyes.

"I got hit with Teal Lady on duty. I'm still recovering. It's my first day back in the office. But I'm still just not me. My brain's foggy. No one's telling me anything. Can't blame them. I tried to brush my teeth with a fork last night."

"Someone got you on duty?"

"Some *girl*," I.P said, as if that only made it all worse. "About our age. We were there for her kid brother. Heard she ran away like a nasty teek—"

I.P. caught himself.

"Uh . . . she's not a nasty teek because she ran away, but because she freaking *attacked* me. Blast it, that junk hurts. Like . . . you have no idea."

Ember. He's talking about Ember.

I was impressed, I can't lie. But also, this wasn't some random T-Force agent she had attacked; it was my friend. It was weird to think about.

"Really haven't talked to my dad since," I.P continued. "You know how he is. And all my mom says is, 'I told ya not to let that boy in the T-Force,' and Dad's like, 'I am the T-force,' blah blah blah. Still a jerk, no surprise there."

I.P. swallowed loudly and painfully, reminding me of Mr. Aaronson.

"But I'm feeling better. They gave me that stuff. It's nasty but it works—stopped me from chucking my guts every minute. I'm just working the desk now . . . probably forever if Mom has her way."

For a moment, I.P. dazed off, stuck in a long blink. Then he shook his head and came back to reality.

"Anyways. Whoa. Why am I blabbing? What the heck did *you* do? You actually left. You freak. You actually left. My dad's out for your blood. He's a stupid jerk, but you know that. But you'll get away with it. You always do. He's after that girl who attacked me now anyways. I probably should have gone with you. But hey—you're back. No pretty ladies in the great unknown?"

The Commander is after me ... and after Ember ... who attacked my best friend ...

I couldn't worry about that now. I had to get Lincoln and Mr. Amos. "Look, I.P—"

"What's Ver–gee–anna?" he said, staring at my shirt.

I wondered what he was talking about, but then I looked down and remembered I was still wearing Mr. Amos's clothes. My T-shirt was navy blue with a red heart and the word "Virginia." I didn't have time to explain, and besides, I had no idea what "Virginia" meant.

"Ian, I need to see the hostages. They just got brought in for questioning."

"Since when do you call me Ian? Besides, you just got back and you're already using me for some scheme? Typical Trot."

I could hear the hint of irritation in his voice. He did have a point, but I needed to insist.

"I know they're in the interrogation room. My card won't let me in there. Please. I'll explain later. I have so much to tell you, but—" I stopped, watching I.P. scratching viciously again. "Look—I'm glad you're okay. Really, I am. I think I've kind of been a jerk to you. For a long time. I don't want to do that anymore, but I need your help today."

I.P. looked stunned to hear me say that.

"Dude ... Yeah, okay. Let's go."

I.P. led me down the hall, zipping past the offices of the administrative staff, who were glued to their Fibonaccis. We took a right and sharp left, and another right ...

"Oops. Dropped my hat. I'll need that," I.P said, scooping up his teal hat.

Another left ... down a long hall.

I saw Lincoln and Mr. Amos sitting in leather chairs behind a floor-to-ceiling glass window. Next to the window on each side was a thick steel wall. I wasn't sure which side of the wall was actually the door and saw nowhere to scan in. As we got within a few feet of the room, the wall on the right slid open.

"You didn't have to scan?" I asked in amazement.

Smirking, I.P. pointed at his hat. "New technology. Pretty cool. Never have to scan in anywhere anymore. They come in handy, these goofy hats."

Lincoln rushed to the door. "Sky!"

I.P. stepped in front of him. "What sky?" He pointed at the ceiling as if Lincoln were an idiot.

Lincoln stumbled backward, and Mr. Amos stood to his feet. I.P. looked at them like a fascinating zoo exhibit.

"Okay, so you saw them," I.P. told me. "Anything else you need to do?"

"Actually," I pulled I.P. aside, "I, uh, need a few minutes to talk to them ... *alone.*"

I.P looked suspicious but reluctantly agreed. "I'll be back in a few minutes. Any more would be pushing our luck. Besides—you owe me some explanations, I'd say."

He turned to leave but only got one foot out the door before he froze in place.

"What?" I said.

"Shh."

He leaned further out the door.

"Blast it. It's Dad. He finds us both here and we're dead meat." I.P. frantically waved his hand in front of the room's back wall, and a door I had no idea existed opened. "In here." He shoved me inside. It was only a tiny closet and was stuffed to the brim with boxes. I stumbled inside and a rain of decommissioned teal hats fell on my head.

"Wait, but—"

"Shup up, man," I.P. said, and the door slammed.

I could hear I.P. on the other side of the door.

"Don't you dare tell him he's here."

I could just imagine Lincoln's face. I.P. had no clue who he was dealing with. Asking Lincoln not to tell the Truth was like asking I.P. not to be so tall. It defied his nature.

I heard multiple people march into the room. I was afraid to breathe, afraid they would hear me.

"Son," Commander Daley said in the same voice he always used with I.P—a voice of extreme disappointment.

I heard I.P. lean up against the door; we were only inches away from each other.

"I was just getting a good look at the teeks, nasty animals. I would sure love to be in the field, catching their *kind*."

I heard the Commander's voice clearly. "Your mother wants you back at the unit for lunch."

I could just imagine I.P. looking at the floor, totally deflated. It was one of the reasons I had always cared for the guy. He had a terrible father.

"Name," Commander Daley said.

"Amos."

"That's it?"

"That's it."

"And you?"

He must be talking to Lincoln. That poor kid.

"My name is Lincoln Freeman. I am twelve and a half years old. I was born on May 22. My parents' names are—"

"That's good, Lincoln," Mr. Amos said, cutting him off.

Lincoln couldn't help himself, and I knew what that meant.

He's going to tell him everything.

"What is your relationship to . . . Sky, I believe you call him," the Commander said.

"Just met him," Mr. Amos said shortly but sweetly.

"And you, *Lincoln Freeman*?"

My stomach tightened.

"Sky is my friend, and I am also Sky's tutor, and he is my student—a very good student. About to graduate him soon, depending on his retention levels of both world wars as well as our westward expansion. Those were his worst areas. He walks me home every day from the—"

"Lincoln," Mr. Amos said.

"No, no." The Commander sounded too happy. "Tell me, Lincoln. Do you always tell the *full* truth?"

"Yes sir."

I heard the other Agents snickering. I was still in the position I had landed in and had an almost overwhelming urge to adjust myself. I thought about how ridiculous it would be to spend my last lucid moments in that tiny closet. I hoped the Commander would at least pull me out into the room before he injected me, at least let me have that much dignity.

I heard the Commander speaking what I thought would be some of the last words I ever heard.

"Tell me, Lincoln—when was the last time you saw *Sky*?"

Mr. Amos interjected. "At least two days. They've been on holiday from studying. It's been at least two days now."

"But—" Lincoln began to say.

"But maybe three," Mr. Amos said, saving my life for just a few more moments.

But then there was Lincoln's little voice again. "It was ... It was ..."

What could he say? He had just seen me a minute ago. That was the first time I ever prayed in my life. I had seen so many people do it in Cherry Harbor; they just closed their eyes and talked. I didn't know what prayer was. I didn't know who I was talking to, but it seemed worth a try.

Please make Lincoln lie.

"It was just—"

"It was many years ago in another part of the world," Mr. Amos proclaimed. "Wallenberg was climbing from train to train, handing out passes. One passenger said, 'But sir, I'm not from the country you listed on this pass.' Wallenberg said—"

I heard the boots rushing through the room.

Why did he stop? What happened?

"That's enough," one Agent growled.

I was so relieved when I heard Mr. Amos again, sounding even more determined. "Wallenberg said, 'For your *life*. I give you this to *save your life*—'"

The Commander spoke over Mr. Amos. "When did you last see him?"

"—and they took the passes. They took them and they lived. Wallenberg was a *hero*. Without a doubt he was a hero."

I knew exactly what Mr. Amos was trying to do, and I loved him for it. It was the question he had asked the pupils.

Is lying to save lives right?

The question was playing out now in real time, and it was Lincoln who would decide the answer.

"One more word and you are going to join your friends in—"

The Commander stopped. I knew he didn't want to give too much away.

"In where?" Mr. Amos asked. "Join them *where*? Is that where you're going to send Sky?"

"He would be lucky," the Commander replied. "He attacked one of my Agents, and I don't believe in second chances for boys like that."

Mr. Amos sounded angry now. "So, you'll end his life? You'll put him away forever?"

"It was last week," Lincoln blurted. "I haven't seen him since last week."

I let out a gasp.

I can't believe it.

That was the end of the interrogation. The Commander stomped out of the room, making one final threat on his way out.

"If you're lying, I'll find out. And like I said, I don't believe in second chances."

I was still afraid to move, afraid to breathe. The few silent moments after all the sound of boots faded away felt like an eternity.

I.P. was laughing when he opened the door to let me out.

"You're gonna cry, huh? You fweeling sad, wittle boy?"

He was taunting Lincoln, who had collapsed into tears in his chair. It was terrible to watch.

"Lincoln, look, I—"

I didn't know what to say.

I.P. got in Lincoln's face, pretending to cry in a cruel and obnoxious way.

"You need a lil' blankie, crying boy?"

I didn't mean to, but I pushed I.P. away.

"Back off."

"Sky," Mr. Amos warned.

"Whoa," I.P. said. "Dude, what did they do to you out there? He's a teek. It's not a big deal."

"He's scared. He's just a kid."

"Who cares?"

"I do."

"Uh, why? You okay, dude?"

"Because he's..."

Lincoln looked up at me with his sweet, tearstained face. He was waiting for me to say it. I knew it would mean the world to him. He had just saved my life, after all.

"He's my friend."

"Serious? This scrawny little teek?" I.P. looked at Mr. Amos and Lincoln, then burst out laughing. "Okay. Good one. That's good. You got me. Seriously. That's funny, dude."

He was about to walk out, but he stopped when he saw my expression. I knew it was a risk to tell him the Truth. He had always been game for any of my schemes, anything to make his dad angry, but this—this was totally different.

Everything in my life was totally different now. I felt like he needed to know that.

"You remember that place we found, under the Interlink?" I asked.

"The one my dad's always at?" I.P. said.

"That one."

"Yeah?"

"Well, we knew all that stuff on the walls was written by ... by teeks, right?"

"Excuse you—" Lincoln called out.

I pointed at Mr. Amos. "This is one of them ... He wrote it. He wrote that one story. You know the one. About the guy who died for that book."

"Yeah, I know it," I.P. said, his body growing tense.

"Well, uh ..." A trickle of sweat fell underneath the back of my shirt. "It's—"

There he was again. Tyndale. I could almost feel the heat of the fire burning him to death. His hand was reaching straight out to me. Through time, through death, it was me he was reaching for. I knew that. I had always known that. But there was my mother too. Yelling at me. *Lies. All lies.*

"It's what?" I.P. asked.

That was the first time I saw Tyndale's face in my mind that clearly. I could see him whisper the words. *I pray their eyes will be open.*

"True," I said. "The story's True."

The words felt like they had escaped from my lips.

It was at that moment I decided it was True. That it was all True.

With just one word—*True*—my whole sense of who I was turned upside down. I was suddenly wandering a world I knew nothing about.

Mr. Amos seemed to buckle in his seat. The look on his face was pure surprise. But at the same time, he looked proud. Proud of me.

Lincoln's little face was glowing with pride. He was my tutor, after all.

Both of them seemed to recognize the fundamental shift that had just taken place; they seemed to feel the same terror and excitement. I thought the whole world must have been on the edge of its seat. That's why I was so surprised by I.P.'s reaction.

"So?"

What do you mean, "So"?

"Ian. It's True," I repeated.

He must not have heard me.

"My mom, your dad —they said it wasn't."

"Mm-hmm," I.P. mumbled.

"I don't think you understand. I said it's True. That means they lied to us." I pointed at Lincoln and Mr. Amos. "It means that they're telling the Truth."

Still no response from I.P.

Does he not understand?

Did he not know that everything in our lives had just changed forever?

I tried to explain it to him another way.

"They said that the teeks were lying. But it's the other way around. They're not lying—*we're* lying. Topos is lying to *everybody.*"

"Makes sense." I.P. turned his back to me and moved toward the door. "Can we go now?"

"You don't even care?"

He whipped back around. "These guys? Are these guys taking over Topos or something?"

"No..."

"Then who cares if it's true?" I.P. scoffed at me. "What's 'true' anyway? So, I'll ask again—are these teeks taking over Topos?"

"No," I said, gritting my teeth.

"Then so what if it's true? That doesn't change anything. Everyone who matters says it's a lie, and anyone who disagrees ends up in Sleep Camp. So honestly, I just don't care."

"I just don't care."

The words were like a punch to the gut. A horrible feeling came over me, like I had just crossed into another universe and, without knowing it, left my friend behind. As I.P. stepped to the door and it opened, I realized I really had picked my side, and I.P. had picked his.

"Stop him!" I yelled.

Mr. Amos pounced, tackling I.P to the ground and dragging him back into the room.

"The hat!" I said. "Get that hat."

Lincoln swooped in from the side and grabbed the hat lying on the ground.

"What are you doing?" I.P shouted. "Are you crazy?"

"I'm so sorry," I took the hat from Lincoln and shoved him out the door. "Mr. A, you just have to get out the door before he does. I'll close him in."

"You're gonna ditch me for teeks? Is that really what you're doing right now?"

I nodded.

"You're picking the wrong side," I.P. warned as he writhed in Mr. Amos's arms, trying to reach his syringe.

Mr. Amos threw him off and ran out the door.

I.P. wasn't able to pick himself up and get to us before I waved the hat, causing the door to slam shut in his face. He stood there, banging on the glass, fury and betrayal on his face. Lincoln read his lips. "He's saying you're going to regret this."

"C'mon." I grabbed Lincoln by the arm and made a mad dash to the elevator. "We're going home."

There was no hope of sneaking around now. The only tactic left was speed. As we ran down the long hallway, turning again and again, we finally reached the receptionist, who yelled at us, telling us to stop. A floor-wide alarm went off just as the three of us were in the elevator with the doors closing. As I pressed the button for the first floor, I could see my hand shaking.

The elevator began to move.

Heading up.

"No," I said, pressing the first-floor button repeatedly. "No, no, no. It's going up."

It stopped on the seventh floor. As the doors opened, Lincoln stumbled backward into Mr. Amos's arms. I couldn't help letting out a gasp.

"Ah, you're back," a silky voice spoke.

It was Azaz Aylo.

I wish I could say that there was a great struggle, that we'd put up a real fight. But the truth was, the Agents had us pinned in seconds. They carried Lincoln and Mr. Amos one way and took me to office 700, the office of the A.O.

"You've caused a great deal of trouble," she said, leaning up against the side of her desk, twirling her pen in her fingers.

"I'm sorry," I told her.

And I was sorry.

Sorry to have been lied to my whole life.

Sorry to be sitting here in this office with yet another liar.

Sorry for myself.

But I was even sorrier for all the people in Cherry Harbor, for Ember and her dad, even for the Oarsmen. I was sorry for anyone who'd ever crossed Topos, because even if they were right to resist, they didn't stand a chance.

"I'll be blunt. The Commander would like to see you in Sleep Camp, and there's only one reason you aren't there right now. Me."

I crossed my arms over my chest. It was freezing in here.

"I'm going to offer you a deal." She sat behind her desk and leaned back as if she were basking in the sun, as if she enjoyed this. "Help us, and you won't go to Sleep Camp."

"What about Amos and Lincoln?"

"What about Ember and her father?" she replied.

I choked. I hadn't said their names on purpose, but she already knew.

She pressed a button under her desk, which triggered the shelf of pastel-colored office supplies to her right to open like a door to reveal a Fibonacci so large that it stretched the height of the wall. I saw Ember and her father climbing a staircase. She was holding him up with one hand and propping herself up on the banister with another. They both looked like something truly terrible had happened to them.

"What did you do to them?" I demanded.

"Absolutely nothing."

"Liar!"

"You want to save them all, do you? Well, Daley will never accept that. He's so angry, he needs to inject *someone*. We have to give him that. One person at minimum. Maybe two."

I hated the way she was talking to me, like each person was only a number in an equation.

"The question is, who? Hmm. Ember?"

"No," I said, too quickly.

"No? Mmm. A crush? Oh, Trotsky. Well, I have good news for you. I also like Ember, and I have every intention of bringing her back to Oasis—back to Oasis with *you*."

I actually laughed at the idea. I had seen the way Ember told her father she was joining the Oarsmen. She would only come back to Oasis as an enemy, not an ally.

I looked back at Ember on the Fibonacci screen. She and her father had stopped and sat down now. Her head was buried in her knees, and he had his arm wrapped around her shoulders. They were both shaking.

"She won't do it," I said.

"Won't she?"

"Neither will I."

Azaz leaned toward me, gesturing for me to lean in as well.

"You will, and your friends will go back to where they're from unharmed. All except one."

CHAPTER NINETEEN

ALL EXCEPT ONE

(Ember and Sky)

"**I**s this it?"

The door slid open without any prompting from us, and the dimly lit stairwell was overcome by the bright light of the hallway. My father winced at the light, and I took his arm. I was determined to help him find this map, determined to help him remember that he was a hero. That was the reason I walked down the hallway with him, expecting to be caught by an Agent at any moment. Not because I personally cared about the map or where it led, but because my father did. He patted my arm in the comforting way only a dad could. To me, that was worth risking everything for.

Above the great wooden double doors at the end of the hall, the word "Welcome" was etched in glowing teal. Lining the walls were an assortment of photographs, perfectly spaced except for one or two photos on the right wall, which were noticeably tilted, with the pictures missing or damaged. I noticed one was a photo of Azaz with a tear down the middle, eliminating whoever had been in the photograph with her.

I breathed in the lingering scent of ocean breeze, although it was very faint—nothing like how I remembered it in Azaz's office. Then I felt my father's hand dig into my arm.

"What? What is it?" I said.

There was an elevator behind us next to where we had come in, and the shaft had started to rumble.

Someone was coming.

My dad turned around and then pulled me behind him. As weak and frail as he was, he still faced forward and waited with his fists clenched. The elevator stopped and the doors opened.

"Sky!"

I was so relieved to see he was okay that I ran to him and flung my arms around him in a hug. Just a few days ago, he had been a stranger in the darkness, but now we were a team, brought together by the coincidence that our lives as we had known them ended for us both at the same time.

I realized he hadn't hugged me back, and I pulled away, feeling a little embarrassed. When I saw his face, his horrified eyes, I knew something was very wrong.

"Th–they took Lincoln and Mr. Amos. I had them, but they took them. You have to help me! They said they were going to hurt them."

"Hurt them?" I said.

Sky was so frantic he could barely string his next sentence together. "No time. Please, now—or else…Lincoln—he's just a kid. We have to go!"

I had never seen him so worked up, so manic. I heard my father take a loud, deep breath through his nose.

"Please," Sky begged. "What am I going to tell his parents if something happens to him?"

My father came and placed his hands firmly on Sky's shoulders. "It's going to be okay."

Sky nodded, looking at me briefly, then back at my father. "I know where they are."

"Where are they?"

"The Administrator's office."

The Administrator.

Somehow I hadn't considered the role the Administrator would play in my life now that I had joined a movement to overthrow everything he'd made. I thought about the picture Henry had standing with him at the Astra Park ribbon cutting. It was probably the happiest moment of Henry's life. But then I remembered the people being tortured in their teal helmets. Was the Administrator, a man I had admired for most of my life, my enemy now?

"How did you find out?" my father asked Sky.

"I heard it."

"From who?" I asked.

Sky didn't answer.

"We'll follow you," my father said. "Do you know how to get to them?"

"Yeah," Sky replied. "Trust me."

I faced the wooden doors.

Am I really going to do this?

I pulled out a new Travel Card, this one colored black. Very few travel cards opened the door to the Administrator's office. Ember and Mr. Aaronson would never have been able to get in, but that wasn't a problem for me. Not anymore.

I scanned the card and the door opened without hesitation. Ember gave me a perplexed look.

"Where did you get—"

I cut her off by talking to Mr. Aaronson. "Thank you for helping me. Really. Thank you."

Anytime someone stepped into the Administrator's office, the first thing they would do was look at the carpet under their feet. You would think the giant circular office with a skylight covering the whole ceiling and a Fibonacci screen taking up half the wall would be more captivating.

But no, it was always the big white carpet with the Topos emblem in the center of it that impressed people, and Ember was no exception. She went and stood over the emblem, in the middle of the three circles, and the light from the skylight washed over her.

It was the effect this office had on everyone. They always forgot their troubles and felt safe here. At least for a little while.

Mr. Aaronson was studying the two desks on each side of the room. The one desk was perfectly organized, with little pastel boxes and pen jars, like it always was, but the other was empty now, which I thought was strange.

"This is beautiful," Ember said. But she was wrong. It looked beautiful, but underneath it all, this was an ugly place. She would understand that soon, but I hated to end this moment for her now. She deserved a second to catch her breath. I wanted her to have that.

Mr. Aaronson wasn't fooled. "We need to keep moving."

"Okay." I walked toward the rounded wall. It slid open to reveal a thin corridor.

I told them to follow me. Mr. Aaronson arranged Ember between the two of us and shuffled across the carpet. The corridor was only wide enough for two people—one if you were Commander Daley.

One of the effects of the hallway was to start making whoever was walking it nervous, like they were running out of space. The doors to the other rooms off the hallway seemed to almost brush against my shoulders. The Envoys Parlor, the Study, the Dream Room, the Contraband Vault.

"Wait," Mr. Aaronson said.

"What is it?" Ember followed her father's gaze to the plaque above the door and read it out loud. "Contraband Vault?"

Mr. Aaronson looked at Ember, then Sky, then back to the door. "Can we get in there?"

I said yes because it was the Truth, but as soon as I did, I wished I hadn't. "Why?"

"It's important."

"The map?" Ember said. "You think it's in there?"

"I know it is."

I had almost forgotten about the map. I was trying to think fast, to come up with some reason why he couldn't go in, but Ember was too excited.

"Sky, let me see your card."

I gave it to her, and I didn't know why.

The door slid right open. I knew it would. Ember was the first to step to the door, but I stopped her.

"I don't know what kind of security they have in there. It may not be safe."

"We have to get the map," she said.

I looked at Mr. Aaronson. "Can you do it alone? We have to find Lincoln and Mr. Amos before something happens to them."

Ember started to protest, but Mr. Aaronson stopped her with just one loving look.

"I can."

I remembered the way Mr. Amos had made me shake his hand before telling me about the Oarsmen. I offered Mr. Aaronson my hand, looking right into his eyes.

"I'll watch out for Ember. When you're done, come down the hall and go through the next door. We'll wait for you there."

Ember grabbed her father's hand. "Please let me go with you."

"No," Mr. Aaronson replied. "Go with Sky. Listen . . . Go with Sky."

Mr. Aaronson looked at me, man to man. "Remember what I told you."

I nodded at him, and he entered the room alone.

The moment the door shut with my father and me on opposite sides, I started to cry. Since we had been reunited, I had watched him constantly to confirm his existence. As soon as I couldn't see him, I had this over-whelming fear he had never really been there at all.

I felt Sky grab my hand. "It's okay. You're going to be okay."

He led me down the hall so gently, but when we reached our destina-tion, and I saw the word "T-Force" over the door, any calm I had found by his reassurance was sucked away by the painted face of the panther-man glaring at me from the entry.

"We're waiting for my dad in there?" I said.

Sky only looked back at me for a second before he averted his eyes back to the door. I hadn't noticed the lights dimming and the floor tran-sitioning to cold concrete. When I looked back, the rounded hallway seemed to go on forever, and I started to panic.

"Do you think he'll find us here? Maybe we should go back. Maybe…"

Sky was ignoring me. Why was he ignoring me?

He didn't wave his Travel Card again but instead pulled out a small slip of paper, which he continually referenced as he entered a series of lengthy numeric codes into a keypad beside the door. His uneasy hand slipped, almost missing a number. He jumped back, as if he were afraid a trapdoor would open on the spot where he had been standing. Then he shook out his shoulders, mumbling to himself, and continued with the code.

"Sky…what's wrong?"

Just as I asked that, a loud clicking sound came from the door. Then another click and a long screech as the heavy door slid into the wall. We were standing in a massive, hollow room with rounded walls and bright screens on all sides.

"Holy Administrator."

In the center of the room, arranged on two separate metal platforms, were Mr. Amos and Lincoln, restrained in thick metal chairs and gagged. Without thinking, I ran straight to Lincoln, who was screaming for help. When I stepped onto the platform, Lincoln jerked and winced in pain. A shot of electricity raced through my body, throwing me to my knees and off the platform.

"A stun floor," Sky said, still standing in the same position near the door.

I writhed on the floor, grabbing my burning feet. "It shocked me. What do we do?"

But Sky stood motionless, his eyes locked on Mr. Amos, who was shouting indiscernibly through his gag while his face turned red. I waited for an answer, but none came.

I stood and circled Lincoln's platform, then placed a hand on it. Lincoln squirmed as I quickly drew it back and checked for wounds. I noticed as I opened and closed my fingers that the pain didn't linger. So, I touched the platform again, this time for one moment longer. Lincoln clenched his teeth around the gag. I withdrew my hand again.

"Does it still hurt?" I asked Lincoln, holding up my hand to him to show there was no damage.

Lincoln tensed his shoulders and shook his head. Mr. Amos was still yelling in Sky's direction through his gag.

"I need help getting them out," I yelled to Sky.

What is he doing?

I circled Lincoln again. The restraints were simple, shockingly simple. I examined the line of buckles, formulating a plan. At least one of us needed to have a plan. I considered warning Lincoln but thought it would be best if he didn't have time to anticipate it...

I jumped.

The platform buzzed as I landed. An electric shock pulsed through my body, making me stumble and twitch. But I forced myself to the chair and unclicked the first two restraints before jumping away. All I thought about was rescuing the boy. As soon as I hit the floor, the pain ended for both me and Lincoln. The kid looked at me tensely but bravely.

"I-I need help," I said, looking at Sky. "It only hurts while you're on it. If we both go, we won't be on as long."

He wouldn't even look at me.

"Sky? Sky!"

He seemed to be growing smaller and smaller in the room, to the point that it threatened to engulf him entirely. He looked more helpless than Lincoln.

What is happening?

Everything was falling apart.

Watching Ember plunge back onto the platform disgusted me. I was disgusted with myself.

She's being so brave.

My insides felt like they were ripping in two.

You don't have a choice here. You can't save them all.

Like Mr. Amos's, Lincoln's feet were elevated off the stun floor by a cold metal bar. To undo the restraints on his calves and ankles, Ember had to lie on her back underneath his legs. I could see that when she lay flat, her spine seized.

"Sky—" she called out.

Ember managed to unclick the final restraints. She and Lincoln stumbled forward together off the platform, heaving and gasping. Ember unbound his wrists and went straight to Mr. Amos on the next platform. Even though the electric shock was pulsing through his body, Mr. Amos never once stopped looking at me.

He knows. How could he know?

I heard something. I turned toward the door. I glanced back at Ember, who had stopped to listen as well.

We both recognized the sound.

Click-clack, click-clack, click-clack.

Azaz was coming.

I remained frozen while Ember leapt onto the platform to undo the final restraints binding Mr. Amos to the chair. As soon as his legs were free, he stumbled off the platform and headed straight for me.

"I wouldn't do that if I were you," Azaz said in a soft, ominous voice as she entered the room.

Mr. Aaronson was walking in front of her, guided by the point of her glowing syringe. He was holding something over his chest.

Everybody stopped. Ember cried out while Mr. Amos, still gagged and bound at the wrist, backed away. Azaz led Mr. Aaronson to the center of the room.

I looked over at Ember.

I need to get out of here. I don't want to watch this.

I hugged the rounded walls and began to creep to the corner, away from Azaz. I wanted the room to swallow me whole so I could disappear into it.

"He'll be here momentarily," Azaz told me, making me stop dead in my tracks.

Seconds later, more footsteps were coming down the hall. I knew who it was before he got to us. His loud voice echoed in the room.

"This better be a good—"

I think the Commander was going to say "surprise," but when he entered the room and saw Mr. Aaronson a skin prick away from Sleep Camp, he was too shocked to say it.

"You wanted Oarsmen," Azaz said. "Here. An Oarsman for you."

The Commander smiled viciously. "Adam Aaronson. You just refuse to die."

Mr. Aaronson didn't flinch. He stared straight into the Commander's eyes with his chin lifted and shoulders back. The Commander met him nose to nose, saying, "What has it been—seven years? Seven years since the T-force dragged you and your wife to Sleep Camp."

Ember's dad remained silent.

"Was it worth it? All this? An entire underground society? Is Topos that much worse than Sleep Camp?"

"Topos *is* Sleep Camp," Mr. Aaronson said.

The Commander circled Mr. Aaronson menacingly. "So, what's it really all about, Adam? Why do the Oarsmen fight us when they know, in the end, they have no chance?"

Mr. Aaronson still said nothing.

"How many are there?"

Still no response.

The Commander pulled out his own syringe. "Tell me."

"You can't do this!" Ember yelled, rushing toward the Commander with a growing look of fury. "I won't let you!"

"Step back, Ember," Azaz said in a grossly motherly way. "Think of your position."

But Ember refused.

"The Administrator is prepared to pardon your behavior and allow you to continue with the T.R.U.E. This doesn't have to have anything to do with you."

"That's my dad!"

Azaz's eyes narrowed into that same beady, nasty look I knew so well. "Listen to me…"

"I'm never listening to you again!"

"Step back, Ember," her father said.

Azaz shook her head. "Disloyalty. I had much higher hopes for you, Ember."

"I'm loyal to my family," Ember said defiantly.

Mr. Aaronson's eyes shimmered with tears. "It's okay, Ember. Step back."

Ember heeded her father, but she still watched Azaz with an unforgiving look of contempt.

"Tell me where the Oarsmen are, or it's lights out right now," the Commander threatened, towering above Mr. Aaronson.

Mr. Aaronson looked up at him as if he were looking down at him.

"The Oarsmen are everywhere."

Even under his cover of anger, you could tell that scared the Commander.

"What you don't understand is that no matter how many you kill, the Oarsmen will never die," Mr. Aaronson said. "Because the Oarsmen aren't people. The Oarsmen are a story. A True story. You can't kill that with all the Teal Lady in the world. No matter what you do, no matter how many dreams you implant, how many people you silence, how much of the past you make disappear, you'll never be able to destroy the Oarsmen. That's the Truth."

"Truth," the Commander scoffed. "You want to know the truth? Because you won't find it in your stories! The truth is, the world changed—forever—and we left your 'truth' behind. No matter what you do, it's never coming back. So, you can try to regather, try to fight Topos, but you can't fight the future, because it comes whether you like it or not, and Topos *is* the future. *That's* the truth."

Mr. Aaronson spoke sternly and plainly. "You're right. We're not going back. But we're not going your way either."

I wanted this to be Mr. Aaronson's victory speech. But I knew it was too late.

He had lost.

There was nothing I could do.

It was at that moment that I recognized what my father was holding in his hands.

My book . . .

It was the oars I noticed first. I had never given much thought to them after seeing them on the corner of my book every day for seven years.

Looking at them now, I suddenly understood. The oars in the Sticking Place, the oars in the hideout, the oars on my book.

Without knowing it, I had been an Oarsman my entire life. Without knowing it, I had been hiding the map to their Armory.

My book was the map.

The Commander spoke. "I am charged with eliminating the Oarsmen. Every single one. And I will complete my mission."

A memory pierced my thoughts. A haunting voice in the night. *We are charged with removing all adult Tenants in this unit.* I recognized the Commander's voice—he had been in our unit seven years ago.

He was the one who had taken my parents.

"It was you!" I lunged toward the Commander but felt someone hold me back.

"Trotsky," Commander Daley said, surprised to find Sky in the room with him. "You dirty, teek-loving—"

"Wait," Azaz said.

We all looked at her.

"I propose a trade."

The Commander grunted at her. "What do you want?"

"Oh, it's not what I want, Commander. It's what you want. You want the Oarsmen to disappear. I've brought you one of their leaders. Isn't it only right you do something for me now?"

"For the kid?" The Commander pointed at Sky, who was still holding me by the arm. "You want to exchange Adam Aaronson for Trotsky?"

Azaz smirked. "You get the credit for catching one of the most powerful Oarsmen, and Trotsky gets full immunity for all of his *behavior.*"

The Commander walked over to Sky and me threateningly, then looked back at Azaz.

"Fine. But I want him to do it."

Sky stepped in front of me. "We did not agree to this!"

"Agree to this?" I said. "What are you talking about?"

The Commander held out his syringe to Sky. "You want to come back to our side? Then prove it."

"He doesn't need yours. He has his own." Azaz pointed to Sky's belt. When I saw him from the back, I noticed a strange outline underneath his T-shirt.

"Sky ... what's happening?"

"I won't do it," Sky said, his voice breaking. "This is not the plan."

I could feel the anger rising in me. "You made a plan with them?"

He looked back at me, reaching his arms out like he was afraid I might hit him. "It's not what you think."

"Did you make a plan with them?"

"He did," Azaz said.

"You set us up?" I yelled to him. "Is that what you did?"

Sky and I locked eyes for what felt like a long time. Without saying anything, he looked like he was trying to explain himself, trying to apologize. I didn't want to hear it, not even from his eyes.

"I won't do it," Sky said to the Commander.

That's when I felt the full force of Commander Daley wrapping his arm around me. I hadn't even noticed him getting into a position to attack me. I saw the tip of his syringe pointed straight at my neck. I heard my father cry out. Mr. Amos shouting, Sky yelling. It was all a blur. All I could see was myself in one of those teal helmets, running from attackers that don't exist, eaten alive by bugs that were never really there.

"Do it or I inject her," the Commander said to Sky.

I couldn't piece my thoughts together. The whole room was pulsing to the beat of my heart and melting into a blurry haze. I could only barely see Sky lift his shirt to reveal the Teal Lady strapped to his belt.

I heard my father tell him, "Do it."

No. No, don't.

I couldn't make the words leave my mouth.

Please don't hurt him.

Just do it and get it over with. Do it now!

I saw Mr. Aaronson's fleshy arm. That's where I would do it. I would strike there. One moment—just one moment and it would be over.

Lincoln had removed Mr. Amos's gag.

"Don't do it, Sky," he said to me.

I took one second to look at Mr. Amos. He had his arms reached out to me, like Tyndale always did in my dreams.

"Drop the syringe. We can help you."

But this wasn't my dreams. This was the real world.

"You're running out of time," the Commander shouted.

Ember screamed.

I have to do it. I have to save her.

I raised the syringe above Mr. Aaronson's arm, and what he said to me the moment before I pierced him will haunt me until the day I die.

"I forgive you."

The syringe hit its target.

I heard Ember shriek in horror and Mr. Amos call my name and Lincoln cry out, but none of that stopped me. As I emptied the last contents of the vial into Mr. Aaronson's bloodstream, I saw Ember collapse.

"*And once he gained their trust, he betrayed them,*" Mr. Amos whispered.

I recognized the words from the story.

Mr. Aaronson was Tyndale, and I was the one who had handed him over to his enemies.

"I tried to tell you," I said. "I'm not like you, and I never will be."

And I knew I never would be like him, no matter how much I wanted to be. Not after that. Anything I thought I could be while I was in Cherry Harbor was reduced to who I was in that moment, watching Mr. Aaronson spasm and collapse. That's who I was now, and I deserved it. I tried to ignore the rising tide of disgust inside me.

I hated myself. Even more than the Commander, more than Azaz, it was me I hated. It was me I wanted to punish. It was me I would never forgive.

"*I forgive you.*"

How could he say that to me?

I couldn't hold myself up any longer. I crouched down on the floor, looking at Mr. Aaronson's face. I was the first to notice that something was wrong. That he wasn't responding to the Teal Lady in a way I had ever seen before.

When he should have been unconscious, Mr. Aaronson rolled onto his back, gasping for air as if it were being forcibly vacuumed from his lungs. He tore at his clothes, as if his skin, too, were suffocating.

The Commander released Ember, and she ran to her father and threw herself over his shaking body.

"Ember," he said, as he clutched the ground beneath him, forcing himself to speak.

"Dad!" she cried.

He tried to say something else.

"What, Dad? What is it?" Ember looked at me. "What's happening to him?"

He shook so violently, Ember had to hold him down. Then his back arched in a piercing inhale before his spine slumped slowly back to the floor.

"Ember," he said.

"Yes? Yes, I'm here, Dad. I'm here."

"I love you."

Ember was sobbing over him, holding his face in her hands. "Don't leave me. Please."

"Ember," he said, his eyes turning to glass. He only said one more word to her.

"Remember."

We all waited for the next breath. But it didn't come.

Mr. Amos ran over to him. "God! No!" He grabbed his wrist. He put his hand over Mr. Aaronson's chest. "God, why? Why!"

"What happened?" I said. "Is he okay?"

Mr. Amos looked at me, man-to-man. "He's dead."

"Dead?" I said. "He can't be dead. People don't die from the Teal Lady. They just sleep. They don't die! He can't be...that's not...people never—"

"He's dead."

I felt the weight of my father's head in my hands, I lowered it gently back down to the cold concrete floor. I put my ear to his chest, shook him, then looked into his eyes. They were wide open, as if at any moment they would turn to me. The passing from life to death seemed too easy for the person who died. There was no effort, no decision, just there and then not there.

I thought the feelings would come all at once, but in that moment, they wouldn't come at all. Nothing came but a full-body numbness, like all of my senses were shutting down. I dragged my palm from my father's chest and grabbed his hand to hold it while it was still warm.

It occurred to me at that moment that Henry had never gotten to see him. He would have loved him.

At the edge of his fingertips, my book lay open. He had dropped it when he fell. When he...

I have no idea what people were doing around me. I have almost no memory of anyone else in the room. I thought of myself as completely alone. That's why I reached for the book.

I turned to the inside of the front cover.

"For our children. May the past guide you into the future."

My father had risked everything for this book, for whatever secret map it contained. When I touched the dried ink, I could hear my father whisper.

"Remember."

I closed the book and pressed it over my chest. I looked back at my father one last time. "I will. I promise."

Then I did the only thing I knew to protect that book.

I ran.

A needle rushed past my head, narrowly missing me.

"Don't touch her," I heard Sky say.

"Lincoln, now!" Mr. Amos said.

Then Sky again. "Lincoln! Take this!"

I heard the doors slamming.

"Run!" Mr. Amos screamed.

Lincoln was sprinting toward me, holding a black Travel Card in his hand. Mr. Amos was right behind him. The rounded hallway rushed past us. We must have set off every alarm in the city, but all I could hear was my father.

"The Oarsmen will never die because the Oarsmen aren't people. The Oarsmen are a story."

That was the story I was holding in my hands as I ran for my life.

The Oarsmen will never die.

CHAPTER TWENTY

TRUTH

(Ember)

"Ember."

The voice whispered, waking me up. I found myself buried underneath a series of blankets, my head throbbing and my clothes feeling damp. I had been having the most terrible nightmares. At least I *hoped* they were nightmares.

"Ember?"

I rolled onto my side, rubbing my chapped lips together and peeling open my heavy eyelids. As I became aware of my surroundings, a sinking feeling filled the pit of my stomach. I blinked as I heard a hushed murmur of many voices in another room. I found myself alone except for a blurry face coming into focus just inches away from me.

"Ember!"

"Henry!" I shot up and almost knocked heads with my brother. "Oh, Henry!"

I wrapped my arms around his neck, then pulled away and grabbed his face with my hands, just to make sure he was really there.

"Whoa, there," Mr. Freeman said, coming into view. He was standing right behind Henry in the corner of the tiny room. His white T-shirt was littered with stains only partially hidden by a warm flannel. Mrs. Freeman was standing behind him in the same clothes I had last seen her in, her thick hair hemmed in by an amber hair scarf.

"Henry is still recovering," she said with a smile. "You have to be gentle."

I couldn't resist giving him one more aggressive squeeze. As I released him, I looked him up and down. It was really him—sitting on his knees—as straight up as his cowlick.

"Welcome to the Outpost." Mrs. Freeman clasped her hands together, looking apologetic. "We couldn't give you a proper tour last night when you came in."

"Wasn't that long ago," Mr. Freeman said, massaging his wife's shoulders to calm her.

"And we had already given Henry something to help him sleep. He was so worried about you," Mrs. Freeman continued in a flustered tone. "But I thought the extra few hours would be good—for both of you. He just couldn't wait any longer this morning."

Henry was smiling as wide as he could without showing his teeth. He looked perfectly healthy. No extended blinking, no scratching, no painful gulps of air; he looked exactly like he had before he'd been injected.

"How did you ...," I began to say to Mrs. Freeman in amazement when I saw Mrs. Hernandez stepping into the doorway behind her. "You ... you did this?"

Mrs. Hernandez nodded.

"It's a miracle," Mrs. Freeman said. "That's what I said when Henry woke up. It's a miracle straight from heaven."

"There's something you've gotta see." Henry took my arm to pull me out of the bed. "This place is great. There're so many kids, and they all want to play. And the food. The food!"

As he dragged me out of the small bunkroom, there was a split second when everything felt normal. Better than normal, even. Henry and I were off together on a fun adventure. That ended when we walked into the main room of the Outpost and I had to walk through a crowd of almost everyone from Cherry Harbor crammed together, looking solemnly at me as if I were a fallen hero and this was my last walk among mortals. The Freeman boys were outside and wrestling when they saw us. They stopped and waved excitedly at Henry, who waved back as if they had been best friends for years. I was happy to see that.

Same old Henry.

The boys ran over to us, and Henry introduced them.

"These are my friends Martin and Will. You guys ready to go?"

"Yeah," Will said.

We walked past Rosa reading to a group of kids and Lincoln leaned up against the trunk of a tree, twirling a black Travel Card in his fingers. He looked like he hadn't slept yet.

"Henry," Mr. Amos called out, jogging up behind us.

"We're going to the boat," Martin announced.

"Oh. I see," Mr. Amos said with a smile to the boys, but his swollen eyes gave away that he probably hadn't slept either. "I'll come watch."

Something about seeing Mr. Amos solidified the reality of what had happened in Oasis. I pictured the look on my father's face when I'd held it in my hands. The way he called my name as if he couldn't see me right above him. Then I heard Sky's voice again.

"This is not the plan."

What was the plan then, Sky? Was my dad supposed to die in your plan? Was that part of it?

I remembered him holding my hand through the cramped hallway. "It's going to be okay," he had said, and I'd believed him. How could he do something like that? I wished I had never touched him, never met him.

"C'mon," Henry said, tugging my arm again.

It was like Henry had absolutely no memory of the last time I had seen him, how I had stood there while the Agents started to inject him. He didn't know it was me who had turned him in; that's why he was smiling at me like that.

But still, Henry was alive, and my father was dead.

The Outpost was similar in many ways to the Sticking Place. It had wooden shingles and a covered front porch and was around the same size as well. But unlike the Sticking Place, the Outpost was not designed to welcome guests, which was apparent by the grounds being lined by a tall, barbed-wire fence.

"I wouldn't poke that," Mr. Amos said to Henry. Then he returned to being silent, thinking about something. The boys had run off ahead of us, playing tag, leaving me and Mr. Amos walking together in a quiet that left far too much space for me to think.

"Say something," I told him.

Mr. Amos, stopped, dropped his shoulders, and shook his head. "In a minute. We're almost there."

The typical confident tenor of his voice had faded into an uncertain whisper.

I heard Henry singing the Fibonacci jingle as we approached the water.

"My friends and me on Fibonacci. Why not just be happy?"

It looked so much like where Mr. Amos and I had sat for my first sunrise in Cherry Harbor, with a stretch of dark water surrounded by absolutely nothing but a few plants trying to start a new life.

Henry and the Freeman boys were dragging a large wooden boat to the water. They were about to run over one of the few tiny green bushes on the dusty shore.

"Go around that—"

They dragged the boat right over it.

Mr. Amos chuckled as the boat slid over the bush, crushing it. But to my surprise, it sprang right back up after the boat passed, like nothing had happened.

"Tough bush," I said.

"Tough boys," Mr. Amos replied, watching them use every ounce of their collective strength to shove off into the water. They pulled something from the bottom of the boat.

Oars.

"What is that?" I asked.

Mr. Amos laughed. "Really?"

"What?"

"You don't know what that is?"

"No."

"Well, my dear Oarsman, that is a rowboat."

Henry had one of the large oars in his hand and faced backward, trying to drag it through the water. The boat turned in continuous circles.

"Did my dad ever use one?" I said, watching Henry.

"You know, it's funny. I'm not sure he did."

Mr. Amos closed his eyes, so I did too. A cool gust of wind rolled over us. The boat crashed gently back onto the shore, and Henry got out.

"Do a lap without me," my brother said to the boys and then helped them shove off again. He came and stood next to me, watching the boys struggle to synchronize their paddling. "Where have you been?"

Do I tell him?

Could I tell him that I had gone with our father to find a map to eventually overthrow Topos and that he had died in the process? How could you tell that to a seven-year-old?

"Do you want to know the secret to rowing while facing backward?" Mr. Amos said.

Henry's face lit up. "Sure."

"When you first start, you have to line yourself up with one point. If you can stay lined up with that point while you row, you'll move in a straight line. You lose that point and you'll end up way off course."

I could tell Henry was testing this theory in his mind. He seemed satisfied with it.

Mr. Amos kept looking at Henry, but I knew he was talking to me.

"Do you remember the book your parents gave you?"

Henry nodded.

"Your book is like that point. If you keep your eyes on it, you can decide where you want to go. But if you lose it, you get lost. It's a gift from the past to the future, and your parents risked everything to give that to you."

"May the past guide you into the future," I whispered.

"That's from your book," Henry said.

"Our book," I told him.

It was another hour before we came back through the front door of the Outpost, where all the adults were standing tightly together around a rectangular wooden table. Over the front door, I noticed, was the same pair of crossed wooden oars as in the Sticking Place, with the same quotations as well, but on this version the author was named.

> *"The Truth laid plainly before their eyes in their mother tongue*
> *or else the enemies of all Truth quench it again."*
> —William Tyndale

I turned around to the sound of Mr. Amos cheering. Lying plainly on the long wooden table, before the eyes of all the adults in the Outpost, was my book. Henry, still very much struggling to catch up, pointed at it with his mouth agape.

"Holy Administrator!" He charged toward the table only to be greeted with a series of affronted faces. "What?"

Mr. Amos chuckled. "Perhaps it's time for a new phrase."

"HALLELUJAH AMEN!" Mr. Freeman said, rushing in the back door. "Is it true?"

"You planning on shouting the house down?" Mrs. Freeman said, rushing in behind him.

"Might could. Is it true?"

"We were just telling Amos," Rosa said, peeling her nose from the open page. Mr. and Mrs. Hernandez pulled Rosa back from the book as if they were worried their daughter might be sucked into it and disappear forever.

"Well," Mr. Freeman said, "let's see it."

Henry and I sidled up next to Mr. Freeman, and we all inspected the open page—one of the first pages in the book. I didn't understand what was happening.

"That . . . *that's* it?" Mr. Freeman said, bewildered.

"It's a piece of it," Rosa said. "My brother told me that the Oarsmen divided the map among their most loyal members. That way if one betrayed them, the location would still be a secret—"

"Brilliant," Mr. Amos whispered.

"—but we have an idea of where to look for the rest now. Now that we know that it's real."

"That what's real?" Henry asked.

"The Oarsmen Armory," Mr. Amos said, causing the room to fall silent.

"So, this," Mr. Freeman pointed at the open page, "is a piece a' the map to the Armory?"

Mr. Amos nodded.

"Gosh . . . I was startin' ta think it was just a myth."

"Can you imagine?" Rosa said, still held at safe distance from the book by her parents. "Once we find it—the Oarsmen Armory—this changes everything."

"Rosa . . . ," Mrs. Hernandez said under her breath.

There was an anxious and excited murmur among the group.

"Why?" I asked, inspecting the seemingly normal page. "What's in the Armory?"

The room fell quiet.

"We're not sure," Rosa admitted. "But the founders of the Oarsmen said that whatever is in there will be . . ."

Mr. Amos stepped forward toward the table and leaned in closely to the page.

"The end of Topos."

As I glanced at the page, I knew my life had changed forever. Wherever that map led, I was going to follow.

If that meant the end of Topos, then bring it on.

EPILOGUE

THE NEW A.O.

Azaz stood in the center of the Topos, Inc. logo printed on the soft white carpet, her face glowing in the sunlight pouring in from the overhead window. Her hands were clasped behind her back, and she watched the large, curved screen in front of her on which the Administrator's cheery face was projected. She allowed her lips to part to a real, true smile.

They tightened back to a thin line again as the double doors flung open and a sleepless and vengeful-looking Commander Daley stomped into the room.

"You have some *real nerve* asking me to come—"

The Commander stopped suddenly, noticing the Administrator smiling at him, his pearly teeth taking up half the screen. The Administrator waited for Azaz to gently glide behind her desk.

"Hello, Commander," he said sweetly.

"Sir." Commander Daley fumbled to pull his hat from his pocket and situate it on his head. Azaz leered at him behind the glowing Fibonacci, which lit her face in an unflatteringly harsh blue.

"I hear we have contraband on the loose," the Administrator said.

The Commander assumed the same position as Azaz, standing where she had stood moments before. "I assure you *I* did everything I could to prevent that, sir." He made sure to emphasize "I" while casting a nasty sideways glance at Azaz.

She gave him a demeaning chuckle.

"Azaz told me everything," the Administrator said. "You were both very brave."

"Yes sir," he replied, his lip quivering with anger.

"So," the Administrator continued, "how will we get it back?"

Commander Daley fumbled over his words. "Well, sir...um...I'll be—"

"I've taken care of it," Azaz said, turning in her chair to face the screen.

The Administrator smiled. "That's my girl. What's your plan?"

"First," Azaz replied. "I have bad news. I told Commander Daley cycles ago that I suspected the Oarsmen were regathering."

"What?! You? *You?*" Commander Daley sputtered.

She spoke over him. "Unfortunately, I was right. It's a weak force, hardly anything to worry about. But I believe it's best to nip these things in the bud."

"I agree," the Administrator said, nodding. Commander Daley looked ready to explode.

"For that reason," Azaz continued, "I'll be taking over a portion of the T-Force."

"You will not," the Commander said, forgetting his place.

"Oh yes, Commander. I will. It will be quite temporary. I imagine we'll end this little regathering in a few cycles, and then your men will be returned to you. Don't worry; you'll be joining the search. I know how much the topic of the Oarsmen fascinates you." Her expression turned into a satisfied smirk. "You will report everything, and I mean *everything*, to me."

"Sir," the Commander said to the screen. "I have to object. Azaz has no experience curbing an active rebellion—she's painfully unaware of the scope of what she's dealing with!"

Azaz returned smugly to her Fibonacci screen.

"I believe that her plan will be best for now, Commander," the Administrator said.

"B–b–but—"

"Yes, I think that plan will be just wonderful."

Azaz gave the Commander a sideways look of delicious satisfaction.

The Commander faced her. His face was turning purple with rage. "And *where* will you look for them?"

"Oh, Daley." Azaz typed on her Fibonacci in a self-righteous and distracted way. "I'll go wherever they lead."

"And what's that supposed to mean?"

"It means," she snapped, "that I put a Tracking Token on the contraband itself."

"You're tracking the book?"

"Good. You're catching up. Yes. I planted the book, knowing Adam couldn't resist, and I let them all go, knowing it would lead me straight to them. I planned it—all of it. And it went exactly as expected."

In his mind, the Commander was throwing Azaz out the window and watching her drop all eight floors, but in reality, he just watched her with hate flooding his eyes.

"It's settled then," the Administrator said as if they had just picked a restaurant for dinner. "But"—he wagged his finger—"you have many responsibilities in Oasis. Who will handle those in your absence?"

"Oh." Azaz waved her Travel Card over the top right corner of her desk, causing the door to the study to slide open. "I have just the right person for the job. I know you will be excited."

A figure emerged from the study wearing fitted black jeans, a teal T-shirt, and an unbuttoned black blazer. The Administrator beamed when he saw him.

"Yes. Oh, perfect."

"And he's already agreed to share his expertise on the Oarsmen to aid in our search. I believe we will find his knowledge on the matter *quite* invaluable," Azaz said, smiling and gesturing to the man to enter the room.

Commander Daley turned his head to see who it was.

"No . . . ," he muttered.

"Yes," Azaz said.

The man strode into the center of the room, next to the Commander.

"My own grandson, taking the reins of my capital city," the Administrator gushed. "You think you're up to the task?"

"Yes," Sky said. "Yes sir. I am."

END

NOTE FROM THE AUTHOR

I have had this series in my head forever.

I first thought of it, surprisingly, while reading Karl Marx. I thought to myself, *The only reason he is so popular is because it's cool to be different.* It's exciting to adopt an idea that feels forbidden. We like to travel beyond the No Trespassing signs of our society.

If that's the case, then when will the writings of brilliant men such as Thomas Jefferson become cool? When you can't read them anymore.

From there, I imagined a world where all the concepts of right and wrong, truth and true history, were forbidden. Erased. But as the insanity began, some started to save books, hide them, memorize them for future generations. Then, perhaps because it was forbidden, the youth would find them and fight for the truth once again.

It was that simple story that I told Mikayla, someone who has been doing research and writing for me for a few years now. I asked her if she could begin to flesh it out. What she has fleshed out is a book series that will take you on a journey through a fictional world that, when you look closely, may not be as fictional as it seems. I think once you read this volume, you, like me, will be hooked.

ACKNOWLEDGMENTS FROM THE COAUTHOR

It's difficult to decide who to thank.

There's my husband, who spent countless hours discussing the world and lore of the Oarsmen with me in great detail. My mother, the first author I ever met. My father, who lay on my couch until midnight reading an early draft of this book. The good people at Forefront Books, who supported and refined *Chasing Embers*; the staff of the American Journey Experience, for lending their historical expertise; the young beta-readers who shared their time and imaginations with me; Travis Thrasher, who enriched this story with his guidance and mentorship; and of course, the team at Blaze Media and Mercury Radio Arts.

The idea for this book was first dreamed up at 7:00 a.m. in Glenn's radio studio. Without his vision, drive, and commitment to inspiring the next generation of truth seekers, this story would not exist.

But it's you, reader, to whom I am most indebted. We created this fictional world, but it's you, turning the pages of this book and the books to come, who will live in it. It's you who will ensure that *the Oarsmen will never die*.

For that, I thank you.